SECOND DOWN Darling

USA TODAY BESTSELLING AUTHOR

LEX MARTIN

Copy editing by RJ Locksley

Proofreading by Julia Griffis, The Romance Bibliophile

Cover by Najla Qamber Designs

Model Photograph by Lindee Robinson

First Edition

ISBN 978-1-950554-10-2

ABOUT THE BOOK

Jake's my best friend and first love. There's just one problem —he belongs to my sister.

I've been crushing on Jake for years, but never had the guts to tell him. One drunken night with my sister and two pink lines later, and he's lost to me forever.

She doesn't care that I met Jake Ramirez first. That he and I were best friends first. That I fell in love with him first. Because what my sister wants, my sister gets.

When she video-calls me and Jake accidentally walks by in the buff, something in me snaps.

Transferring to a different college might seem like a copout, but I have to get away from Jake and my sister before I say or do something I'll regret. In an act of desperation, I ghost my old life.

For the next two years, everything is great—until I come face-to-face with Jake and his son, who my sister abandoned.

Jake's the new wide receiver at my school, and he wants *nothing* to do with me, which is fine because I plan to keep my distance. Except we're thrown together in the most dire circumstances that bring back all those old feelings.

They say everyone deserves a second chance, but my heart can't handle breaking one more time.

∼

Second Down Darling is an angsty, friends-to-lovers, forbidden romance, featuring a sexy single dad who's a down-and-out college football player and a nerdy girl determined to overcome her wallflower ways. It has major second chance vibes and lots of steam! *Second Down Darling* is a dual POV stand-alone in the *USA Today*-bestselling series Varsity Dads.

"There could have never been two hearts so open, no tastes so similar, no feelings so in unison, no countenances so beloved. Now they were as strangers; nay, worse than strangers, for they could never become acquainted. It was a perpetual estrangement."

—Jane Austen, *Persuasion*

PROLOGUE

CHARLOTTE

"JAKE, DO YOU WANT—?" I stumble in the doorway of the baby's room.

"Shh." Jake Ramirez, my best friend, local football god, and the object of all my high school fantasies, shoots me a boyish grin as he drags a finger over his sleeping son's perfect nose. Asher, his almost-one-year-old, is sprawled across his father's bare chest. "Just got him to sleep."

"Sorry!" I whisper, desperately trying to ignore how handsome Jake looks. His dark hair is in disarray, damp from the shower he took when he got home. The muscles in his shoulders bulge enticingly as he cradles Asher, but it's the sweet, soft look in his beautiful brown eyes as he stares at his baby that really does it for me.

No, Charlotte Darling. We do not ogle this man!

When I can't remember why I came into the nursery, I scramble to say the first thing that comes to mind. "How did your econ exam go?"

"Great. Those flashcards you helped me make did the trick. You're a genius."

His compliment makes me jittery like I'm on a sugar high. I finally remember the question that prompted me to search him out. "I'm making sandwiches. Do you want one?"

"Thanks, Charlie. You're the best." His smile goes crooked, and my heart batters my rib cage.

No, I'm not the best. I'm actually the worst person on the planet, and I'm likely going to hell.

Or maybe I'm already in hell.

Because the thoughts in my head are so, so wrong.

For a flash, for just a second, I'm staring at *my* boyfriend.

Who's cradling *my* baby.

And not my sister's.

I shake my head, ashamed and embarrassed. Thank God no one can hear what I'm thinking or I'd have to move to Bolivia.

It was so easy to fall for the charming, epically handsome Jake Ramirez.

With dark, soulful eyes, a smile punctuated by dimples, and a body like a Greek god, Jake has been my quiet obsession for years.

To be fair, he was my friend first.

My best friend. The reason I got up in the morning and dragged myself to high school.

But that was before he met Kota at a party our senior year, and everything changed.

My stunningly gorgeous older sibling sidles up to me and lets out a huff of annoyance when she sees Jake. "Are you seriously still trying to get him to bed?"

The baby jerks awake at the shrill sound of his mother's voice, and Jake glares at her. "I'm doing my best here, Dakota."

"But does it really need to take an hour? I've barely seen you this week. I thought shit was supposed to get easier once football season ended. The second semester is almost over, and if anything, you've been busier."

Actually, Jake's been around quite a bit, but if I butt in, she'll bite my head off.

His nostrils flare as he whispers harshly over Asher's head. "Just because we don't have games doesn't mean I can sit on my ass. I've explained this. I still have daily conditioning, a heavy class schedule to make up for the easy one I had last fall due to football, physical therapy on my shoulder, finals..."

As their voices get louder, I tiptoe out of the room and distract myself by making ham and cheese sandwiches.

"Please don't tell me you're going to be a gym rat all summer!" My sister streaks out of the baby's room and crosses the hall into their bedroom, slamming the door behind her. A minute later, Jake follows without the baby. It's miraculous the kid isn't wailing right now, but Jake is so good with him. I shouldn't be surprised he was able to put him down despite the ruckus.

I sigh. This is what they do. They bicker all day, but when the lights go out, they bang like the world is ending. Or at least that's what my sister tells her friends. I make a point to *never* spend the night. Because the *very last thing* I want in this world is to know whether Jake and my sister fuck like fiends.

After I plate two ham and cheese sandwiches and some steamed veggies for my sister, because God forbid she consume a carb, I wait for them to join me. My attention snags on the photos next to the flatscreen TV. Most are pics I took of Kota for her social media, but my favorite is the one of me, Jake, and my sister at our high school graduation last May. We're wearing caps and gowns and smiling like loons. Towering over us, Jake has us wrapped in those big, strong arms.

My sister is super pregnant in that pic, but still so gorgeous. She has a natural charisma that's hard to miss.

Kota and I couldn't be more different. Where she's outgoing and fun, I'm quiet and shy. Where she's adventurous and loves to party, I prefer to stay home and read a book. Where she loves being the center of attention, I'd rather blend in and not cause a fuss.

Or as my mother tells everyone, I'm the wallflower and Kota's the prom queen.

She's not wrong.

My sister and I are only ten months apart, but she got held back when we were young because she got really sick for a while, which landed her in my grade. It's been a blessing and a curse.

A blessing because despite my current heartache, I love my sister. I'd do anything for her. Almost losing Kota when we were young screwed us both up, and I'm not immune to the difficulties she faced.

A curse because...

I look down the hall, my stomach clenching.

But then I remember how sick she was, how we almost lost her, and I feel like the lowest scum of the earth.

Doctors could never pinpoint what caused Kota to projectile-vomit and waste away. It was terrifying. All those machines and needles. The antiseptic smell of the hospital. The way my sister would cry so desperately when they came to draw blood.

Kota's illness is what kicked off her reality show stardom.

It happened one day when a producer was trolling the pediatric ward, looking for a story.

Well, he found one.

Who could resist a sick seven-year-old with a smile like hers? I'll tell you—no one. Kota was an immediate sensation, even with an oxygen tube taped to her face and IVs hanging from her scrawny arms. The show, *Little Darlings*, which featured stories of sick kids but centered around my sister, smashed all kinds of records.

Once she got healthy and landed on that other show, *Winchester Prep High*, she skyrocketed to superstardom.

I know what you're thinking—I sound bitter. I *know* I'm a terrible person. Because who begrudges their sister happiness and success after everything she's been through?

It's just that sometimes, when I'm lying in bed at night and thinking about Jake, I wonder if my sister is as innocent as she claims to be.

I'm grateful Kota is alive, I remind myself. *I can deal with anything, even my dreadful case of comparisonitis. Her health is the only thing that matters.*

I pick at my sandwich, wondering how long the argument will last.

Glancing down the hall again, I'm about to ask if I should wait for them when I hear a giggle. "*Stop*, Jake, my sister is going to hear you and then she'll know you've got a huge dick."

My heart stops, then plummets to the floor.

Jake's low voice mumbles something in response, but I can't make out what he says.

Nor do I want to.

I'm frozen for the next two seconds before I spring out of my chair, grab my backpack, and fly out the front door. But not before my sister wails, "Fuck me harder, baby!"

Jake texts me later that night. All it says is, **Thanks for dinner. Sorry about... you know. It wasn't what you think.**

Um, sure.

I'm so tortured by what I overheard, I can't sleep or eat. It's so pathetic, I want to bury myself in a deep hole and wallow in shame.

For the next few days, I can't bring myself to go over there. I bail on babysitting twice, but make sure someone fills in so it doesn't screw up Kota's schedule. It's not her fault I'm in love with her boyfriend.

Deep down, I know I can't go on like this. I can't deal with their sex life or references to Jake's giant member or the fact he trips all over himself to do things for Kota, who acts like he owes her.

If I'd gotten knocked up at a party, perhaps I'd feel the same way, but as a bystander and his friend, it's hard to watch.

I grab the envelope I hid under my laptop.

Charlotte Darling, welcome to Lone Star State University! Attached you'll find everything you need to make your transition to our fine institution.

Lone Star State has always been my dream school. Jake's too. But after my sister got pregnant, she argued we should stay close to home so our families could help with the baby. Even though I resisted for a while, I couldn't really say no when Kota begged me to attend North Texas U with her and Jake.

If all that babysitting I do is any indication, my nephew is my Achilles' heel. Because the last thing I wanted was to tag along while the guy I'd been infatuated with for years dated my sister.

And yet that's exactly what I did.

But no matter how frustrated I am, I'm not sure I can pull the trigger. Can I really bail on my sister, nephew, and best friend?

Maybe if I set some clear boundaries and make sure I'm never at their apartment in the evenings, I can decrease the odds of overhearing Jake and my sister having sex.

I'm so torn up about everything, I take a shower and cry into the tile until the water runs cold. I don't have anyone I can talk to about this. I obviously can't tell my sister, who used to be my main confidante. I can't tell my best friend I'm in love with him when he's very seriously committed to Kota. And my mother would freak out if I even suggested I had feelings for Jake.

Plus, I'm not a home-wrecker. I would never do anything to come between Jake and my sister.

But I need someone to talk to.

It's a depressing thought—I've been at NTU for an entire year and literally have no friends here. I've been too busy babysitting my nephew to have any kind of social life. I'm gone so much I barely see my suitemate.

You know how you can erase your computer and reset it to the factory settings? That's what I need to do with my life. I need to start over.

But how?

~

A FEW DAYS LATER, my laptop chimes. Without looking, I know it's my sister. It's much earlier than she usually calls, but I've been MIA lately, so maybe it's thrown her off too.

Every week, we video-chat so Kota can plan out her social media. You'd think having a kid would slow her down, but if anything, it's only made her more focused on building her online following, which is now two million strong.

I prefer doing our calls by video so I don't have to haul my crap over to her apartment. She gets mad when I forget to bring one of her calendars or social media planners, and the last thing I'm in the mood for is an argument.

As much as I shudder at the thought of displaying my whole life online, I admire her focus and drive. It's probably why Kota and Jake got together. He's been singularly focused on playing D1 football since he was a kid, and now he's living his dream. I'm so proud of him. Both of them, really. They have a bright future ahead of them, and I'll always cheer the loudest for their success.

After taking a deep breath, I accept the call and my sister's face fills the screen.

"Hey, loser. Did you edit those pics? I need them by noon." She leans over her dressing table and flicks on some mascara. She's wearing some kind of sheer, lacy lingerie and her boobs are spilling out.

I manage to stop myself before glancing down at my modest chest. *Comparison is the thief of joy, Charlotte. You'll never be Dakota. That's okay. You do you.*

"Yes, I uploaded the pics to your drive last night."

"Did they include the ones of me and the baby napping? The ones where the light is filtering in from the window? It made my skin look really good."

"Yes."

She pauses applying her makeup and turns to face me. "Are you over... your stomach bug?"

The look she gives me makes me think she knows the real reason I bailed, and I feel horrible for lying, but I needed to tell her something plausible. Something that would help me save face the next time I see Jake, which I hope isn't for a few weeks because I need to lock down my emotions first. "Mostly."

"Good, because I don't want you to give me the shits."

Feeling my ears go hot, I'm grateful no one is around to overhear her. I swear I'm the only person she talks to like this. With everyone else, she's as sweet as pie. Well, she's snarky with Jake, but having a baby just before college and then trying to get through freshman year as a parent while your boyfriend plays D1 football is not a cakewalk.

Still, she was never mean before she starred in three seasons of *Winchester Prep High*. I swear those producers turned her into a snob.

I miss my sister. The one who always shared her toys and clothes with me. The one who gave the neighbor kid a shiner when he kicked sand in my face. She's in there somewhere, and I'm not giving up until I find her again.

We talk about the plan for the week. She keeps glancing backwards and eventually angles the screen until she's mostly cropped out.

"Kota, I can't see—"

"Hold on." She mutes herself. I can see her profile. She's saying something, but I can't hear the words.

That's when it happens.

The bathroom door behind her swings open, and Jake steps out through a billowing cloud of steam.

Freshly washed and *completely* naked.

I blink, a strangled whimper lodging in my throat.

Holy crap. He's perfect.

I knew he was beautiful, but my fantasies fall short of the reality. His wet hair falls in his face as he towels off. First his damp locks. Then his wide, muscular chest. Down his washboard abs. And finally his groin where an enormous erection bounces against his stomach.

I'm frozen until the sound mysteriously pops back on again, and his deep voice fills my room. "Let's make this quick, Dakota. I gotta jet."

They're definitely going to fuck.

"Oh God." I slam my laptop shut. My hands are shaking as I fling it away from me.

Nausea sweeps over me so hard, I barely make it to the trash can before I lose my breakfast.

Five minutes later, my phone buzzes from my nightstand, but I ignore it. The calls and texts keep coming. I don't bother to check them because nothing my sister or Jake say will change my pathetic situation.

Later that afternoon, Jake knocks on my door, calls my name, apologizes for not knowing I was on a video conference with my sister. My suitemate thinks I'm home, but since I don't answer, they decide I must be out. I don't budge from where I sit on the floor with a box of tissues.

The sun sets and rises again. My suitemate comes and goes as the dorm comes alive, and by the time I finally dust myself off and stand, I've made my decision.

I'm going to transfer schools.

As quickly as possible.

1

JAKE

Two years & three months later

SOME BETRAYALS CUT DEEPER than others.

Expectation is everything. Knowing shit's headed your way and preparing for the tackle keeps a man's spirit intact despite whatever gale force sacks him.

It's the difference between staying down and getting back up again.

The film flickers against the screen, filling the room with the familiar crunch of player smashing against player. It's a sound I love. A sound I live for.

Or at least, I used to.

My mind is a million miles away. It should be on the upcoming game against Alabama. It should be on their killer defense that could pound my ass into the turf come next week. It should be on leading my new team to a victory.

Instead, I see my ex, Dakota, bare ass up, face down on our bed as my best friend Troy railed her from behind.

While our baby sat in a dirty diaper and cried in the other room.

Mentirosos. Liars. Both of them.

I'll admit I wasn't excited to have a kid. Not at first. But despite my party reputation in high school, I would never let my responsibilities slide. Unlike my father, who eventually left us, I promised myself I'd be there for Dakota.

She and I were a hookup after I'd seen my parents get into another screaming match on my mom's front porch, one that almost made me come to blows with my father.

I was pissed off at the world, drank too much, and banged the bombshell blonde at the party who straddled my lap and told me it was my lucky night.

There was nothing lucky about that night.

I rub the ache in my chest.

No, it feels wrong to think that. I got Asher, and he'll always be the highlight of my life even though his mother has made my life hell.

I changed everything for her.

She planned to attend North Texas U, so that's where I went even though I'd gotten a full ride to my dream school, Lone Star State, which was four hours away. I wanted to support her and be near our son. I committed myself to her in a way I'd only ever done for family and football.

And cheating was the thanks I got.

Dakota finally admitted she'd been fucking Troy Snyder almost the entire time we were at NTU.

At least Asher is mine—the DNA test confirmed it.

Sometimes I'm tempted to pick up the phone and call Charlotte to vent before I remember she doesn't give a shit.

That's a whole different level of betrayal. I don't even know where the fuck she went. Dakota and her mother Waverly won't tell me anything, and Charlotte changed her number, so it's not like I can ask her. And even though she took pics for her sister's social media, Charlie never posted any of her own online. After being on that reality show as a kid, she hated being in the spotlight.

Charlotte was my best friend from high school, the girl who never asked for tickets to games or wanted my help getting into hot parties or grilled me about my college prospects. I had a little thing for her when we first met. With her light blonde hair, big blue eyes, petite frame, and quiet ways, she drew out all of my protective instincts.

She was in my English class freshman year, and one day our teacher randomly picked her to be Juliet. Charlie had to lie there while I, Romeo, reacted to her death. Even though we'd never spoken at that point, I could tell she was terrified. I hooked her pinky finger with mine to help steady her, and from that point on, we became the best of friends.

So when guys were dicks to her, I made it clear they'd have to go through me if they ever thought to mess with her. When I saw her sitting alone in the cafeteria, I pulled up the seat next to her. When she seemed sad, I invited her to hang out.

But she never looked at me all googly-eyed like the other girls. She never flirted or found reasons to touch me. She actually made me do my homework when we studied together. I figured she wasn't into me like that and moved on. But she was still my best friend. Even when things got awkward between us after I started dating Dakota.

And no, I'm not that dick who goes around fucking friends' siblings. To be clear, I didn't know Dakota was Charlie's older sister when we hooked up. One, we weren't real big on names that night. Two, Dakota had been off recording a reality show at some ritzy boarding school in New York. She'd just moved back home after one of her classmates partied too hard and overdosed, resulting in the show getting cancelled and the school nearly closing. And three, Charlotte called her sister Kota, and being a drunk dumbass, I didn't put it all together until it was too late.

In my head, I run through all the reasons Charlotte might've taken off two years ago.

Initially, I'd thought she was upset after I accidentally walked in on that conference call in the buff. Dakota had called out to me, demanding we talk *that very minute*, and I waltzed out of the shower with my dick and balls hanging free like an asshole. Honestly, things between me and Dakota had been so strained, I thought it would be funny. A way to break the ice, I suppose. We hadn't had sex in months, despite the dumb shit she told her friends—probably because she'd been screwing my teammate—and some stupid part of me wanted to show her what she was missing.

Instead, I gave poor Charlie a full-frontal show, just barely stopping short of giving my dick a tug.

Chingao. I don't get embarrassed easily, but that's definitely not my proudest moment.

Dakota laughed her ass off. Almost as hard as she'd laughed a few nights before when she'd pretended we were fucking in the other room.

She stopped laughing when Charlie refused to return her calls. Or respond to her texts. Or do her social media posts. That's when shit got real.

Dakota swears her "jokes" weren't the reason Charlie went MIA. She says they got in an argument, but refused to tell me what it was about.

I didn't get a chance to ask Charlotte before she took off.

Not knowing really fucking bugs me.

I just don't understand why Charlie would ghost me too. I thought our friendship meant more to her. Thought she loved Asher and wanted to watch him grow up. Thought we were family, for better or worse.

Guess I was wrong. But I'm wrong about a lot of things, I'm realizing.

The lights flip on, and Coach Santos returns to the podium.

Coach, whose nickname from his NFL days is the Saint, is only in his early forties, but he has the authority of a much older man.

"Gentlemen, our first game of the season is around the corner. The challenge won't be physical. You've done the workouts and routes and training. You're elite athletes at one of the best programs in the country. Some might say *the* best." Lone Star State lost in the championship game last year, and everyone knows Coach Santos spent the last several months recruiting his ass off.

The guys let out a roar of approval, and Coach cracks a rare smile before his eyes go squinty. "The challenge will be in here." He taps his temple. "Football, like life, is a mental game. Broncos, we can go all the way this year if you want it badly enough, but it starts with mental fortitude. Tonight, when you're lying in bed, envision those killer tackles you're going to make. Feel the ball in your hands after you catch that miraculous throw."

The guys around Ezra Thomas, our cocky quarterback, slap him on the back. I suppose I'd be cocky too if I'd taken my team to the championship game as a sophomore, which has ESPN calling him the next Trevor Lawrence.

Coach's voice grows louder. "See yourself relying on your teammates and trusting your instincts." His eyes meet mine briefly before he scans the team.

The insinuation is there—my instincts are shot to hell. It's why my last two seasons at NTU were utter shit, which sent me scrambling to transfer to Lone Star and hopefully get one last shot at the NFL.

After Charlotte took off, Dakota and I eked out a few more months of misery, months that left me sleeping on the couch.

Once my father remarried and barely bothered to talk to his four sons, I was bound and determined not to be that guy. I would stick around, come hell or high water.

Maybe I shouldn't have been surprised when I found Dakota in bed with Troy, but it hit me like a Mac truck. I had the worst season of my career. Dakota took off for LA, dumping me with Asher full time while I juggled football and school. I was a mess.

I wish I could say I regrouped junior year, but it was only marginally better. It was hard to get my head on straight with that fuckwit Troy on our team. But I couldn't exactly go around and explain to the media that our QB had fucked my baby mama behind my back and that's why my stats were in the shitter.

It's a miracle Lone Star State considered me, but it makes me that much more committed to doing whatever Coach Santos asks of me. That man has given me a lifeline, and I don't intend to squander it.

Billy Babcock, our safety, quips, "Do I have to be alone in bed to do this vision quest, Coach?" He chuckles. "Because I might need some company to help me handle my balls."

Idiot. You don't joke with Coach like that. I've only been here since July for training camp, but even I know this.

Coach rolls his eyes as a few of the guys with a death wish laugh. When everyone quiets down, he leans forward. "For the love of God, please wear condoms. I don't want to have to remind you—again—about the consequences when you're irresponsible."

I flinch, the reminder I fucked up always in the back of my mind. I didn't realize the condom had busted until after we were done. Dakota waved it off like it wasn't a big deal. She said she'd get the morning-after pill, patted me on the head, and took off. I didn't think much about it again until she tracked me down one day after football practice and told me the pill hadn't worked and she was pregnant.

There's a five-percent failure rate with those pills.

Lucky me.

But Dakota is a beautiful woman. Smart. Ambitious. I figured we could make a go of things and try that whole "committed relationship" route, something I hadn't really considered in my life up until that point. My family is devoutly Catholic and supported my decision even though they weren't crazy about Dakota. Hell, my oldest brother David supported that more than he ever did my football career. In his mind, I should get my business degree and join him and our other brother Elijah at their garage.

I'd rather drink motor oil than live the rest of my life under the hood of a car. I've seen how our small town treats the men in my family, like the grease under their nails and our address near the train yard means we're not worthy. I aim to prove them otherwise. If anyone deserves a nice house with a picket fence in a safe neighborhood, it's my mother, who has dealt with her fair share of bullshit from me and my siblings.

After the divorce, my older brothers, David and Eli, tried to help Mom with her mountain of bills and two other boys to raise, but she still struggled.

That's the main reason I couldn't bail on Dakota, even if she treated me like shit. I saw what my mom went through, and there was no way I was doing that to another woman. It's probably why I stayed with Dakota long after I thought it was a good idea.

The truth is we never should've gotten together. We would've been better off trying to co-parent. Maybe learn how to be friends. Learn how to work together. What is it they say? Hindsight is twenty-twenty.

Coach's pep talk turns into a lecture about partying. After

the team got busted for a naked swimming party last year, I don't blame him for his concern. Some of the guys play fast and loose around here. If I didn't have a son, I might have the same attitude, but my family's future is on the line. I'm not here to fuck around.

When the meeting is over, he calls my name.

Praying I haven't screwed up already, I gather my things and head to the podium. "What's up, Coach?"

"How's the new apartment? You settled in?"

"Yes, sir." It's in a shitty part of town, across the street from some run-down condos and college kids who party too much, but it's not a terrible hike to campus, and I can afford it with my housing stipend.

Most of the guys live with teammates. I can't exactly join them with a three-year-old kid tagging along. It sucks to miss out on a central part of the college experience, but Asher needs me to be my best self, and that doesn't include living in a party house like the Stallion Station.

Coach lowers his voice. "And the babysitting situation is working out?"

Not so much, but there's still time. "I'm hammering out the kinks." My mom stayed with me during training camp so she could watch Asher, but she went back home, and I've been scrambling to make sure I get decent people to watch my son.

"Good. Did you receive the money from the student assistance fund to help you pay for childcare?"

"Yes, sir. Thank you. I really appreciate everything you did to make that happen."

He nods solemnly. "No thanks necessary. It's my job. Just want to make sure you're equipped with what you need to be successful this year."

NTU never gave me a penny to help pay for childcare. I sold my grandfather's old coin collection so I could contribute to what we paid Charlie to watch Asher. Yes, the Darlings are flush, but I never wanted to be that guy who mooches off his girl-friend's family. "It's going to help tremendously."

"I was already in the NFL when I had my daughter, but I remember what it was like to be a rookie and have a baby at home. And let me tell you, Roxanne was a handful. She still is." He chuckles. "Having solid childcare will give you peace of mind so you can focus on the game. Have you called Michael Oliver yet? He knows what you're going through."

Oliver was last year's star running back who had twins late last fall with his girlfriend. He was drafted to Chicago.

"Yes. He had some good advice." Mostly to trust Coach, because he didn't at first, and it bit him in the ass.

"And what about the girlfriend situation? Do we know what kind of show to expect? I want to brace myself for the worst."

This was the hardest part—getting the call from my first-choice college and needing to tell them my ex might blast my shit on national TV. Because of course her new reality show kicks off in a few weeks.

Thankfully, Coach took it in stride.

"*Ex*-girlfriend." He knows this, but I feel the need to remind him that whatever Dakota does on that show should not reflect on me. I swallow and nod slowly. "It's called *The Hot House*."

"Let me guess. Because all of the contestants are hot?"

"Yes, sir."

"God help us. Okay. What else?"

"It's one of those big fall lineup shows that start in October. A new episode every week." Which is almost worse than a series you can binge. Because I'd prefer to rip off the Band-Aid and watch it all at once.

Coach must see something on my face because he pats me on the back. "Breakups are tough, but maybe this was a blessing in disguise. You don't need a girlfriend who airs out your dirty laundry in public. You'll need to work hard to block out the noise."

I swallow past the thick knot in my throat. If my relationship with Dakota has taught me anything, it's that I'll never be the idiot who trusts a woman like that again.

For the next year, I have two goals: Take care of my son and kick ass at football. There's zero room in that equation for girlfriends.

I was a fool to go there with Dakota.

"Coach, thanks for taking a chance on me. Especially with all this other stuff going on."

He nods. "You know what sealed the deal for me? Your honesty. The fact that you leveled with me from the beginning. Because I can't help my players if they don't trust me to do right by them."

Aside from my parents and brothers, this man is about the only other person I trust in the world.

"Hang in there, Ramirez," he says as he gathers his stuff. "When you have your priorities straight, life has a funny way of working out when you least expect it to."

It reminds me of something my mom always says. *Cuando Dios cierra una puerta, abre una ventana.* When God closes a door, he opens a window.

I hope Mom and Coach are right. I need to stay focused on football this fall, but with Dakota doing who knows what on *The Hot House*, I'm not sure what to expect.

If I know my ex, it has the potential to be bad.

Really bad.

2

CHARLOTTE

DOWN ON MY hands and knees, I coo at the despondent fur ball huddled in the corner of his cage. "Come on, Duke. You have to eat."

The speckled Australian shepherd with haunting pale eyes ignores me and lets out a whine.

A lot of animals have trouble when they land at the shelter. They keep looking to the door, waiting for their owners to return. They don't eat. They don't want toys. They don't understand why they were abandoned.

It's a feeling I'm well acquainted with. Now that I've gotten some space from my sister, I realize my family deserted me a long time ago. I was just too blind to see it.

"The vet says he's fine," Sheryl calls out from her desk. "Physically, there's nothing wrong with him. He got an IV 'cause he was dehydrated, but he won't go near the kibble." She pauses. "My hands are tied if he won't eat, darlin'."

Meaning Duke will be put down because the shelter can't afford the feeding tube. She's already explained the vet will do the first treatment pro bono, but anything beyond that, Second Chances Animal Rescue will have to foot the bill. And since they can't afford that, they'll hand the dog over to Animal Control, which will euthanize him.

My eyes sting at the thought this beautiful animal might lose his life because some asshole mistreated him.

I reach out my hand, with my fingers curled in so he doesn't nip one off. Duke jerks back, like I'm going to strike him, and my heart clenches.

Witnessing the aftermath of abuse is the worst part about volunteering at a rescue shelter.

"It's okay, buddy," I say softly. "I'm not going to hurt you. I know what it's like to not have anyone you can trust. I just want to be your friend."

I shrug off my camera and tuck it carefully into the second-hand padded case. Duke's headshot will have to wait. I don't let myself consider how he might not be here later this week when I return with the new adoption flyers.

For the next few minutes, I try my best to forget what might be on this floor and slowly sprawl out on the ground and wait for Duke to get used to me.

Sheryl's footsteps echo on the concrete floor. She pauses when she sees me lying down in Duke's cage. Lifts a brow.

"We're bonding," I whisper as I creep my hand closer to Duke. I keep my eyes down because I don't want him to think I'm challenging him. I'm a huge pushover, something I'm working on, but the terrified dog doesn't know this.

"You're crazy, Charlie, but I dig that about you." Sheryl's husky laugh wanes as she continues to the break room, where Merle's low baritone voice joins hers.

Sheryl's in her forties. Divorced. Has a smoker's cough and is secretly in love with Merle, who runs this place. She's never come out and said she has a thing for her boss, but I can tell.

After all, I'm an expert when it comes to unrequited love.

For a second, I let myself think about Jake and his captivating eyes fringed with long lashes and the way they crinkle at the corners when he smiles.

I hope he's doing well. That he's kicking ass at football and that he and my sister have worked through their challenges. I say a prayer for him and Kota and baby Asher every night. I might not be in their lives anymore, but they're always in my heart.

Despite moving four hours away, I'm still obsessed with Jake. Not in the way you think. Just... he's who I compare every man to, especially the datable men around here. And, well, they always fall short.

At least Jake didn't know I was in love with him. That's a level of humiliation I wouldn't have been able to stand—him knowing how I felt and still choosing my sister.

A scratchy, wet tongue licks my wrist, and it's my turn to jerk in surprise. Duke stares back at me and whines. He bows his head, and I reach up to pet him.

"Look at you. Aren't you a sweet boy?"

I relish the distraction. Transferring colleges two years ago to get away from the Jake and Dakota sex-fest helped, but once in a while, those old ghosts haunt me.

Mostly I worry about my nephew. My sister isn't a great mom, something she admits. Kota's just not that present when she's with Asher. I'm sure Jake will hold down the fort, but he plays football, so he can't fill in *all* the gaps.

I miss Asher so much some days it's hard to breathe. He's three now and probably doesn't remember his aunt Charlie anymore. The heartache of not seeing him is what brought me to Second Chances originally. I needed something to fill that crater in my heart.

The worst part is I can't even ask how he and his parents are doing because I changed my phone number when I took off. I left Kota and Jake notes to explain, sorta, so they wouldn't think anything horrible had happened.

And I called my mother so she'd understand why I couldn't go to NTU anymore. All she did was scream I was ruining everything before she told me not to bother coming home for the summer and hung up on me. Since my father goes along with whatever my mom wants, I didn't bother calling him because I know he doesn't care.

My mother was just pissed she'd have to start babysitting instead of dumping that responsibility on me.

I've been on my own ever since.

With a sigh, I drag myself off the floor, but I can't shake the idea that if I don't do something, Duke won't make it.

Sheryl and Merle are reviewing some paperwork when I pop into the break room. ESPN is on in the background. Merle is obsessed with sports. That's the only drawback to helping around here. I try to avoid anything that might mention North Texas U football and Jake.

Leaning on the doorframe, I wave behind me to the kennels. "I took everyone's photo except Duke's. I was afraid the sound of the shutter would freak him out."

Merle shakes his head. "It's his second day of not eating, Charlie. Not sure how long we can hold out."

I chew the inside of my cheek, hesitant to ask the question. After a minute, I work up the courage. "How much would the vet charge to do the feeding tube?" My bank account is getting low, but I want to help.

Sheryl clicks her tongue. "Sweetheart, I know you don't have any money. You can't save every dog that comes through here. Plus, don't you have your hands full with Winkie?"

It's scary how well Sheryl knows me after I've volunteered here for only a year. Winkie is the one-eyed kitten I adopted last fall.

"Winkie's not a problem." He finally stopped tearing up my clothes. And curtains. And bedding. Mostly.

Merle leans back in his chair. "Just because we save Duke in the short term doesn't mean he'll make it. He'll have to want to get better." His face darkens. "Wish I could beat the tar out of whoever did this to him."

My throat gets tight. I can't let this happen. "What if I fostered him? What if I took him home and loved up on him? You know being around so many other dogs is stressful."

Merle's haggard eyes meet mine. "We're supposed to stabilize the animals before we foster them in homes, Charlotte."

"What does that matter if you're just going to give him to Animal Control in a few days? I know what I'm signing up for." Duke might not make it. I'm not good with confrontations, but the fear of this dog being euthanized forces me to dredge up the courage to fight Merle on this.

He rubs the bridge of his nose. "For every instance of neglect, you need ten times more affection and care to offset the damage that's been done. You've got school and your photography. You sure you're up for the task?"

I nod quickly. "My schedule this year is great. I have a break in the middle of the day and plenty of time to take Duke for walks." I can't believe I'm already a senior.

When Merle doesn't say anything, I fold my hands like I'm praying. It's a tactic straight out of my sister's playbook, normally not something I'd attempt, but I'm desperate. "Please. I promise I won't ask to do this again. I just can't let him die without trying."

"You're still gonna do that calendar, though, right?"

"Absolutely." With the tough economy last year, Second Chances lost several major donors, and they've been on the brink of closing their doors ever since. I suggested doing a calendar to raise funds, and since photography is the one area of my life where I excel, I want to help.

Now I just have to persuade a few athletes to take cute pics with some homeless animals.

Sweat gathers under my arms at the thought of talking to so many people. This is why Dakota is our mother's favorite. Kota is great at public speaking and knows how to ham it up for the cameras. Not me.

Despite being a photographer, I have a tendency to blink whenever I'm photographed. My shrink explained it's psychosomatic and caused by stress. My mother rolled her eyes and declared that was a nice way of saying it's all in my head.

Yes, my mom took me to a psychiatrist to see if she could cure me of this "ailment" and turn me into another media sensation like my sister.

Newsflash: It didn't work. As the dumb memes people made of me when I was little indicate.

You can do this, Charlotte. You're not a wallflower anymore.

Fake it till you make it, right?

I clear my throat. "I'll start coordinating the photoshoots this week."

Since I never go on dates, I'll have the time.

Merle winks at me with a nod. "Then you got yourself a deal." He points to the TV mounted on the wall, which is highlighting a Bronco game from last year. "Gonna have a hell of a season."

When he starts talking football, I usually duck out. Lone Star State's team is one of the best in the country, so it's a popular subject around here. I even went to a game with my friend Maggie, who just got engaged to one of the former players, but the topic bums me out, so I try to avoid football altogether.

Before I can return the conversation to taking Duke home

with me, Merle smacks the table with a grin. "Coach Santos has built a helluva team this year. That transfer portal is a game-changer. We're getting two new wide receivers, and..."

His voice fades as my pulse races.

Jake's a wide receiver.

It was his lifelong dream to play football here.

But what are the odds Jake would transfer his senior year of college? I can't imagine a scenario that would have Kota excited to move down to the Hill Country.

I shake my head. I'm just being paranoid.

A tidal wave of guilt settles in my belly at the memory of leaving the way I did, but I didn't think I had a choice. I was dying inside. I had to do something.

Jake never called, Charlotte. You don't owe him anything.

In a moment of weakness, I gave him my new number. My note said if he ever had an emergency, I wanted one person to know how to reach me.

With the way I left, I shouldn't be hurt that he never called or texted, but I am.

And before you say I'm a nutcase—because who changes their phone number but then hands out the new one?—I agree with you. As my psychosomatic photo blinking likely proves.

But there's no way I could leave my sister with a way to contact me. Even if I blocked her, she's relentless when she wants something. She'd have no qualms about using her horde of fans to harass me until I did her bidding. And if I caved to her demands *one more time*, I'd never be able to live with myself.

I can't stop thinking about it, though. *Jake wouldn't transfer his senior year, would he?*

I'm so tempted to Google his name and low-key stalk him until I can confirm he's staying put at NTU, but I'm on a two-year streak without that man, and I don't intend to backslide now.

If Asher is my Achilles' heel, Jake is my favorite drug. And as everyone knows, you don't give an addict a shot of alcohol.

Mentally, I high-five myself for staying strong. I'm done being that sad loser who's always moping around in her famous sister's shadow.

I love Dakota. I'd give her a kidney if she needed it. The problem is Dakota only loves herself.

I wonder if Jake has figured that out yet.

So no more pining over my sister's boyfriend. I deserve better. Someday I'll find a man who wants me and will put me first, and until then, I have an Australian shepherd who needs my help.

Resolved, I smile at Merle. "So how do I spring Duke from this joint?"

3

CHARLOTTE

THE SOUND of a key in the door breaks the standoff. Once again, I'm sprawled on the kitchen floor, one hand full of warm, shredded chicken that I hold out to Duke, when my new roommate Roxanne Santos walks in.

"You're going to spoil that dog."

I must look ridiculous, but Duke is worth the inconvenience. "He needs a little convincing sometimes. I won't do this forever." It's only been a week. He's still super freaked out around people, but at least he's eating.

Tentatively, he licks my fingers, and I babytalk to him. "You're a good boy. Yes, you are."

My roommate snorts, but she's smiling.

Roxy is a junior. She has thick, dark brown hair and a criminally dirty mind. She's the opposite of me in all the best ways. In other words, like my sister minus the attitude and self-importance.

Getting distance from Dakota was the best thing I could do. I see now how I let her boss me around. I worked my ass off for her and never even got a thank you. I think I let myself be manipulated out of guilt because I had feelings for Jake.

I refuse to be a pushover anymore.

This is the year I take charge.

I direct this ship. I'm queen of my castle.

"Are you sure I can't talk you into coming to the Baylor game this weekend? I can get you great tickets." Roxy is the daughter of the football coach, Richard Santos. She's also a cheerleader, a really good one who gets flipped into the air and does death-defying moves every day.

I would never say this to her because I'd hate to hurt her feelings, but she wasn't my first choice of roommates. But the friends I made at Lone Star State were all seniors who graduated last May, and I was starting to panic because I can't afford this place solo even though it's located in one of the shadier areas in town. I met Rox when I was hanging out with my friend Maggie, who just moved to Chicago with her boyfriend Olly and their twins.

But Roxy is fun and outgoing, and I definitely need someone to push me out of my comfort zone. She makes me laugh, and I could use more laughter in my life. Like me, she's a transfer to Lone Star, and I get the feeling she could use a friend. Plus, she was cool with me having a one-eyed demon cat and now a freaked-out Aussie.

"We had a deal, Miss Santos. You don't talk about football, and I won't nag you to get up when your alarm goes off in the morning."

She snickers. "The right to snooze should be in the Constitution."

"But if you don't keep up your grades, your father is going to move you back into the pool house, and that's no fun." I hate being the voice of reason, but I want her to do well.

"Ugh, don't remind me. Dad can be such a hardass."

Roxy partied a little too much last year, and her parents put her on lockdown for a while. I'm surprised she isn't living somewhere swankier, though. Our neighborhood is full of crazy college kids, and some of the buildings around here are run-down. But it's affordable and not too far from campus.

Duke finally starts nibbling his dinner, and I slowly back out of the way. If I get up too quickly, he gets scared, and I'll have to start all over again.

Once he's done eating, Roxy gets down on her knees and holds out her hand to Duke, who takes a quick sniff of her hand before he licks it. He even lets her scruff his fur, but then he gets skittish and backs away. "It's okay, Duke. I'm not gonna hurt you."

"He's learning to trust again. It takes time."

"Meow-eow!" Winkie rubs against Roxy's leg, but runs off before she can pet him.

"Your cat has the funniest meow." She laughs and tries to lure him out from behind the couch, but pauses when she spots my eight-by-ten black-and-white prints on the coffee table. "Holy shit. Are these yours?"

"Yeah. I'm obsessed with the darkroom." Something I discovered when I transferred here.

Using film is so much more rewarding than taking digital shots. Don't get me wrong, digital offers immediate gratification. Plus, you can see right away whether you have the photo or not. That's obviously important.

But old-school film photography has its own allure. It demands attention to detail. Is the aperture correct or will the shot be blurry because it's not well lit? Am I using the right film speed or will it be too grainy? Will I find the perfect way to crop the image under the enlarger or will the composition be boring? The whites in your final print should be crisp with detail, as should the blacks, which is not easy to do on the same image.

I love the challenge of getting everything *just right*. In the darkroom, I call the shots, and that's a new feeling for me.

The animals at the shelter are the perfect subject for black-and-white photos, since the flyers won't be in color. And my secondhand Nikon FM2 takes beautiful pics. "I'm going to give the prints to the families who adopt them."

"That's a great idea. You're so sweet."

"Thanks. I love these little guys."

"I can tell. It comes through in your images."

"Hey, do you smell that?" I sniff the air. Is something burning?

"It's just the potpourri crock pot downstairs. Those girls never turn it off." She keeps flipping through my pics. "So are you a photo major?"

"A photojournalism major, yes." I could've chosen the art degree route to study photography, but I love capturing people in their natural surroundings, which is the opposite of every contrived pic my sister ever had me take for her.

Maybe now is a good time to ask Roxy for that favor. "Any chance you'd like to be in a calendar I'm putting together for the shelter? I'm supposed to get 'hot' athletes—my boss's description, not mine—to take pics with the animals so we can raise money." I explain how Second Chances is in trouble and might not be able to stay open next year.

By the time I'm done, Roxy's eyes are wide. "Of course I'll help! Are you sure you don't want to just use male athletes, though? A shirtless football player might sell better."

Unbidden, the image flickers in my mind.

Jake.

Shirtless.

Wet.

And very, very hard.

Everywhere.

I blink and shake my head to clear my wayward thoughts. Unfortunately, it's not easy to purge the image of Jake emerging naked from his shower, no matter how much time has gone by.

"They don't need to be shirtless. I need athletes, and you work your ass off for several hours at every practice and game, not to mention those workouts I see you post online. Plus, you're beautiful. I think you more than qualify."

"I *am* kinda cute." She buffs her nails on her shirt.

We laugh and make plans to do the shoot. "I could use your help finding some other athletes, though." I hold my hand out. "They can't all be football players." Preferably none, but if I say that, she might get suspicious. She just thinks I'm not into sports. It's hard to bare my soul about what happened at North Texas U.

"I got you, girl. I know everyone, and there are some fine-looking men on the team this year. I might even be tempted to break my own rule about not dating one."

"You don't date football players?" She's one of the head cheerleaders, and I assumed they got first pick of the players since they're always around each other.

She gives me a look. "Have you met my father? He terrifies everyone, and his athletes would probably prefer a rectal exam than his scrutiny. Deep down, he's a teddy bear, although I don't think I'd be doing the player any favors if we dated. But I might be tempted to bang one of them."

I fold my lips as I hold in a chuckle.

She waves her hand around my face. "Your ears just went bright red. I should have warned you before I moved in—I don't have a filter."

"I don't mind." It's refreshing. I never feel like Roxy is playing games.

I'm not sure what it is about her—maybe it's her bubbly personality or the way she's jumping in to help me with the calendar or just me needing a friend—but I'm so tempted to tell her about Jake. Instead, I blurt, "Maybe you could help *me* get a date."

Then I slap my hand over my mouth.

That makes her stand up straight. "Of course I can get you a date. Maybe we could go on a double. I just found out there's a drive-in theater here. Wouldn't that be fun?" The thought of going out with someone practically makes me hyperventilate. "Wait. What's going on? You're freaking out right now, aren't you?"

I nod and lean over to take several deep breaths. "This might sound weird, but I've never gone on a date."

"What?" She yanks me up. "Are you serious? Do you mean you've never had a boyfriend, but you've gone out with a few guys once or twice? Or do you mean you've *never ever* gone out with anyone?"

"Never ever." Maybe that's part of the problem. If I dated and got out more, perhaps I wouldn't still be fantasizing about Jake.

She gasps. "How did this happen? You're so beautiful. How have you managed to go this long and not get snatched right up?"

How do I explain this? I hate how everything jumbles in my head like a bad *Jerry Springer* episode. "I had a thing for my best friend for years. But he didn't see me like that, and then he started seriously dating someone else. We all went to college together, and as much as I wanted to be social and go out, I ended up being the third wheel in this other relationship." Which sounds so pathetic, I want to reach back in time and slap myself.

Roxy nibbles her bottom lip. "Is that why you transferred here?"

"One of the reasons, yes."

"You musta really loved the guy."

With my whole heart and soul. "When I transferred to Lone

Star two years ago, I had every intention of putting myself out there, but leaving my friends and family behind was harder to deal with than I expected. I needed some time to get my bearings."

"Why did you have to leave your family? Do you just mean relocating was tough?"

I shake my head as nausea flips my stomach. I've said too much, but I've already come this far, and I could really use someone to talk to. If I don't tell her Jake's name, maybe I can share more. "This guy... was dating... my sister, so yeah. I basically had to leave my family too."

Once again, Roxy's eyes widen. "Your sister?"

"I know it sounds terrible, but I'd been best friends with him for three years before they met. Except I was a wimp and never told him how I felt. By the time I dredged up the courage, it was too late."

I knew Jake didn't have a date for homecoming, so after the game, I finally worked up the courage to tell him how I felt.

But he wasn't home.

He'd gone to a party.

The one where he met Kota.

So many what-ifs dart through my mind.

What if I had told Jake how I felt when we were in high school?

What if I hadn't been such a big chicken and I'd flirted with him when he was single and I had the chance?

The worst one, though, the one that still keeps me up at night, is—what if I hadn't told my sister I had a huge crush on my best friend?

Because despite her claim she didn't specifically seek out Jake at that party, I sometimes wonder.

"Fuck, that sucks." Roxy throws her arms around me, and I pat her back awkwardly. "I'll be your family."

Her words bring tears to my eyes. Now that I've shared some of my past, the weight on my chest feels lighter. "Thanks, Roxy. I'd love that. I could use a sister." I miss Dakota fiercely sometimes. I don't know why. She treated me like shit more often than not.

When we break apart, Roxy puts her hands on her hips. "I'm gonna find you a great guy too. Just watch."

I nod, a little embarrassed.

Then she lowers her voice to a whisper. "Does this mean you're a virgin? No shame if you are, but if so, you might want to think about getting on birth control if you're not already. Also, some guys are fuckboys, and I don't want to set you up with anyone who's just DTF."

Birth control. Right. That's important.

Hold on. "DTF?"

"Down to fuck. You know, someone who just wants to hook up."

Maybe that's what I need to get over this hump. A hookup. I've been romanticizing dating and men for far too long, and now that I understand the reality, I kinda just want to have sex and get it over with. Maybe that would demystify dating, and it would freak me out less.

Because it's dumb to wait for the perfect guy when he doesn't exist.

There's no such thing as Prince Charming.

There never was.

4

JAKE

Exhausted from class and practice, I toss my crap by the door and set my to-go box on the counter. "Hey. I'm home. *¿Dónde estás, pingo?*" *Pingo* means "little scamp" or "rascal" in Spanish and describes my son to a T.

My babysitter's faint voice calls from the bedroom. "We're back here, Jakey."

I can't tell Miss Louisa's age, but she has to be pushing seventy. That's the only reason I allow her to call me Jakey, because Dakota's nickname always made me cringe.

Miss Louisa was my last resort, but at least she's kind and treats my son well. But I don't know how much longer she'll be able to keep up with my hurricane, who just turned three over the summer.

"Daddy!" Asher howls, torpedoing across the room until he rams into my legs.

I scoop him up in my arms and kiss his sweaty forehead. "How's my little man? Did you have a good day?"

His smile vanishes and he wraps his arms around my neck to whisper in my ear. "I peepeed my pants."

My eyes meet Louisa's, and she gives me a patient smile.

"He'll learn. Asher got too excited about building sandcastles and forgot to let me know he had to go potty."

This is tough because he'd pretty much nailed potty training with my mom, but since we moved to Charming, everything's new for him, and he's having a tough time acclimating.

"Aww, Ash, it's okay, bud. Everyone has accidents when they're first learning."

His head pops up and those big blue eyes stare up at me. "You peeped your pants?"

I chuckle. "Not recently, but I'm sure Nana would tell you I had a few accidents in my day. So did your uncles."

His head jerks back like I just revealed a national secret. "Weally?" He means *really*, but we haven't nailed the R sound yet.

"I promise. We just gotta take one day at a time. Tomorrow will be better." I hug my little stinker, wishing I could be home more. It's late. After eight. I still have to give him a bath and get him to bed before I hit the books. He should probably already be asleep, but I'd rather spend some time with him every day and let him snooze late in the mornings.

Louisa grabs her purse. "He ate chicken nuggets and some applesauce. Did you already eat dinner, or do you want me to make you a sandwich before I leave?"

For a second, I hear another voice asking me if I want a sandwich. It makes something in me ache. I don't know why I'm not over Charlie ghosting me. It's fucked up, but I miss her more than Dakota.

Once I realized what my ex had been doing behind my back, she was dead to me. Charlotte, though... It's weird as hell not having her in my life anymore. And as much as I thanked her for taking care of Asher, I'm seeing now that I didn't appreciate how she took care of me too. Always feeding me. Always helping me if I needed a study buddy. Always knowing how to cheer me up after Dakota reamed me out for something stupid. Just being an amazing friend.

Did I run Charlie off? Did I do something to hurt her? Was Dakota lying about why her sister left? When I'm not pissed about her leaving, I'm still tormented. It keeps me up at night. Is Charlotte okay? Does she have friends? Is she still in school? Her family doesn't give a shit about her, and it makes me wonder who's looking out for her now.

Realizing I never responded, I muster a smile. "Thanks, Miss Louisa. I brought some dinner home from the cafeteria." I love this sweet woman. She's been such a blessing in our chaotic lives.

I have to admit the athletic amenities at Lone Star are top notch. There's a late-night athletic dining hall that caters to jocks. They have mountains of takeout boxes ready to go at all hours. If I missed the cafeteria hours at NTU, I was shit out of luck.

Ash sneaks a few of my fries as he watches me gobble down my meal. I was running late and grabbed whatever was closest. Typically I wouldn't be tossing back a cheeseburger during the season, but considering it's my second week of classes, right before another big game, and I'm stressed as fuck, I figure I'm doing okay.

After I wrangle the kid into the tub, I sit on the toilet seat as he plays with his toys. He's wearing a mask my brother got him, and he periodically dips his whole body under water so he can pretend he's snorkeling.

"Ash, let's take that off so we can wash your face, buddy."

He tosses it over his head, and it goes crashing into the corner where it knocks over the shampoo and body wash. Jesus. How the hell did my mom deal with four of us?

After I scrub down my hellion, he holds out his arms while I wrap him in a towel.

"Use the hairdriver!"

Hairdriver? I chuckle. My kid always entertains me. "You want me to blow-dry your hair?"

"Yeah!" He shakes his head like a wild dog coming out of the rain.

By the time he's dry and I've wrangled him into some pajamas, I'm ready to pass out, but I still have homework. I'll need to make some coffee if I want to get more done tonight.

I tuck Asher into his big-boy bed, his birthday present from my mom. "Listen, bud, I know we haven't spent a lot of time together since we moved here, but I have a treat for you this weekend."

His eyes light up. "A tweet?"

"How would you like to go to the park on Sunday? There's a playground we haven't gone to yet, and there are supposed to be dogs we can pet. I have to take photos for something, but that will probably only take a few minutes. Then we can play."

Coach Santos asked us to help his daughter with a fundraiser, and I'm so indebted to the man, I'll do anything he needs me to.

"Dogs?" Asher leaps out of bed and starts jumping up and down. "I wuv dogs!"

He's been asking me for a pet since he learned what they were. It sucks we can't have one, but I have my hands full as it is. My first order of business when I get drafted is getting my son a puppy.

Ash howls with glee as he flings himself on me.

I hug him, smiling but exhausted. I never should've brought this up at bedtime because now he's hyper—lesson learned—but it makes me happy to see my kid so excited even though it's gonna take him longer to go to sleep.

Definitely gonna need that coffee now.

5

JAKE

Ash and I cruise down the street with the windows rolled down and classic rock blaring from the stereo. Charming, Texas, is one of those small towns that belongs on a postcard.

The downtown area has cobblestone brick along the main drag and Bronco-colored flowers on every corner. Locals say 'howdy' or nod in greeting, not just to me but to everyone. And the baristas at the Rise 'N Grind Coffee House remember my name and how I like my coffee and save me empanadas on Sundays. It's hard not to fall in love with this place.

Once we get to the park, Asher swings from me like I'm his personal jungle gym. We trek under the giant brick archway and onto a grassy hill. It's warm and sunny, and I have the whole afternoon to love up on my kid. It's gonna be a good day.

I switch Ash to my other arm because I'm sore.

Yesterday's game was close, but we pulled it out in the end. We're now two and oh. I got a little game time. Not a ton. Not as much as I was hoping to get, but it's still early in the season. Coach knows what my goals are, and I just have to trust him.

It's a scary concept. I don't want to trust anyone anymore, but Coach Santos is basically the only person in my life besides my mom who thinks I can hack D1 football, and I aim to prove I was a good bet.

Across the field, I spot my teammates. They're waiting around under some trees next to several dog crates.

"Hey, bud. Race you to that tree." I point it out and watch my kid streak across the park. I chuckle and jog after him. I have every intention of wearing him out so he goes to bed early.

After I scoop him up and toss him over my shoulder, I join my teammates Cameron Fletcher and Billy Babcock, whose eyes are glued to the ass of some blonde who is bent over one of the dogs.

"I didn't know we were supposed to be wearing our football gear," I say. The guys are sporting white t-shirts, football pants, and cleats.

Billy shrugs like he can't speak and check out a chick at the same time. Cam points over his shoulder. "I only heard about it today."

One of the cheerleaders I've seen around the field house jogs up to me. She's decked out in her cheer outfit and full makeup. She looks like a young Zoe Saldana with thick, beautiful hair and a winning smile. "Hi, I'm Roxy. I think you know my dad."

"Yeah, I know the Saint."

She rolls her eyes playfully and grabs my shoulder. "Don't call him that. It'll go to his head."

This girl is definitely flirting with me. She's a stunner, but there's no way I'll go there with Coach's daughter. I'm not a dumbass.

And after that fiasco called Dakota, I'll never do another hookup. Hell, I might never date again. Yes, I'm at risk for a serious case of tendonitis in my hand from all the jerking off, but if it keeps me from ever engaging another drama queen, it's worth it.

I smile politely and turn my kiddo around so I have a reason to move away from Roxy. "This is my son, Asher."

"Oh my God, you have a son! He's gorgeous just like his daddy. Hi, cutie!"

Roxy is definitely a cheerleader. She's loud and excited and her energy makes me nervous.

That's when the blonde stands up and whips around, her ponytail flying.

Stunned blue eyes meet mine.

Eyes that look exactly like my son's.

And my ex's.

What the fuck?

I open my mouth. Close it.

It probably takes me a full minute before I can say anything. "Charlotte?" I'm so shocked, I almost drop Asher. "What the hell are you doing here?"

She flinches like I've slapped her, and I'm suddenly so fucking mad at her for how she disappeared, I can barely breathe.

How does your best friend of five years up and leave without a word? Why couldn't she tell me what was going on? Leave me a message. Something. Anything. Even if it was to tell me to fuck off.

When she doesn't say anything, I turn to leave. I can't do this.

"Wait! Jake, wait. Please." The pleading in her voice makes me freeze.

In the back of my mind, I hear my grandmother. *Ten paciencia, mijo.* Be patient.

Sorry, 'buela. She's been gone for a few years now, but when I lose my temper, I try to remind myself of her. *Abuelita* never got mad at me and my brothers, even when we were little dicks, which was often.

Staring at the ground, I take a few deep breaths until Charlotte's beat-up Reeboks enter my peripheral vision. She got those for her birthday in high school. Dakota would never wear anything but the latest and greatest clothes that companies sent her to model on her social media. It annoyed me that she couldn't just wear generic shit. That she always had to be so put together.

I don't know why the hell I'm thinking about Dakota right now. If I could bleach her from my brain forever, I would.

"Asher, hi. It's your aunt Charlie. Remember?"

I close my eyes when I hear her voice. Conflict wars within me. I can't explain why it feels so good to be near her.

And so fucking maddening.

Suddenly shy, my son burrows his face in my neck, and I lift my head.

Charlotte's light blonde hair is tied up, which makes her blue eyes huge. She's wearing a t-shirt and jean shorts with those old tennis shoes and her face is free of makeup. She's gorgeous in a natural way I've always loved. She's always been slender, petite, but now she's rocking a few more curves.

My dick sits up and takes notice.

What the fuck am I doing? This is my ex's sister, asshole.

I tilt my head back to stare at the sky. Seeing Charlie again after all this time is like taking an unexpected tackle and getting the wind knocked out of me. It pisses me off that I have any reaction at all. She disappeared without a word. It devastated me in a way I hadn't expected.

I finally turn to her. "No. He doesn't remember you. Because you left."

Her eyes tear up, and I feel like an ass. I sigh and look around. Everyone who's here for the photoshoot is staring at us. Dakota always made a production wherever we went, and it makes my skin crawl. Ironic given how much I loved being the center of attention in high school. After games, I felt like a god, strutting around campus like I owned the place. Now I keep my head down and try to get shit done without screwing up. It's a tall order.

I stalk off about fifteen feet until my teammates can't over-hear. Charlie is frozen in place, but when she realizes I'm waiting for her, she runs over.

"Is my sister here?" she asks, her voice wavering as she glances around nervously.

"Why the fuck would she be here? We broke up two years ago." I could handle breaking up. What I couldn't deal with was the way Dakota took off to Los Angeles without skipping a beat, never once bothering to see Asher. Her mom Waverly stopped by to see him sometimes, but even that tailed off.

The shock on Charlie's face seems genuine, but I'm not inclined to trust one of the Darling sisters. Fool me once and all that.

"What happened?" Her soft voice, so full of compassion, really would've had me collapsing like a deck of cards a few years ago.

"Don't pretend you care."

"Of course I care, Jake."

I laugh. It hits me out of nowhere, and I can't stop laughing. It's an ugly sound, and I kinda hate myself for being so cold, but I've been through hell thanks to Charlotte's family. I'm not ready to play nice. "Really? So disappearing off the face of the planet without a word is how you show people you care? Good to know."

"Without a word?" Her eyebrows pull tight. "I left you a note."

"Was something wrong with your phone? You couldn't text like one of the other seven hundred times you messaged me?" My eyes narrow. "I didn't get a damn note. You left campus and changed your number." I know because, like an asshole, I called and called until I broke down and asked her mom what happened. Waverly flicked her manicured fingers over some invisible lint on her tailored dress and said Charlotte was being a brat and changed her number.

I've never known Charlie to be a brat, but then she'd never ghosted me before.

"I swear I left you a note. I waited until you went to the gym and Dakota had left for the day, and I used the spare key y'all gave me to get into your apartment. I left you both notes."

It pains me to hear that she deliberately avoided me. "Where? Where did you leave them?"

Her brows furrow again. "I put hers by the coffeepot with the spare key and yours under the playbook on your nightstand. I swear, Jake. I would never leave without saying something."

"Well, I never got it." Dakota swore up and down she hadn't heard from her sister. Although I do remember coming home one day and finding several trash bags by the front door. Dakota had been in a cleaning frenzy, which was unusual because she was not a tidy person. "What did you say in this alleged note?"

Charlotte's cheeks fire up like she's sitting under a heating lamp. "I, uh, well..."

"Spit it out, Charlotte," I say as Asher wiggles, tired of sitting still.

"It's just... I needed some space."

I wait for the rest, because what the hell does that mean? But when she doesn't say anything, I let out another unamused laugh. Un-fucking-believable. "So you take off, change your number, and ghost everyone you know because you *needed space*. Totally reasonable. And you've been here the whole time?"

She looks down. "Yeah."

Coach Santos always says we have to talk through things. That not bottling up our feelings when we're butthurt is the key to working through our issues.

But after this conversation, I sure as shit don't feel better.

Roxy trots up to us. "Sorry to interrupt, Charlie, but we'd better finish our shoot before we lose the good light. Plus, some of the dogs are getting restless."

Asher grabs my face. "Puppy dogs?"

"Yeah, bud. Puppy dogs." Damn, as much as I wanna bail, I promised the kid. I turn to Charlie. "Can I show Asher the animals?"

She nods, her eyes lighting up. "Sure. Of course."

"We won't be staying, though. Hope you have someone else you can shoot."

That light dims, and once again, I feel like a dick, but what the hell am I supposed to do? Sit there and smile for the camera like an asshole? Pretend Charlotte didn't torpedo our friendship because she *needed space*?

Roxy looks back and forth between us before she frowns and wraps her arm around Charlie. As they're walking back to the others, Roxy yells over her shoulder. "No worries, dude. The baseball team is coming next weekend. We'll be rolling in hot guys. We don't need you."

That's when I remember who I'm dealing with.

Coach's daughter.

Damn, I hope I didn't screw myself by bailing on this.

6

CHARLOTTE

I'M SO SHAKEN, I can barely hold the camera. Roxy steps up to me and whispers in my ear, "You're doing great. This is the last guy for the day."

I nod, grateful to have Roxy. I try to focus on Cameron and the bulldog he's holding, but it's tough to concentrate. Somehow I manage to get through the shoot. In a daze, I thank him and Billy, who nudges me with his elbow. "Wanna grab a bite to eat when you're done here?"

After chugging some water, I roll my eyes. "That's an improvement. Usually you just ask if I wanna bang." I wipe the sweat off my forehead. I'm exhausted. Hungry. Embarrassed. No, humiliated.

Because even though Jake tried to keep our discussion from prying eyes, I get the impression everyone working on the calendar heard us talking—cheerleaders, football players, bystanders at the park.

Billy hums. "Just thought you could use a pick-me-up after..."

I appreciate him not spelling out what he witnessed. "Billy, are you trying to be nice?" He and Cam used to rent rooms from my friend Maggie because she has a huge house, so I got to know them a little over the summer. Billy's attractive with dirty blond hair, scruff along his chin, and several intricate tattoos along his muscular arms. He's a decent guy, but a total horndog. And if the rumors are true, he and Cam sometimes tag-team their dates, which will never be my scene. I'm a one-guy kind of girl. Not that I've ever had a guy.

Billy chuckles. "I'm trying to turn over a new leaf. Take girls out instead of just asking if they wanna fuck. Besides, I told Maggie I'd keep an eye out for you. Keep your cute ass out of trouble."

"I still won't sleep with you." Despite my better judgment, I turn to where Jake and Asher are playing on the jungle gym on the other side of the park. It hurts to know Asher doesn't remember me, but what did I expect? He was a baby the last time I saw him.

"Really don't want Ramirez to beat the shit out of me, so I get it. That's fine. But I'm starving, and I figure you are too. Cam and I want to take you and Rox out." He holds out his hands. "Just as friends. I swear."

"Trust me, Jake won't care." It's like we were never friends. My eyes sting, but I can't be upset with him. I did this to myself. I was too chicken to tell him how I felt in high school, and I only compounded everything when I left NTU without talking to him first.

"I don't know about that." Billy's voice lowers. "Aww, hell, Chuck. Don't cry."

I sniffle and blink several times. "I'm not crying. It's allergies."

Jake stops playing with Asher to glance over at us, and my heart sinks at the cold expression on his face. There are icebergs in the Arctic warmer than the look he gives me.

Billy makes that humming noise again before he slips his

beefy arm over my shoulders. "Doesn't care, huh? I might regret this later, but how 'bout we give him something to care about?"

"What?"

That's when the doofus pulls me into his chest and kisses me out of the blue. There's no tongue, thank God. Just the hard press of his bristly mouth against mine.

It's fine, I guess.

When he pulls away, he smacks his lips. "You taste minty."

I sigh, and it's not because he swept me off my feet. "That was my first kiss." I don't mention I was saving it for someone special.

His eyes widen. "Like, ever?"

"Yes, and now I need to go home and write about it in my diary," I say sarcastically before I turn to pack my gear, a little upset my first kiss wasn't more magical.

He yells, "I can't tell if you're pulling my leg right now."

"Life is full of mysteries," I yell back as I check on the dogs we brought today, but after a few minutes, once the shock wears off, I trot after Billy and tug on his jersey. When he turns to me, I whisper, "Maybe ask next time." When he doesn't seem to know what I'm talking about, I add, "Before you kiss someone. I'm okay with it, but someone else might not be. You know what I'm saying?"

He freezes and rubs the back of his neck. "Shit. Sorry, Chuck. Didn't think of it like that."

I give him a patient smile. Billy is really clueless sometimes, but since he's trying to be a better person, I figure he needed to hear that.

When I get back to the animals, I give them all fresh water and treats. It helps get my mind off that very public fiasco with Jake. Merle pulls up with his enormous van, and we start loading up the animals. I was a little worried this would freak them out, but they've loved all of the attention. I swear some of them were smiling when we took their photos. One of the cheer-leaders is even going to adopt one of the dogs, so I consider today a success despite that very public conversation with Jake.

After Merle takes off, I scroll through the images on my camera. Roxy peeks over my shoulder. "Those are awesome!"

"Thanks. We have way more pics than pages in the calendar. Especially if we do more shoots." Roxy really did schedule half the baseball team next Sunday.

"That's a good problem, though, right?"

I nod. "It'll be hard to pick."

"Maybe we should use them all. We could make flyers for the shelter with the images that don't go in the calendar. Does the model clearance you used cover that?"

"I'll look it over again tonight just to be sure, but it should be cool."

Roxy waits until we're home to bring up the neon-pink elephant in the room. "So you and Jake Ramirez? That's who you were talking about the other day? Your sister's boyfriend?"

Shame burns my face as I nod.

"And he's her baby daddy?"

"It's as bad as you think it is."

"Did you guys, um, ever sleep together?"

I recoil. "God, no. Never. We hugged at graduation, and he's given me noogies from time to time. Trust me, the infatuation was completely one-sided." Roxy must think I'm full of shit to be crying about never having dated or been kissed.

Scratch that. Because now I've been kissed. I'm not sure what got into Billy today to plant that on me.

Roxy pauses, her lips pursed. "Are you sure? Jake seemed really riled up for a guy who doesn't feel anything for you."

"I swear. He was very committed to Dakota. You probably overheard us talking, but they broke up. So I think he was extra pissed about that."

The lightbulb goes off. "Holy shit. You're *Dakota Darling's* sister?"

Here we go. "Yup."

"And you were in that show *Little Darlings* when you were a kid? Aww, were you the one who sucked her thumb?"

Much to my mother's horror, I became an internet sensation when I was a child, but not the kind she was hoping for, all thanks to an image of me sucking my thumb. So while Kota charmed the masses, I was the butt of all the jokes. When someone's sad they lost a promotion or the big job or their girlfriend, their buddies send them this meme—a tear-streaked Charlotte Darling, sucking her thumb like a loser. I mean, I was six years old. You'd think people would have some compassion.

Growing up, I preferred being invisible to being mocked.

Except I became invisible at home too. I was always the odd one out in my family. It didn't help that Kota and my mom had so many secrets. Secrets they never bothered to share with me. I'd see those two whispering, almost angry with each other, but the second I walked in, they'd stop talking. Every time.

Roxy grimaces. "Sorry I flirted with Jake. I did that whole arm touch thing."

"What arm touch thing?"

"This one." She steps up to me and grabs my arm while she stares up at me, all doe-eyed.

"Wow, that's pretty good. I'd totally bang you." We laugh, and I give her a hug. "I don't have any claim to Jake, so there's no need to apologize." And if I'm a tiny bit jealous she touched him, I'll get over it.

That interaction gives me pause, though. Roxy is so good at interacting with guys while I'm always so awkward.

"Um. This might sound crazy, but could you maybe show me how to do that? How to flirt?"

She claps and jumps up and down. "I can definitely teach

you that. By the time I'm done with you, you'll have Jake down on his hands and knees, begging you to give him a shot."

"*No*, I'm not doing this for Jake. In fact, I'm more determined than ever to move on." Jake obviously hates me. As painful as that is, maybe it's exactly what I need to shore up my heart. If I had just attended Lone Star State right out of high school, we could have avoided all the drama. But I never got a chance to get over him because I tagged along with Jake and Kota to NTU. "Except I don't know anything about flirting or relationships. I'm pretty sure you saw Billy lay one on me out of the blue? That was the first time I'd ever been kissed."

"Oh, hell, honey. That's completely unacceptable."

"Right? I'm a senior in college. By the time I graduate, I'd love to at least have some experience with men."

She gives me a wicked smile. "You've come to the right person. I can definitely get you *experience*."

7

JAKE

With a grunt, I finish my last set of pull-ups before I release the bar and drop to the floor. I nod at Cam, who's on the machine next to me, before I reach for my water bottle. I usually enjoy early morning weights before class because it helps me focus, but today my head is all over the place.

I tossed and turned all night. Couldn't stop replaying my conversation with Charlotte. Couldn't stop seeing the hurt in her eyes. Couldn't stop feeling pissed about the way she left.

And for some fucked-up reason, I couldn't stop seeing Billy fucking Babcock pull her into his arms and kiss her.

Now that I think about it, I've never seen her with a boyfriend. In high school, she hung around a couple of guys, but they were nothing serious. I can't remember her dating anyone in college.

I'll admit I'm conflicted. Part of me wants to protect her like I always have, and the other part feels strangely possessive. Which... I don't understand.

I gather my stuff and head to the locker room, which means I have to pass Billy on the leg press.

"Hey, man," he calls out. "Got a minute?"

I clench my fist. "What's up?"

He sits up and wipes his face with a towel. "You were a dick to Charlie yesterday. Just wanted to point it out. I know we're all supposed to be nice to you or whatever 'cause you've got a kid and you're a transfer, but I don't understand why you had to shit all over that girl when she was busting her ass to do something cool."

I take a deep breath and will myself to react calmly. "You don't know my history with Charlotte, so maybe you should mind your own damn business. And for the record, I was there to help Coach's daughter."

"You're right. I don't know your history. But what I do know is that Chuck barely spoke when I first saw her around campus. She was quiet and withdrawn and reminded me of a ghost. It's taken a lot to draw her out of her shell. I don't know why you had to be an asswipe to her."

Chuck? His little nickname irks me in a way I can't describe. "Funny that you use the word 'ghost' to describe her, because that's exactly what she did two years ago when she took off without telling anyone."

He lowers his voice. "Bro, I will readily admit I'm a fuckup. Ask anyone. As the president of Team Fuckup, I always recognize this trait in others. But I have to tell ya, I don't see that in Chuck. So if she bailed on you, there had to be a good reason."

It's what I've been telling myself this whole time. That Charlotte had a good reason to leave. She must've. But what? And why didn't she tell me what it was when I saw her yesterday?

I'm not gonna share my thoughts on this with Babcock, though. "What's it to you? You guys dating?"

He smirks. "Now why in the world would you care?"

"I don't." It's a lie. I obviously do care. Not sure why. "Just curious."

"Hmm. Interesting."

I hate the smug look in his eyes. "Treat her well, asshole, or you'll have to deal with me."

His smile widens. "It's good to see the stoic has some emotions in there. You'd best channel that on Saturday." We play Texas Tech this weekend.

My attention snags on that word. Stoic? Me? I feel like the whole world can see through me, see that I'm a volcano ready to spew lava everywhere.

Against my better judgment, I decide to ask him about Roxy. They seem to be friends, and I don't want her to be upset with me and go to her father to complain.

"Listen, I didn't mean to bail on Roxy. Can you tell her that for me? Tell her I'm sorry for taking off before we took the photos?"

"You know it's not Roxy's project, right? It's Charlie's. She's trying to keep that animal shelter open. She can't adopt more of them since she already has two." He chuckles, and I hate that this douchebag knows more about Charlotte than I do.

"Charlie's doing the calendar?"

"Yeah. She's been volunteering at Second Chances for the last year. I think it's been good for her. It's drawn her out of her shell."

I'm still thinking about Charlotte and her shell and the fact that Billy is all wrapped up in her business when I get home that night. I could really use a long shower, beer, some pizza, and a hard fuck, none of which are plausible at the moment.

I pick up my wiggle worm and smooch Asher's sticky face. "Hey, bud. You have a good day?"

He's rambling about his Legos and sandcastles as I hoist him onto my shoulders so we can walk Miss Louisa out to her car. It's getting late, and this isn't the best neighborhood.

She's unusually quiet. After Miss Louisa opens her car, she turns to me. "Jakey, I have some bad news. My son wants me to move down to San Antonio next month so he can keep an eye on me. My hip's been giving me trouble, and I can't get up and down steps like I used to. He has a nice one-story with a spare bedroom that he's going to set up for me."

Fuck. "Next month?" I rub my throbbing temple. I knew I was going to have to find more babysitters. Just didn't think I'd need to do it so quickly.

"Maybe six weeks. It depends on my son." She pats my shoulder. "I'm so sorry to do this to you right now. I know how busy your schedule is."

Inside, I'm freaking out, but the rational part of my brain knows I need to chill. As much as I want everyone to make my football season the center of their universe, it isn't. "I'm not gonna lie, this poses a challenge, but nothing's more important than your health. I understand. We're gonna miss you, though."

She opens her arms, and the kid and I give her a hug.

Asher and I watch her drive away until her taillights disappear.

What the hell am I gonna do now?

8

CHARLOTTE

I FLINCH when Roxy gets too aggressive with that curling iron.

She lets out a little huff of annoyance. "Hold still or I'm going to burn you."

"Is that a threat?" I tease.

"I'm almost done, I swear. Your hair's gonna look fab."

I'm sitting on the edge of the tub while she does her thing. I'm not great with hair and makeup. That was my sister's domain. I can't count the number of times I milled around taking photos of Kota while she was getting ready to go out.

With Jake.

I close my eyes and give in to the temptation. Let myself think about Jake at the park last weekend. When I first saw him, I wanted to drop everything and fling myself into his arms, but the expression on his face stopped me cold. I'd secretly imagined our reunion and all the things I'd say to him, all the things I'd apologize for, but that's not what came out of my mouth. Just like every other time, I fumbled—big time—and made things worse.

That was new. Jake's never been upset with me. He and my sister would have crazy arguments, but he's never once raised his voice with me. Not that he yelled at me last weekend. No, this was worse. There was a hurt in his eyes I hadn't expected. Hurt and so much anger.

At this point, I don't know how to make things right with him. I used to think I was doing him a favor by leaving. No man needs his girlfriend's sister mooning over him.

But how do I say that to him? Do I just confess that I've been in love with him for years and seeing him date Dakota was slowly killing me?

I'm curious how Jake and my sister worked out custody. Does she visit every few weeks? Does he take Asher up to NTU?

My nephew is so big and beautiful. I want to hug him and never let go.

"Hey, what's going on? Your eyes went glassy, and if you cry, I'm going to scrub your face and do your makeup all over again."

I laugh and sniffle and carefully wipe my lower lashes so I don't smear the mascara. "I'm fine. I swear. Although I'm not sure I'm ready to go on a blind date."

"Well, it's not *totally* a blind date, but I think you'll feel comfortable with this person, which will give you a chance to use those moves I taught you." Roxy holds up a hand. "Before you freak out, you should know he understands you're just friends. He's not at home right now counting his condoms."

I chuckle. "That's good to know."

I'm not completely surprised when Billy shows up at my door. The bouquet of flowers, though, that is a surprise.

"I have to be honest, Billy," I say as I smell the pretty roses. "I didn't have you pegged as a flowers kind of guy."

"I'm really not. Besides my homecoming date in high school, you're the only woman I've ever gotten flowers for."

"I'm honored. Thanks. These are lovely."

He clears his throat. "You look hot. I'm digging that shirt. Makes your tits look amazing."

"Um, thanks?"

Roxy pops into the living room. "Have fun, kids! Be sure to use protection!"

I roll my eyes because I know she's teasing and push Billy out the front door. "Ignore her. We're not having sex."

"You've mentioned this before. I don't know why I'm getting ruled out. I'm a nice guy, I have a big dick, I—"

Reaching up, I shove my hand over his mouth. "No. Whatever you plan to say, just... no."

He's laughing as he bites my hand. "Just teasing, Chuck. I like ruffling your feathers for some reason."

"What exactly did Roxy say about tonight?" I ask as I wipe my palm on my jeans.

He tosses his arm over my shoulder. "I'm supposed to let you use your moves on me. Teach you how to flirt." Billy winks.

"Ugh." Hanging my head, I cover my eyes with my hand. "This is humiliating."

"We'll up your game. Don't you worry. And I have the perfect place."

After all the buildup, I'm caught off guard when he parks in front of the Rise 'N Grind. "This is your big plan?"

"Patience, grasshopper. If my sources are correct, this will all make sense soon."

We grab two iced coffees and some cinnamon cookies and camp out in the corner. I'm busy shoving food into my mouth—I'm not excited to spill my lackluster dating history to Billy—when Jake walks in with two drop-dead-gorgeous girls. One has beautiful, thick blonde hair like my sister, and the other one has dark tresses piled up on her head.

They're batting their eyelashes at him and flirting as they order drinks. Jake puts his hand on the blonde bombshell's back as they walk to a nearby table.

Is he seeing someone already? Am I going to have to watch

him date someone new? Or worse, what if he turns into a manwhore and screws his way through our class?

He glances up and our eyes meet. I look down and wait until he's seated to return my attention to Billy, who's watching me carefully.

"I can't do this," I whisper and blink back the sudden sting in my eyes.

"Do you trust me?"

"No." We stare at each other a second before we start laughing. I dab at my eyes and tilt my hair, grateful it hides me from the other side of the coffee house.

"Look, Chuck, you wanted to practice flirting. Don't let Ramirez being here turn you into a coward. No offense, but you're always a little pill with me. Why don't you show him what you're really made of?"

"Has anyone ever told you that you're kind of an asshole?"

"Every day." He sips his drink. "So what's it going to be? You gonna show me your sexy moves or what?"

I smile, embarrassed, and tuck my head down. "I don't have any sexy moves. That kiss the other day really was my first one."

He clicks his tongue. "That thing you did just now was pretty sexy."

"What thing?"

"You blushed and looked up at me all sweet and soft. I dig it."

"But I don't know how to do that on command."

"That's probably what's so enticing. You don't even realize you're a little morsel."

"What if I do something dumb? I'll be embarrassed."

"Stop caring about what everyone else thinks. You're wasting your energy on that shit. Do you think I care what people think about me?"

I shake my head.

"Exactly. Now do exactly what I say." Pretty sure I'm going to regret this, but I nod. He glances over his shoulder at Jake's table. Jake is facing us, and the girls are sitting on either side of him. It gives us a clear view of him, unfortunately. "Okay, Chuck. I want you to thread your fingers through mine and laugh like I'm funny. I mean, I *am* funny, so this should be easy."

"What exactly is this supposed to teach me?"

"Stop stalling and do it."

God, I'm going to regret this, but I do as he instructs. Reaching across the small table, I thread my fingers through his and try not to squirm from the awkwardness.

He smiles, lifts my hand to his mouth, but pauses. "This okay?"

With an embarrassed smile, I nod.

After kissing the back of my hand, he motions to me. "Now laugh. Remember that I'm a handsome dude, the coolest, funniest guy you know."

I chuckle, and he shakes his head.

"That was pathetic. Do it with gusto, Chuck."

I resist the urge to roll my eyes and force out a laugh. It reminds me of Dakota and how her loud laugh always gets everyone's attention.

I don't need to look to know Jake is staring at us right now.

Squeezing Billy's giant paw, I whisper, "Did you do this on purpose? Did you know Jake would be here?"

"Remember how I said Jake cares?"

"Yes."

"If you could see his expression right now, you'd believe me, but don't look now or you'll ruin the moment. Keep staring into my eyes. Make me believe you like me."

"Don't make this weird."

He studies me so intently, it makes me uncomfortable. "If you just had some confidence, Chuck, you'd be a stone-cold fox. You have gorgeous eyes. A beautiful face. A hot little body. A sassy personality that bites back when provoked. All good things. How's that for weird?"

My face heats, and I look away, another awkward chuckle leaving my lips. "Stop pretending you like me."

"I'm not pretending at all. I'd totally fuck you through your headboard if given the opportunity, but I get the feeling you're into someone else."

Ugh. "Roxy told you?"

"She didn't have to. It's written all over your face. You don't give *me* those sad puppy dog eyes. Ramirez is the lucky bastard, huh?"

I brave a glance at his table. The blonde has her hand on Jake's arm. He's smiling at her, and she laughs. It's so loud, everyone, predictably, turns to look at her. Then she leans close to him and whispers something in his ear that makes his cheeks flush.

Seriously, fuck Jake and all the reasons he's made me cry over the years. I'm so done.

Exasperated, I turn to Billy. "I'm not waiting around for Jake. I'm more than ready to move on."

"We'll see about that. Oh, shit. Come on. Hurry." He yanks me out of my chair and hustles me to the door, where we practically ram into Jake and his two dates. "Ramirez, hey. Funny seeing you here."

"Remarkable, really," he says dryly. "Did you sign up to babysit too?"

Billy chuckles. "No, but I'm thinking Charlotte here would be great with your kid."

I close my eyes. Right now, I truly hate my life. Why would Billy say that? "I don't know, Billy—"

"Nah, we're cool," Jake says, interrupting me. His expression is cool as he tilts his head toward the girls. "Buffy and Yvette have offered to watch Asher."

Billy leans forward. "Did you say your name is Buffy? As in, *The Vampire Slayer*?"

She giggles and leans into Jake. "What can I say? I'm good with big sticks."

"Of course you are, lovely." Billy winks at her, and I roll my eyes as he turns to Jake. "Buffy and Yvette look like they have a *ton* of childcare experience. Kudos, man. Looks like you have two very responsible babysitters. You and your big stick will be all set."

He did not just say that.

Yvette, the blonde, steps up to Jake and winds her arm through his. "Don't worry. We'll do *whatever* Jake needs."

I laugh, unamused. "I bet you will," I say under my breath as I drag Billy through the door.

I've practiced flirting enough for one night.

9

CHARLOTTE

FOR THE LOVE OF GOD. "Duke, please poop. Please." I swat at the mosquito gnawing on my arm.

Duke and I have been walking down the road for the last forty minutes, and he's yet to do number two. If he doesn't take a dump now, he'll do it tonight in the corner of my bedroom. I speak from experience.

I've been so wrapped up in my own head, thinking about seeing Jake at the coffee shop with his two *babysitters* last week, that I don't realize how far we've gone until I look around and realize the road is deserted. There's a housing development on one side that's still several months from being done, and a forest on the other. Except for the sound of crickets, it's silent. Still. And *very* dark.

"Duke, this is creepy. Hurry and poop, so we can go home." I turn him around and cross the street to the forested side. Maybe he'll sniff out a good place to crap on the way back.

He finally squats and does his business.

"What a good boy!" I break out the treats and reward him with one. Duke's doing much better. He's putting on a little weight, and he's not quite as shy as he used to be. He now greets me and Roxy with doggy kisses and a wagging tail when we get home from class, but he's still super skittish around strangers.

Behind us, the sound of an approaching car breaks the silence. I speed-walk toward the lone streetlight and pray that's not a serial killer. Damn my sister for making me watch all of those killer clown movies. I'm glancing around, wishing we hadn't gone so far, when a familiar blue Dodge Avenger pulls up.

"What are you doing out here?" Jake's gruff voice instantly has me relieved and irritated. I can't see him because he's yelling through the passenger window from the driver's side.

"What does it look like I'm doing?" I pull on Duke's leash, and thankfully, he follows.

"It's dark."

"Thanks for the heads-up, Sherlock. Hadn't noticed."

"I'm serious, Charlotte. You shouldn't be walking around bumfuck by yourself in the middle of the night." The gravel crunches beneath his tires as he follows me. I'm hoping he's done with the lecture, but nope. "Let me give you a ride home."

He must really be worried I'll be strangled by a psycho. Still, I'm too proud to accept the handout. "I can manage fine, thanks."

"Don't be stubborn."

"Don't be overbearing."

Blissful silence greets me. Then... "I don't remember you being such a smartass."

"I don't remember you being such an asshole," I yell back.

When he doesn't respond, I fully expect him to hit the gas and leave us in the dust, but that's wishful thinking because he shuts off the engine. *Damn it.*

I flinch at the sound of his car door slamming shut. Jake stalks up to me. His hair is damp and in disarray. He's wearing a fitted t-shirt and joggers that cling to his muscular thighs, and he smells like he just stepped out of a shower. Why does this man have to be so freaking attractive?

He points behind him. "Either get in the car and let me drive you home, or prepare for me to follow you all the way back."

"Honest question, Jake. Why do you care? I've been getting a strong 'fuck off' vibe from you since our reunion in the park. Why are you doing this?"

Blowing out a breath, he runs his hand through his hair. "I might be pissed at you, but I don't want you to die. Is that a good enough reason?"

Stop with the swoony words, Jake. "You tried, and I declined. Your conscience is clear. I'm really and truly fine on my own."

His rugged square jaw tightens as he speaks through clenched teeth. "Charlotte, my long-lost friend. I would be devastated if you were hurt. Now please get your little ass in the car."

I chuckle at his serious expression and how it contrasts with the absurdly sweet tone of his voice. "And if I don't?"

My skin prickles under his intense stare.

Those beautiful dark brown eyes travel up and down my body in a way they've never done before. "I could always toss you over my shoulder," he says with a cocky smirk.

Don't read into this. Don't. "That's called kidnapping, Jake, and you could get two to twenty." I'm about to walk around him when he crouches at my feet and starts petting Duke. "He doesn't... like... strangers."

But Duke is licking Jake's face and wagging his tail excitedly.

Traitor.

"Come on, Duke. We have a frozen dinner calling our name."

Jake looks up at me and smiles. His dark eyes crinkle in the corners, and his dimples pop out. It's a lethal combination. God, I've missed his smiles. "He's beautiful. I remember how you always wanted a dog, but Dakota was allergic."

"He's not my dog. I mean, he is momentarily, but I have to return him to the shelter once he's rehabilitated." It's going to tear me up. I see the question in Jake's eyes. "I can't have dogs in my apartment. I'm kinda breaking the rules right now, but it was either that or let him be euthanized because he wouldn't eat."

"He's doing better now?"

"Yeah. He's doing great."

Jake's eyes go soft. "You've always had a big heart."

Don't. Read. Into. This. Because the moment he remembers why he's upset with me, he'll yank back those charming smiles, and I'll be devastated all over again.

Wanting to get this interaction over as soon as possible, I pull Duke toward the passenger side of Jake's car and get in. Duke hops in my lap without prompting.

Jake smiles again, and it makes my heart catapult painfully.

We drive in silence through the winding, desolate road that leads back to my subdivision.

There's one benefit to the darkness, though. It makes me brave.

Jake deserves to know the truth about why I left. Billy is right. I have to stop being such a coward.

I motion toward the white apartment building. "There, on the corner."

"This is where you live? Because I'm just down the street."

Of course he is. Always so close but so far away.

And then, with my heart pounding in my throat, I say the words I've been dreading. "I had feelings for you, Jake. That's why I left." I've been in love with him since we were fourteen, but I'm not brave enough to go that far.

When he doesn't say anything, I glance at him. His lips part, like he's about to say something but forgot what it was. I decide to put him out of his misery and fill the uncomfortable silence. "I couldn't sit there one more day while my sister bragged about all the times you guys screwed. Or listen to you guys fuck in the other room. Or watch how she treated you like crap while you accepted it like it was your due. So I left."

Stunned. That's the only way to describe his expression.

He swallows, his eyes remorseful. "I—I didn't know. Truly, I had no idea."

"Now you do." I reach for the door handle and spit out the next words as quickly as possible. "I left you my new phone number in that note. I know you don't believe me, but I did."

"Wait. There's a lot to unpack there, and I have some things... things I need to tell you too."

I shake my head. "Don't make this more awkward. You finally got the truth now, okay? Let me go dig a hole and bury myself in it. Feel free to ignore me the next time we run into each other."

"Charlie." His voice is soft. Gentle. It sends chills up my arms.

"It's late, Jake. Isn't Buffy or Yvette waiting for you at home?"

Without waiting for a reply, I jump out of the car, and fortunately, Duke follows. I bump into the girls on the first floor as they head out, the smell of potpourri wafting from their apartment. Too upset to speak, I wave as I frantically rush up the stairs. Fortunately, Roxy isn't home, so I'm free to wallow in my own stupid misery.

Once I'm locked in my room, I fling myself on my bed and let out all the tears.

Then I swear to myself this is the last time I let myself fall apart over Jake Ramirez.

10

JAKE

THUNDERSTRUCK, I sit there and watch Charlie race into her building. A light eventually appears on the second floor, and I catch a glimpse of her blonde hair streaking across her apartment through the sliding glass door on the patio before she disappears again.

What the hell just happened?

I don't remember driving home, but all of a sudden, I'm in my driveway.

Charlotte had feelings for me. That's why she left. I'm still so shocked, I turn off my car and sit there and stare into the darkness.

A million questions race through my mind. First of all, how was I so fucking clueless? Charlie always gave me such neutral, almost emotionless looks over the years we were friends, but tonight, it was like seeing behind that wall for the first time. There was so much pain in her eyes, I wanted to lift her onto my lap and hug her until her beautiful smile returned.

I think back to our year together at NTU. At all the times she'd look away when Dakota threw herself on my lap. At the way I'd sometimes catch Charlie staring at me, but then she'd act like she was just spacing out. How she'd go quiet when Dakota joked about her never dating.

Jesus, I was an idiot.

What else did I miss?

I force myself to concentrate on the week before Charlie left.

Oh, shit. Dakota pretended we were fucking in the other room. She thought it was hysterical. We argued about it afterward when I opened the bedroom door a minute later and realized Charlie had taken off.

And then Dakota baited me into walking out into the bedroom right after a shower while she was on a video call with her sister.

I was naked.

And sporting wood.

I groan and lean my head against the window and close my eyes. I'm not easily embarrassed, but that moment definitely goes down in my personal hall of shame.

At that point, my relationship with Dakota was hanging by a razor-thin thread. If it weren't for Charlie, I'm not sure we would've lasted that long. She was the buffer between me and her sister. Always being the peacemaker. Always doing things to ease our stress. Always helping however she could. Making us dinner. Babysitting Asher. Running our errands. Helping me study.

If the roles were reversed and I had to watch a woman I had feelings for be with another man, watch her walk into the bedroom naked, clearly to have sex, it would fuck me up.

And Dakota rubbed it in her face. Christ.

Did her sister know how Charlie felt?

Now that I think about it, Dakota's snide jokes that I spent too much time with her sister make sense. Maybe she never believed that we were completely platonic. Never believed that

Charlie and I really and truly were the best of friends—but that's it.

If I'm being honest with myself, I kept waiting for the kind of friendship I had with Charlie to take root with Dakota.

It obviously never did. By the time we broke up, I pretty much hated her. That's a horrible thought to have about the mother of your kid, but Dakota wrecked me, one small criticism at a time, and hammered the last nail in our coffin by fucking one of my teammates.

My mind snags on the letter Charlotte says she left me. She said she gave me her phone number.

I sit with that a moment... and I believe her.

I'm guessing Dakota found the note and figured her sister must've left me one too and tore up the apartment to find it. Then she pretended like she was cleaning to explain why everything was out of place.

I close my eyes, wondering how different the last two years would've been if I'd been able to reach Charlie. Just to make sure she was all right. Shit. She must've thought my silence meant I hated her. That I didn't call her 'cause I was pissed.

And I was, but only because she ghosted me and Ash without a word.

Suddenly, all the anger I've been harboring since Charlotte took off deflates. I get it. I do. Sweet, shy Charlotte couldn't deal, and since she didn't feel she could talk to me or her sister, she did the only thing she could—she left.

Without that veil of anger, I can see everything more clearly. Charlie probably thought she was doing us a favor. By taking herself out of the equation, she was protecting me and Dakota.

I close my eyes. *I was a total dick to her at the park. And the coffee shop.*

I'm an asshole.

I need to apologize to her.

It's possible she'll want space right now. Hell, she moved four hours from home to get away from me, and now we're living down the street from each other. If that's not ironic, I don't know what is.

I drag myself out of the car and up to my apartment where Buffy greets me with way too much cleavage on display. I swear she was wearing more clothes when she got here earlier. Averting my eyes, I drop the keys on the kitchen counter and check on Asher. He's sleeping soundly in his bed, sprawled out like a starfish.

When I return to the kitchen, I lean back against the counter. "Thanks for watching him, Buffy. How did things go?"

"So great! After dinner, he played with his Legos. I read him a few books before bed, and he went to sleep without a problem."

That's promising. Asher doesn't always go to bed without a struggle. "Perfect. How much do I owe you?" This was a trial run. Just two hours to see how things went before I put her on any kind of permanent rotation.

She trots up to me and puts her hand on my arm. "Want to hang out a bit? I don't have to be anywhere tonight."

Buffy is beautiful. A solid ten by anyone's measure. But I'm not going to fuck the babysitter. That spells disaster.

I gently remove her hand. "I have a busy morning, so I have to call it a day." I really hope I don't have to deal with this every time she watches Asher. I'd be more discerning in who I hire to babysit, but I don't have a lot of options at the moment. At least my son is safe. That's all that matters.

Jutting out her lower lip, she pouts, her fake eyelashes fluttering. She has no idea how much that turns me off. Dakota did shit like this. Not that I plan to date anytime soon, but if I eventually do, I want a woman who doesn't play games. Someone who says what she means. Someone who won't try to lead me around by my dick.

Once I pay Buffy and make sure she gets to her car safely, I flop on my bed. I replay that conversation with Charlotte in my head. Even though I'm exhausted, a part of me wishes I could run back to her apartment and make her listen to me. So I could explain a few things and apologize for my shitty attitude.

It'll have to wait.

She looked gorgeous tonight. Makeup-free. Just wearing a tank top and shorts. Her hair in that ponytail. Looking so damn cute with that dog dragging her down the street.

When I close my eyes, I'm suddenly assaulted with the memory of Charlotte taking Babcock's hand. Him kissing it and her blushing. Him mauling her in the park.

My chest goes tight, and I force a breath into my lungs.

Fuck. Please don't tell me I'm jealous.

Charlotte Darling is the last woman I need to have feelings for. Even if I am harboring some fondness for her, likely because I haven't seen her in so long, I could never get involved with her.

Because if Dakota finds out, she'll burn us both down to the ground.

No, Charlie and I will never happen. It looks like she's moved on with that asshole Babcock anyway.

That's a good thing, I tell myself as I unclench my fist. It'll give me time to get over whatever weird possessiveness I have about her. And we'll both get on with our lives.

What I don't understand is why he'd bring her to the Rise 'N Grind when he knew I was interviewing potential babysitters there. I'd been talking about it at practice, asking if the guys had friends who might be interested. Giving out all the details.

It's almost like he wanted me to see them together. Am I throwing off jealous vibes and he wanted to rub it in my face? What a dick.

Regardless of my feelings about the guy, I need to apologize to Charlotte for how shit's gone down since we ran into each other in the park. I'll give her a few days to cool off and then I'll track her down again. Maybe she'll even let me do that photo-shoot. If it'll help that animal shelter she obviously cares about, I'd like to help.

Even if that means I have to sit by and watch her date that asshole Babcock, I'll do it for her.

11

JAKE

"You okay, man?" Cam asks.

"Yup," I mumble as I try to shake off my latest fuckup.

Ezra Thomas throws the perfect spiral pass over traffic, and I'm the idiot who drops the ball. Worse? It was third down, so now we have to punt and lose possession to Iowa.

I unclip my helmet and brush the sweat out of my eyes.

"Ramirez!" Coach shouts. "Get over here."

Fuck. I prepare myself for an ass-reaming.

He doesn't look up from his clipboard. "Son, what's going on in your head? You're a mess."

"I'm sorry, Coach. That won't happen again." I refrain from telling him how Asher wasn't feeling well this morning and didn't want to stay with Yvette. I was so tempted to beg Miss Louisa to swing by before I remembered she's out of town.

But I can't get my son's teary expression and desperate wails out of my head.

And underneath it all, I keep thinking about Charlotte. It's been nine days since I gave her a ride home. Is that enough time for her to get her bearings?

Coach finally faces me. "I'm giving you one more shot today. Don't screw it up."

"Yes, sir."

Thankfully, I gain twenty on the next possession, but I'm disappointed shit's still not clicking for me with my new team. Most of the guys have the advantage of playing together three years, but I can't blame my fumble on their camaraderie. This is the fifth game of the season. Shouldn't I have my act together by now?

We win. Barely.

I'm the first one out of the locker room, on a mission to get home. Asher's whole face lights up when I open the front door. "Daddy!"

I scoop him into my arms and kiss the top of his head. "You feeling better, buddy?"

Yvette steps out from behind the kitchen counter where she's covered in jam. "We, uh, we had a little accident, but everything's okay."

After I help her clean up, pay her, and send her off, I grab my wallet and offer the kid my arm. Like a baby monkey, he instantly attaches himself to me, kicking up his feet so he dangles off the floor. "Wanna go grab some ice cream?" I think his tears this morning were from not wanting to stay with someone new rather than an illness, which is a relief. The last time he was sick, I walked around covered in puke for a week.

His little face grins up at me. "Can I get Wocky Woad?"

"Sure thing, bud. A scoop of Rocky Road sounds great. Let's go." I could use the pick-me-up after that atrocious game. It's getting late, but I think the kid could use some time together, just the two of us.

We're on the way home after enjoying our ice cream when we near Charlotte's place. I slow down when I spot flashing lights and smoke.

What the fuck?

I park on the corner, unbuckle Asher, scoop him up, and run toward Charlotte's apartment. Cops are on the scene and pushing people back, but the fire department hasn't arrived yet. I scan the lawn, hoping to spot Charlie, but I don't see her.

Thick black smoke starts billowing from the unit beneath hers.

"Do you guys know Charlotte Darling?" I ask a group of girls huddled on the sidewalk as I bounce Asher in my arms. "Did she get out? She lives on the second floor." I describe her, and my heart sinks when they say they haven't seen anyone come out yet.

Is she up there? It's hard to tell with the smoke.

But underneath the chaos, I hear barking. Fuck, that's Duke.

In the distance, sirens blare, but if Charlotte's up there, will they get here in time to help her?

I turn to the nearest girl, who looks familiar, like we had a class together at some point. "Can you watch my son for a minute? I need to see if my friend got out."

She nods and takes him. When the cop turns to talk to someone, I race up to the building. There's a small overhanging porch on the second story. I don't stop to think. There's no time. Charlotte could be up there, choking to death.

I leap up and grab a hold of the overhang and drag myself up. The barking gets louder. The apartment is dark, but that doesn't mean anything. I try to pry open the sliding glass door, but it's locked.

Duke frantically paws at the other side.

"Hang in there, dude."

Behind me, cops are yelling for me to get down, but fuck that. There's no way I'm going to stand around if there's a possibility Charlotte's trapped in her apartment.

Holding my arm over my face, I kick in the glass. Or at least I try to. Duke has the smarts to move back once I start. It takes three attempts to finally shatter.

I shove away the splintered glass and cover my mouth with my arm. "Is Charlie in here, boy?"

He whines and backs into the room, which is full of smoke. I take a deep breath of fresh air, cover my face again, and follow him into the darkness.

On the bed, I spot a blonde head of hair. "Charlotte! Wake up! Don't you fucking die!" I lift her into my arms and head down the hall. Coughing, I move toward the front door, but there's black smoke coming in from the bottom that makes me think that's a bad idea. Plus, the floor feels like lit coals.

Turning, I move back toward the shattered sliding door. I step through it, careful not to get Charlie snagged on any glass. Firemen are running toward the building. Across the way, they're unloading their gear.

"Drop her," one of them yells. "We'll catch her."

It's not that far, but fuck, I'm not crazy about this idea. Except there's no time to debate it because the temperature skyrockets. The building groans and somewhere behind me, glass shatters.

"Don't die on me, Charlotte. I need you," I whisper against her sweaty forehead before I dangle her limp body over the ledge.

The firemen catch her easily and whisk her away from the building. Behind me, Duke barks frantically.

"Not gonna leave you behind, buddy." In between coughs, I whip off my t-shirt and tear it so it hangs in one long piece and scoop him up. Swear to God, that dog wraps his paws around my neck. Using the shirt, I wind it around us like a sling and tie a knot. "Hold on, Duke. This might be scary."

I carry us over the metal railing. After a second, I let go and land in a crouch, but the weight of the dog throws me off balance, and we tumble to the ground. Somehow I manage not to flatten him in the process. He licks my face as I cough.

Firemen drag me away from the building just before an explosion takes out the bottom unit. Glass flies everywhere and people scream. Through it all, I'm coughing until a paramedic puts an oxygen mask over my face.

"That was brave," the paramedic says. "Stupid, but brave. You likely saved your girlfriend."

I yank down my mask. "Is Charlotte okay? Where is she?"

"In the ambulance. We're about to take her to the hospital."

Scrambling off the grass, I look around and spot them loading her up.

But I can't just take off. Where's Asher? I scan the crowd. There he is. Thank God. I thank the woman and hug him to my chest before I run toward the ambulance. It's already pulling away. "Wait!"

But I'm too late.

I flag down a fireman. "Where are they taking her? Which hospital?"

He unclips the walkie-talkie from his chest and asks. "Charming Memorial."

"Thanks." I race to my car and load Asher. Then I run around to the driver's side, hell-bent on getting to the hospital as quickly as possible, when a bark stops me.

Duke. Shit. I can't just leave him here.

"Come on, boy," I say. He hops into my lap and scrambles over to the passenger seat. "Let's go check on your mama."

I claim the first spot I see at the hospital, grab Asher, and hightail it inside. I'm freaking out by the time I get to the reception area.

The nurse behind the counter holds up her hand. "Sir, you can't bring a dog in here."

I'm so unglued, I didn't even notice Duke following me out of the car.

Fuck. Why didn't I think of this? "He's, uh, he's a service dog. He's very well behaved." I look down at Duke. "Sit." His butt instantly hits the floor. "See?"

I feel bad for lying, but what am I supposed to do with a dog?

"Aww, he's beautiful, but I can't allow him in without a leash or harness." She eyes me up and down, and that's when I remember I'm not wearing a shirt.

I catch my reflection in a mirror behind the credenza. My face and torso are covered in soot. Asher is sucking his thumb. Poor guy. He's probably spooked too. I kiss his forehead before I turn to the nurse again.

"Listen, we were just in a fire, and my friend's dog barely escaped. I only want to check on her, and then I'll drop Duke off at my apartment and return. Is there any way I can make this happen?"

"What's your friend's name?" She types it into the computer. "They brought her in, but I don't know much more than that."

"I just want to see her for a moment. Make sure she's okay. I don't even know if she was breathing when I pulled her out of her apartment."

Fuck. What if she doesn't make it? We never really cleared the air. I never had the chance to apologize. To tell her how much she means to me.

"I'm so sorry. That's terrible." The nurse glances around. "I could get in trouble for this, but it's been a slow night. If you swear you won't be longer than ten minutes, I'll put him in the break room while you check on your friend."

"Thank you so much." Once I get Duke situated, I take off

with Asher through the large doors. It takes me three tries before I finally find the correct emergency room pod.

I take a deep breath, scared as hell of what I'm gonna find on the other side of the divider.

Please, God, let her be okay.

And then I swing back the curtain.

12

CHARLOTTE

MY LUNGS ARE ON FIRE. I try to yank away whatever's on my face, but a huge hand wraps around my wrist.

"You need the oxygen, Charlotte. Leave it alone."

It takes me a minute to realize who's speaking. "Jake?" My throat is killing me, and his name comes out a rasp.

I crack open my crusty eyes to find the haggard-looking man sitting next to my bed.

My *hospital* bed. "What happened? Why am I here?"

"There was a fire. I just spoke with the fire department. They think some electrical device in the unit beneath yours caused it, but they're still investigating."

A fire? Oh my God. "Is Roxy okay?"

He nods. "I didn't know you guys were roommates, but thankfully she wasn't home. She just went to her parents' house to change. She'll be back in a little while."

"What about Duke and Winkie?"

"Duke's fine. I got him out, but..." He rubs the back of his neck, a pained expression on his face. "Shit. I forgot you had another pet."

"Winkie's my cat." My little demon fur ball might not have made it. A tissue appears before me. I didn't realize I was crying.

Grateful, I accept it and wipe the tears streaming alongside the oxygen tube and into my hair.

"I'm sorry, Charlie. I didn't see him, and after I got Duke, there wasn't time to sweep your apartment again."

"When? When was the fire?"

"Saturday night. It's Monday morning."

Holy crap. "I've been asleep all this time?"

"You've been out of it. This is the first time you've been really lucid."

I start coughing, and he holds a cup with a straw to my lips.

"Take small, slow sips."

Our eyes connect as I drink, and I'm caught off guard by the emotion on Jake's face. That's when I remember what he said.

"*You* got Duke out? Not a firefighter?"

He sets down the cup and rakes his fingers through his hair. "I'm told I have a future with the company if football doesn't work out for me. Which, after my game last weekend and missing practice, is a strong possibility."

Shocked, I spill the water. "Why are you missing practice?"

Jake has never, in all of his years playing, *ever* missed practice.

"Kinda hard to play when I'm being observed for smoke inhalation." He sighs. "Coach's orders. I told him I'm fine, but apparently you can have complications up to thirty-six hours later. I have to check in with the team doctor tomorrow to see if I'm cleared yet."

"Because you jumped in my apartment to save Duke?"

He looks me over, a strange smile forming on his lips. "Among other things."

I'm so confused, but before I can say anything, the door

swings open and the doctor enters. "Miss Darling, good to see you're awake. I'm Dr. Holland."

He checks my pupils. Looks down my throat. Feels the lymph nodes in my neck. Listens to my chest.

"You're still a little wheezy. We'll get you another lung treatment. You'll want to do them every four hours until you can get in to see the pulmonologist next week. We'll send you home with a kit."

A respiratory tech sets up everything next to the bed, and then places a mask with a cool mist against my face.

The doctor smiles. "We're going to keep you one more night to observe you. Let me know if you experience any nausea, vomiting, or severe headaches, but your oxygen levels and labs look pretty good considering everything you've been through. Rest is the best medicine, though, and you'll get more of that at home than here."

When he leaves, I lie there, frozen.

Home. I turn to Jake. "Is my apartment..."

He winces. "It's gutted from the fire and water damage. I'm not sure there's much to salvage."

"My camera. All of my work." I rip the nebulizer off my face and try to sit up.

"Charlie, take it easy."

"Take it easy? Jake, I don't have the money to replace my equipment or clothes or textbooks. I'm skating on fumes as it is." I'm out of breath and start to pant. The respiratory tech covers my mouth with the nebulizer again.

Jake frowns and leans forward. "What about your royalties from *Little Darlings*? I thought those were supposed to last you for years."

Sniffling, I shake my head. "My mom was pissed when I left NTU, so she cut me off."

"But I thought that was your money?"

I wait until I'm done with my treatment and the respiratory tech leaves before I respond. "It is my money, but because I was a minor when I was on *Little Darlings*, she's the trustee on that account. I don't know what she did, but I can't withdraw funds from it anymore. She said if I want that money, I'll have to take her to court."

"That doesn't sound legal."

"It's not like I have the funds to contest it, or that there's a ton in that account these days. But, ugh, I definitely can't afford to get another camera." I bite my lower lip to stop it from quivering. Photography is the only thing I have. It's been my life raft through so many difficult times.

"Hey, it'll be okay." Jake sits on the edge of the bed, and when he opens his arms to me, I don't think. I just tuck myself against his chest and close my eyes. His strong arms wrap around me, and I cry until I can't anymore.

"What am I going to do?" Photography has been my entire plan to support myself after graduation. The small jobs I've done so far have built my portfolio, but without the camera gear, I won't have the income to support myself. The few school loans I took out won't cut it.

"It'll be okay." Jake's hand runs up and down my back. "We'll figure out what to do."

"Well, well, well. Isn't this cozy?" Billy smirks at us in the doorway.

"Don't make this weird, Billy." I sniffle and wipe my eyes. "I'm told I almost died. That gives me free rein to bawl my eyes out. What are you doing here?"

Jake stands and backs away. "Thought you'd want to see your boyfriend. Although, dude, you could've swung by sooner. She's only been here two days. Nice of you to rush on over."

"Hey, asshole, I tried, but they said only family could come up here. Apparently her *boyfriend* was already visiting her."

Jake jams his hands in his pockets. "One of the nurses assumed that early on, and I figured if it allowed me into the ER with her, then it's not a big deal. I just didn't want Charlie to be alone."

"Just giving you shit, man. I don't care." Billy chuckles and gives me a look like *I told you so* before he reaches over to hug me. "Glad you're okay, Charlie, baby. Would've sucked if you'd been burned to a crisp. Good thing Ramirez jumped into a burning building to save your cute ass."

Jake did what? I turn to him, but he's gathering his stuff. "Jake? You saved me too? I thought you only rescued Duke."

Billy whips out his phone. "It's all over the news. Your boy's a hero. He carried you out of the inferno. Even Coach is impressed, and nothing impresses that bastard. Check out the video." He slides his thumb over his phone, taps, and shows me the screen.

Someone recorded the fire. Black smoke billows from the unit beneath mine. There are sirens and cops and a crowd, but I don't see any firefighters.

A female voice shouts, "Someone is going into the building!"

"Doesn't that look like Jake Ramirez, our wide receiver?" someone asks.

"Holy shit. It is." The response comes as Jake hops up and clings onto my patio before he swings himself up and over the railing.

I sit there in awe as he kicks in the sliding glass door. Smoke gushes out of my apartment as he heads straight in and returns a minute later with me limp in his arms. He slowly lowers me to the firefighters on the ground who just arrived.

And then he strips off his t-shirt, rips it apart like the Hulk, and straps Duke to his chest before he hops over the railing and drops to the ground. People cheer as firemen drag him away to give him oxygen.

Holy thirst trap. That's the sexiest thing I've ever seen.

Then the bottom floor explodes.

I flinch as my apartment building flies apart.

Open-mouthed, I stare at the screen when it ends.

"Are you crazy? You could've been killed." My eyes sting, and I blink until I'm sure I won't start blubbering again. I might be upset with Jake, but some part of me would die if anything happened to him.

"So you wanted me to leave you in a raging fire?" Jake slings a backpack over his shoulder. "You were passed out on your bed, Charlotte. I tried waking you up, but you didn't budge. Two minutes after I pulled you out, the floor collapsed. If I'd waited for the firefighters, they might not have known you were there. You didn't answer when I called out."

I reach for another tissue and wipe my nose. "I've had a tough time sleeping, so I took a few shots of vodka before I went to bed."

"Well, that definitely worked." He rubs his forehead. "The one thing I can't figure out is why there weren't any fire alarms. Aren't apartment buildings supposed to have them?"

Maybe that's why rent was so cheap—my landlord sucked.

"Where you staying, Chuck? Wanna crash with me?" Billy grins mischievously. He must know I'll decline the offer.

Although... where *am* I going to stay? "Thanks, but I'll figure out something. Don't want to encroach on your nighttime activities." The last place I want to live is at the Stallion Station with half the football team.

Jake stares at us like we've lost our minds. "Aren't you two dating?"

"I wish," Billy says as he winks at me.

I feel my face flame and roll my eyes. "Billy, you're a Lambo on the Autobahn, flashing down the road at two hundred miles

an hour. I'm an economy car. I like slow, steady, and reliable."
Don't look at Jake. Don't.

"My loss, dollface. But if you change your mind about bunking down with me, let me know. I'll always make room in my bed for you."

"Go charm the panties off another girl, Billy. I'm planning to keep mine on for the time being."

"You wound me, Chuck." He surprises me by leaning over to kiss me on the forehead. "Holler if you need anything. I'm still available if you want to practice your moves. And hey, I'm glad you didn't die." With a toss of his chin toward Jake, he struts out of my room.

Jake's quiet, and I wait for the inquisition.

He clears his throat. "You guys really aren't dating?"

"No."

"So... y'all were more of a friends-with-benefits situation?"

Pretty sure you need benefits to qualify for that. "We were more of a practice situation."

An adorable crinkle forms between his brows, but we're interrupted when a cute nurse walks in. "Good to see you up, Miss Darling." She turns to Jake and grins. "Hey, here's my number."

Of course the nurses are throwing themselves at him.

Closing my eyes, I flop back in bed, disgusted, but I really must be messed up because the motion makes my lungs hurt.

"Uh, thanks. I'll call you. Maybe we can set up some time later this week."

I wave my hand at them. "Can y'all go set up your date somewhere else?"

The room goes silent, and I crack open an eye just in time to see a flush creep up Jake's face. "Matilda offered to babysit. That's all."

It might've started as an offer to babysit, but based on the way she's checking him out right now, that's not the only thing on her mind. "Whatever. Just do whatever you're doing in the hall." I curl up on my side, which makes it difficult to breathe, but I can't stand to watch this go down right under my nose.

They step out of my room, and the ache in my chest grows. When will I learn? Just because a man pulls you out of a burning building or drives you home late at night doesn't mean he's in love with you. It means he doesn't want you to die. Big difference.

The door creaks open again, and Jake clears his throat behind me. "That really was about babysitting."

"Not my business." I pull the blankets up closer to my chin. "Thanks for saving me, Jake. I'm gonna nap now." I'm sure I sound ungrateful. I don't mean to be, but my emotions are all over the place, and I'm afraid I'll start blubbering again.

"Everything will work out, Charlotte. You'll see."

I don't have an apartment, my cat died, all of my possessions went up in flames, and I have no way to support myself.

Sure, everything will be okay.

As we wait in the drive-thru of a burger joint, Roxy shakes her head. "Just think. All those times we smelled potpourri wafting from downstairs foreshadowed our fiery demise."

"Roxy! Don't talk like that."

"I'm just mad. Things could've gone so differently that night. All because of that girl's dumb electric potpourri warmer."

Roxy's dad spoke with the fire department this morning and confirmed the cause of the blaze.

"I know what you mean, but she didn't do it on purpose. I'm just grateful no one got injured." Roxy gives me a look when I cough, and I wheeze out, "You know, besides me." I grab my inhaler and take a puff.

Despite feeling a little crappy still, I'm grateful to be alive. To not be hooked up to any more machines or prodded by nurses all night, checking my vitals.

After Roxy gets our order, she hands me the milkshake.

I take a sip. "This is so good. It's been a million years since I've had any decent food. Thank you."

She slurps her drink as she pays through her window. "I'm trying to butter you up."

"Why do I need to be buttered up?"

We head out of the parking lot. "Remember I told you I have a place where you can stay?"

"Yes, and I'm so thankful. I hope it doesn't bother your parents to have me crash in their pool house." She suggested it yesterday, and while I'm not crazy about staying with Coach Santos and his family, I know it'll be a safe place.

When she doesn't say anything, I turn to look at her.

"Well, about that..." She gets really focused on her driving, but I already know it's bad news.

Bummer. I knew it was too good to be true. "Don't worry about it. I knew this was a long shot. Who wants a stranger and her rescue dog living in their pool house?"

"It's not that. Usually my parents would be cool with it, but after I moved out, they decided to renovate everything back there because there was a plumbing issue. I hadn't been home since I moved in with you, so I had no idea."

"It's okay. I understand."

"You can move in the main house. Stay in my old room. My mom is allergic to dogs, though, so you can't bring Duke."

I'm not ready to give him up yet. What if he gets adopted by another negligent family and stops eating again? I have to make sure he's fully recovered before I return him to the shelter.

"I can probably swing a few weeks in a motel. That one by the highway accepts pets." I stayed there a few nights when I first moved to Charming. It'll tap me out, but it's not like I have a choice. Because I'm really not comfortable staying in her parents' house, especially without Roxy, since she's moving in with other friends.

"Don't be silly. I've seen that motel. It looks straight out of a slasher movie. Like Leatherface is gonna hop out from behind a dumpster and murder you. No fucking way am I dropping you off there." She takes another sip of her drink. "I have another place you can stay. It's just that..."

"Just that what?"

She pulls up in front of our old place. Our side of the building is totally gutted. It's ash and soot and rebar. Everything I own went up in flames. I literally have nothing except a bag and a few outfits Roxy loaned me that she dug out of her old bedroom at her parents' house.

We get out and make our way around the debris. "Winkie!" I yell, pausing to cough.

Roxy helps me look for my pirate cat, but there's no sign of him. Just charred particles blowing in the wind.

She hugs me as I cry in the back parking lot. "He loved to tear up my socks."

"Sorry, boo," she says as I start coughing again. She tugs me to her car. "Let's get out of here. This air can't be good for you to breathe."

As we walk, I glare at my old clunker on the other side of the parking lot. It won't turn over and is basically useless. Will I be able to get anything for it at a junkyard? Why couldn't that have burned up and my apartment been spared?

I feel like I'm starting all over again, like I did two years ago. Except this time I'm broke.

Look on the bright side, Charlotte. You can still do the calendar for Second Chances.

In all the chaos of the fire, I forgot that while I lost my camera equipment, at least my negatives and hard drive with all of my digital photos are at school. I have a locker down by the photo lab where I store that stuff. It used to annoy me that I couldn't afford editing software and had to do that work on campus, but I guess it's a blessing in disguise. Otherwise, I would've lost those images too.

"I'm so glad you're okay, Charlie. When I saw the video of

Jake pulling you out, you looked like a rag doll. I've never been so scared in my whole life." Roxy starts her car as I tug on my seatbelt. "I'm sorry I wasn't home that night."

"So you could've been endangered too? No, I'm glad you were off causing mischief and mayhem."

She giggles. "Shh. Don't tell my dad about my mischief. He's pissed we were living in such a shithole."

"Why was that? Why did you want to live there with me?" Surely her family can afford better accommodations.

"It's what I could manage without begging my parents for money. I have a little college fund, and I'm trying to stay within those financial parameters and prove to them I'm responsible."

I get that. "I'm sorry about your stuff. About your cheer outfits going up in smoke."

She shrugs. "It sucks, but clothes are replaceable. Most of my important things are at my parents' house. I'm just grateful you're okay."

"Did your dad freak? I know he's pretty protective of you."

"You should've heard the lecture I got about fire alarms. Even though you won't be staying with my parents, they still want to have you over for dinner sometime."

Hope they don't mind if I roll up in sweatpants and a t-shirt that belong to their daughter, because that's all I have.

"So about this other place where you can stay..." She lets that statement hang as she pulls into an apartment complex two blocks from our old place. "First, you should know that Duke is welcome here."

That's great. "But...?"

"But nothing. You're welcome to stay here as long as you need."

"That's amazing. What's the catch?" I glance up at the building. "Whose place is it?" Roxy and I have a few mutual friends. Well, they're mostly her friends and my acquaintances.

I can't imagine any of them offering to let me couch-surf indefinitely.

"The catch is... you might need to do some babysitting in return."

I only know one person who has a kid in Charming. "Roxy, I don't think..."

The door to the apartment upstairs opens and out step Jake and Asher. Behind them trots Duke. Jake gives me a huge smile and whispers something to Asher, and the kid waves at us as his father carries him down the stairs.

Roxy grabs my hand to keep me in the car and whispers quickly, "Jake barely left your side for those first two days in the hospital. He was worried sick about you. I know you guys have a messed-up history, but maybe this is what you need to work it out. A second chance to talk about things and be friends again."

"He didn't want me to die, but that doesn't mean he wants me to stay with him. Not after everything we've been through."

But then Jake reaches my door and opens it. Before I can get out, he hands me Asher. "Give your aunt a hug, buddy."

Pudgy little arms wrap around my neck, and my nose stings. "Hi, Ash. I've missed you."

My nephew leans back, and his eyes widen excitedly. He's Jake's clone with dark hair and olive skin, but he has my sister's startling blue eyes. "We got a dog. I wuv dogs."

Jake chuckles and picks him up again. "Buddy, Duke belongs to Charlie, but since she's staying with us, we get to enjoy Duke too."

My pooch sticks his nose in the car and rests it on my lap. "Hey, handsome." I scruff behind his ear, and he wags his tail.

I chew on the inside of my cheek. "You don't have to do this, Jake," I whisper. "You don't owe me anything. If anything, I owe you for dragging me out of my apartment last week."

"We'd love to have you," he says easily. Almost like he means it. "If you don't mind sleeping in Asher's miniature-sized bed, that is. He'll sleep with me, and you can get his room. He doesn't mind. Do you, bud?"

Asher shakes his head frantically. "Can Duke sweep wit us?"

Jake chuckles. "In case you haven't noticed, the kid is obsessed with your dog." He tickles Asher. "Pretty sure Duke wants to sleep with Charlie."

Roxy nudges me with one eyebrow hiked high. "Won't that be nice, Charlotte? You can keep Duke *and* visit with your nephew. Win-win. Plus, I got you a job. It's nothing sexy or anything, so don't get too excited."

"I'll take anything at this point." Especially now that I need to replace all of my equipment and clothes.

"How do you feel about roller skates?" she asks as she grabs my bag out of the back seat like this is a done deal.

But where else do I have to go?

14

JAKE

I WISH I could say I'm excited to be back, but my stomach is in knots. I've never missed practice before—for any reason—but Coach didn't give me a choice. I should've been cleared for yesterday's practice, but I had some congestion, and Coach didn't want to take any chances, so I got sent home one more day until it cleared.

Still, I can't help but feel like I've screwed up.

Strangely, the locker room is empty when I arrive, and that feels ominous. Am I late? Fuck.

I rush to change and then beeline for the conference room, where everyone stares at me. Damn it.

"Sorry I'm late, Coach. I didn't know practice time got moved up."

"You're not late, son. Come up here." He smiles, waving me to come to the podium.

My teammates' expressions are solemn, like someone just died. It doesn't mesh with Coach's rare smile. I feel like I'm about to get punked.

I brace myself to get my ass reamed out in front of the team for being late. Irresponsible. For letting everyone down. It's the kind of lecture my high school coach would've leveled on anyone who was tardy.

Coach faces the guys, and I stand there next to him like a dumbass.

He leans toward the mic. "Fellas, college football is about two things—winning games and molding y'all into respectable humans. Because if the latter isn't part of the equation, it doesn't matter how many games you rack up. Do I want to win a championship? Of course. It's in my blood. Lone Star State wouldn't have hired me if I didn't eat, sleep, and breathe football. Just ask my wife. It annoys the hell out of her."

The guys chuckle, and I start to relax. Maybe he isn't about to eviscerate me.

He taps on the podium. "But if you're all dirtbags, getting arrested for DUIs and womanizing and partying like fools, I'm not doing my job either. College sports are rife with examples of talented athletes who get in trouble for doing dumb things."

Here it comes. I did the dumb thing.

At least that's what my brother yelled into my ear for half an hour the other day. He said our mom cried when she saw the video of me jumping into a flaming building, and because the Ramirez brothers have a standing policy to kick each other's ass if one of us makes our mama cry, I've got a reckoning coming.

Coach continues, his voice taking on an almost religious quality. "I think of all the little kids who watch our games, who cheer us on. Who wear your jerseys. Who paint your numbers on their faces. They look up to you. Every one of you. So you have to be on your best behavior on *and* off the field." He pats my back. "Last weekend, I watched a video of this young man charging into a burning building to save a friend. He didn't hesitate. Just leapt up there like some guy in an action movie."

"That's right, Ramirez! You kicked ass!" Babcock howls.

The team starts clapping and stomping their feet.

"Don't forget he saved the dog too!" someone else yells, and Coach chuckles.

"Yes, he also saved a dog. But Jake Ramirez is a prime example of how to be a role model. Now, I'm not saying you should put yourselves in danger—that's not my message. But I am asking y'all to model his selflessness." I'm so stunned, I could topple over with a stiff breeze. "We have a lot of ego in football. Some of it is warranted. Some isn't. But let this be our high-water mark of character. Let us strive for greatness on and off the field."

Babcock, the ass, starts chanting my name—"Ra-mir-ez! Ra-mir-ez!"—and everyone joins in. It's ridiculous. Moving, but ridiculous.

My face is hot, like I've been scorched by the sun.

When our little powwow is over, Coach pulls me aside. "The media has been on me since they got wind of what happened. I told them you're recovering, but could answer their questions after Saturday's game."

I nod, already loathing the press conference. *Lo odio.* I hate that shit.

"I didn't realize Charlotte was Roxy's roommate. I'm relieved you were there in time to help her." He glances around and lowers his voice. "I almost lost my lunch when I heard Roxy's apartment building caught on fire. I know my daughter wasn't there when it happened, but I'm relieved to know y'all are friends. She says Charlotte is a good girl, and frankly, Roxy needs more solid friends."

"Charlotte is an old friend from high school." I don't know why I offer this information, but I always feel like I'm about to confess my darkest sins to this man for some reason.

"How's her recovery? Roxy says she's on the mend."

"Yes, sir. She's doing better."

"Glad to hear that." I follow him out to the field and he turns to me. "You ready to practice? You feeling good?"

"I got a clearance from the team doctor, and my lungs are fine."

"That's what I want to hear." With a hard pat on my shoulder, he motions to the line of scrimmage where the team is setting up drills. "Get on out there. Let's see what you got."

There's a natural rhythm to playing football. An ebb and flow. A give and take. When everything clicks and the camaraderie between players starts to gel.

I've never had that here.

Until now.

For the first time since I got to Lone Star State, everything goes my way. I hit my marks and catch every ball thrown during practice. It's exhilarating.

And I don't know if it's the fact that our QB is in the groove or if it's me, but I'll take what I can get.

I just hope I can maintain it through Saturday's game against Kansas. Because catching a few throws during practice doesn't mean shit if you turn into a fumbling idiot during a game.

WHEN PRACTICE IS over and I'm standing under a hot stream of water in the shower, it hits me. I wasn't worried about Asher today. He's with Charlotte, and I know she'd never let anything happen to him. He's safe at home, likely wrapping her around his little finger.

Having that confidence put me in the right frame of mind so I could focus on football. I didn't realize how out of whack my concentration has been until now.

I find myself rushing to get to my apartment. Charlie only moved in yesterday, but I'd be lying if I said I wasn't excited to have her around. She's always been a calming force in my life, and I'm hoping we get back to a good place. That we can be friends again.

When I get home, I find Charlie and Roxy chatting on the couch. I barely get a greeting out before Asher charges at my legs. I let him tackle me to the ground—it's his favorite thing to do.

"Dude, you have a future as a linebacker if you keep that up." I scoop him into my arms as he giggles. Glancing at Charlie, I ask, "Did he behave today?" Miss Louisa watched him until this afternoon, and then Charlotte took over. I wanted her to wait until next week to give her more time to rest, but she insisted. I refused until she said Roxy would help too.

"He was great. We ate lunch in the park. Roxy took him and Duke for a long walk around the playground. We stopped off at... the store... so I could get some clothes. Don't worry—he wasn't out of my sight for a minute. Asher should be exhausted, honestly."

She's embarrassed about shopping at the Goodwill. I overheard her talking on the phone last night. She should know I don't care about brands. With two older brothers, I wore hand-me-downs my entire childhood and then handed them down to my youngest bro.

"Asher will conk out after his bath." I consider everything she did today. Shit. "Should you be running around like this so soon after you got released from the hospital?"

"I'm fine, Jake. I'm still doing my lung treatments. I get a little out of breath sometimes and cough, but I have my asthma inhaler in case I'm out and about."

Roxy slings an arm around Charlotte. "I can testify that she didn't overdo it."

I nod, but I'm still concerned. "If I gave you too many shifts this week, let me know."

I move into the kitchen to check the schedule. Miss Louisa is still watching Asher in the mornings, but Yvette is covering tomorrow afternoon, and Buffy is doing the next day. At least that gives Charlotte a few days off.

Roxy and Charlie are whispering back and forth before they burst into laughter. Roxy holds her ribs and points to me. "You can practice on Jake!"

"Practice what?" I ask as I get a glass of water. I'm taking a long drink when Roxy says, "Flirting," making me choke.

When I can breathe again, I clear my throat. "I'm sorry. Did you say flirting?"

"I did. Our girl here is taking charge of her dating life, and she needs to practice flirting."

I think back to a few days ago. "Is that what Babcock meant when he visited you in the hospital?"

Charlotte turns an adorable shade of pink and looks down at her lap when she nods.

Roxy pops off the couch and gives me a teasing look. "Our girl needs to go out on dates, so I plan to set her up. Isn't that great? Half the baseball team is in love with her, so it shouldn't be a problem."

That's right. They had another photoshoot.

The thought of Charlie dating some douchebag baseball player makes my chest tighten.

Roxy is right, though. Why wouldn't any red-blooded man want to date Charlotte? She's always been a pretty girl, but now? She's beautiful. Maybe because she's not quite so painfully shy anymore. All of that photography has probably given her confidence, and she makes more eye contact than she used to.

God, her eyes. Charlotte's are almost crystal blue with little flecks of amber. I've always thought they were stunning.

I find myself staring at her as she chats with Roxy, and I wonder...

It's something I haven't let myself dwell on, but I'm curious —does Charlotte *still* have feelings for me? The question is a Pandora's box, because even if she does, there's nothing I can do about it. Dakota would murder us both. She might be in Los Angeles, but she has a powerful online presence, and the last thing I need before the draft is Dakota flinging about our dirty laundry online.

Wake up, idiot. The girls are literally planning dates right in your face. There's your answer.

Gotta say, I'm strangely disappointed to be back in the friend zone.

Roxy gathers her things. "Plus, if she practices flirting, it'll help her with her new job at Toasty Buns."

"That's the place where the girls run around on roller skates, right?" I ask. *And really fucking small skirts.* The guys love that burger joint. "Kinda like Sonic carhops?"

"Exactly. They blast classic rock and the girls wear these cute little outfits and deliver food on roller skates."

That sounds dangerous. "Charlie, do you even skate?"

She shrugs. "How hard can it be?"

Roxy chuckles. "I brought her a pair so she can practice. She doesn't start for two weeks because I know she needs time to recuperate."

When Roxy leaves, I get Asher bathed and ready for bed. When my son is asleep, I slip out of bed and close the door. I find Charlotte doing the dishes.

"Hey, you don't need to do those."

"I don't mind. I want to help out to thank you for letting me crash here. I swear it won't be forever."

I hold out my hand and dry the next dish when she finishes washing it. "Stay as long as you need. Ash and I are happy to have you."

She's quiet for a long stretch, but she's tense and keeps

glancing at me. Finally, she takes a deep breath. "When, uh, when is Dakota coming by to see Asher? I just want to know so I can make myself scarce."

I'm a little shocked at the question. I don't know why. She told me she didn't talk to her family, but I didn't realize she'd gone completely no contact. "Dakota doesn't visit. Especially not now with her new show."

Charlie pauses washing a glass to look at me, her brows pulled together. "Ever?"

"Ever. She basically abandoned Asher to go 'find herself' and audition in LA. She gave me full custody two years ago if I agreed she didn't owe me any child support."

"Wow. Okay, so she *never* sees Ash?"

"Never." I clench my jaw at the thought Dakota could be so heartless.

"That's crazy. And my mom was okay with this?"

"She's the one who said Dakota would sign anything if it meant your family didn't have to pay child support."

"Oh, Jake. I'm so sorry. That's terrible."

Charlie's slender arms immediately wrap around my waist. I rest my chin on the top of her head. "We're getting by. It's okay."

"It shouldn't be like this. You shouldn't have to do this alone."

I think about that a lot. What raising a kid would be like with a real partner. Someone who always had my back. It's obviously a pipe dream. I'd need time to find and date this hypothetical person, which I don't see happening in the foreseeable future.

Charlie lets go of me and gives me a sympathetic smile as she turns to the sink. "What kind of show did she land?"

"*The Hot House*. It's a reality show. Starts airing next week."

"Oh God." Her shoulders slump. "What are the odds she won't drag us into her drama?"

If I know Dakota, slim to none, but I don't want to freak out

Charlie. She's had a rough week, and the truth is anything is possible, so why not be optimistic? "We're not in her life. She probably doesn't even think about us anymore."

Her head tilts. "That's kinda sad, but also the best possible outcome if it keeps us out of her dumb show."

We continue washing dishes. I finally nudge her and ask her the question that's been on my mind since Roxy left. "You gonna tell me why you need practice flirting?"

Her neck turns red and she sputters. "Just... I'm terrible at it. Guys never know I'm interested in them because my whole face goes blank. Some girls have resting bitch face. I have disinterested bitch face."

I'd laugh, but something about what she describes reminds me of all those times we had class together in high school and I'd catch her looking at me. But she never gave off interested vibes. And yet she just told me she left NTU because she had feelings for me. *How far back do those feelings go?*

But I guess... yeah, she should work on that.

"You are pretty bad at flirting." I nudge her again, and her mouth drops open.

"That's mean. You're supposed to say, 'Aww, Charlotte, you're not that bad.'" She flicks me with soapy water.

"Oh, no, you don't." I get a scoop of bubbles and fling them at her. They smack her in her neck and chest.

She squeals and pulls her white t-shirt away from her chest where her nipples pebble. I look away as soon as I realize I'm checking her out. But it's hard to forget those perfect breasts. Round. Perky. Just the right size.

Don't think about her that way. She's your friend, asshole.

"I'm gonna get you back for that." With a cup of water in hand, she growls. I laugh and take off around the counter.

When her arm pulls back, I cut in the other direction. Water goes flying, but it misses me. Spotting an opening, I charge at her, hoisting her over my shoulder.

She laughs as she pounds on my back with her little fists. "Put me down right this instant, you savage."

I'm about to spin her around when she starts to cough. That drops the smile from my face.

I slide her to the floor gently and pat her back. "Sorry. Are you okay?"

Her head turns up to me. She barely comes up to my chin. We're so close, I can see those gorgeous amber flecks in her eyes. "Yeah. Just need something to drink."

I grab a bottle of water from the fridge and open it for her. She takes a few sips and nods. "See, I'm okay. And I'll do another breathing treatment before bed."

Seeing her out of breath reminds me of how much she's been through. How I almost lost her.

I rake my fingers through my hair. "Charlie, I've been meaning to tell you this for a while, since I drove you home that night, but I'm sorry for the way I treated you at the park. I get it now. I get why you did what you did, and I'm pissed at myself for not being more sensitive when we were at NTU. You did so much shit for me and Asher." And for Dakota, but I don't want to say her name. "I don't think I ever really thanked you for being amazing."

My throat gets tight when I think about that fire. It could've killed her, and I'd never get another chance to tell Charlotte what she means to me and how much I've always treasured our friendship.

"For the record, if I'd had your number, if I'd gotten that letter, I would've called." Her eyes get teary, and I hook my pinky into hers. "Just wanted you to know I've missed you and I'm really glad you're staying with us. Maybe this will give me a chance to kick your ass at chess again."

She blinks, her eyes still misty. But she cracks a smile as her pinky squeezes mine. "You wish, sucker."

I chuckle and pull her into my arms. Holding her feels like coming home. I kiss the top of her head and whisper, "Get ready to lose, cupcake."

15

CHARLOTTE

ROXY CLASPS HER HANDS EXCITEDLY. "You're going to love me when you hear my news."

"I already love you," I mutter as I squint at the computer screen. We're in the bowels of the communication building, down in the photojournalism lab. With a few clicks I burn in an underexposed portion of the image until I can clearly read "Lone Star State Baseball" on the athlete's t-shirt.

She ducks her head next to mine. "Ohhh. He's hot."

The guy holding the German shepherd and staring into the camera is attractive, but he doesn't give me butterflies.

Unlike my current roommate, who runs around the apartment shirtless and gives me heart palpitations.

On one hand, living with Jake is like being on a perpetual high. Seeing him rumpled first thing in the morning when he snuggles Asher is my personal catnip.

On the other, it's also my personal hell. Because as sweet and accommodating as Jake is, he can never be mine.

The closer we get to the airing of my sister's new reality show, the more afraid I am she's going to say something to humiliate me or Jake. The first episode is three days away. Pretty sure I'm going to have an ulcer by the time the season is over.

Needing to get out of my head, I swivel my chair to look at Roxy. "Tell me what's going on."

"I found a camera you can use."

I sit up straight. "Are you serious?"

"It has some strings attached, so hear me out before you get too excited. It belongs to the athletic department. The new athletic director wants a student to shoot the football games so he has content for his newsletter and whatnot. He has a camera and some pretty awesome lenses you could use. Plus, I'm guessing the school newspaper might be interested in those too. AD Armstrong said that was fine as long as he got first pick of those images."

My shoulders slump. "Rox, I've never shot sports. That's a whole genre. I'm used to setting up shoots and making sure the lighting is good. I'm more of a human-interest photographer. You know, the man on the street or that stray cat sitting in someone's backyard. Football is really unpredictable and fast."

"Think of it as a challenge. You said you needed a camera. Well, I found you one."

She's right. I can't do any of my photojournalism assignments if I don't get some equipment ASAP.

"Do you think Mr. Armstrong would let me do a trial run? And if he's not happy with my shots, I can just return the equipment?"

She gives me a look. "Charlotte Darling, look at your work." She points at the monitor. "You're amazing. Own it, girl. I mean, sure, you can return the equipment if you bomb, but come on. You're not going to screw up. You're too conscientious. Besides, he took one look at your online portfolio and said you have the gig if you want it."

By the time I get home later that night, I'm so excited to talk to Jake about this opportunity, I'm practically levitating.

Until I open the door to his apartment.

It's late, and I'm guessing Asher is already in bed, but I don't want to make any unnecessary noise, so I quietly turn the key.

I find Jake and Matilda sitting side by side on the couch, looking cozy. She's touching his arm and gazing up at him like she's hoping he rips off her underwear with his teeth.

Jake's sporting a backwards baseball cap and looking so freaking sexy, I almost can't blame Matilda for drooling.

She jumps back when she sees me, a guilty expression on her face.

But Jake gives me a wide smile. "Hey, Charlie. How was your day?"

"Sorry, am I interrupting something? I can leave."

"Don't be silly. Matilda was just looking at my wrist. Took a hard tackle today, and I was icing it." He points to the ice pack in the bowl in front of him.

"Isn't that nice of you, Matilda? Good of you to take such good care of Jake." I'm being a snarky bitch, but it goes over Jake's head, because he just reaches for that bag of ice.

Matilda, though? She gets what I'm saying. Eyes narrowed at me, voice syrupy sweet, she says, "We just ordered dinner."

Jake scoots over to make room between him and Matilda and pats the seat, his attention on ESPN. "Join us. I ordered pizza. Pepperoni and black olives. That's still your favorite, right?"

I smile victoriously at her before I plop down between them. "That's really sweet of you to remember, Jake. Thanks. I'd love to join you."

She rolls her eyes and grabs her purse. "I probably need to get going."

Don't let the door hit you on the ass, lady.

After the pizza arrives, I nibble on a slice before I turn to him. "You know she's hoping to be the next Mrs. Ramirez, right?"

His expression is incredulous. "What are you talking about?"

"Jake, I might be terrible at flirting, but you've always been clueless about the women lusting over you."

"Matilda? She was just being nice." Sure. Nice. I'd agree if she didn't look like she was minutes away from doing a naughty nurse striptease. "And even if she was flirting, I have no intentions of dating anyone this year, much less one of the babysitters. I have to focus on football or I can kiss my dream of the NFL goodbye."

I should be happy to hear this, but some small part of me is crushed.

He never said much about my big declaration that I left NTU because I had feelings for him.

What, Charlotte? Did you think him letting you move in here was some ploy to make his move on you? He had three years to try something with you before he met Dakota. He never did. There's your answer about how he feels about you. He still sees you like a little sister. His pal. His partner to play chess.

Jake shovels away his food, unaware of my inner turmoil.

When I return my plate to the sink, I catch sight of the babysitting schedule this week. Miss Louisa is a sweetheart, but Yvette, Buffy, and Matilda? I'll go crazy if I have to come home every day and find one of them seconds from scaling Jake.

And just because he gave me that politically correct response about not dating doesn't mean he won't hook up with anyone. Jake's friends have always been horndogs. I'd be an idiot to think he's any different.

I definitely need to find somewhere else to live as soon as possible.

"You okay?" he asks as he throws away his trash.

"Great." The new Charlotte, the one who wants to take

charge of her life, is tempted to share how I'm sick with jealousy and see his reaction, but that will make living here awkward.

I'm not sure what else to say, but my tumultuous thoughts are interrupted when the sports announcer says Jake's name. He and I rush back to the TV.

"Here's another look at that daring rescue made by Lone Star State's wide receiver Jake Ramirez." Seeing him storm into the burning building and carry me out makes me emotional.

"You made national news." I sniffle and try to swallow past the knot in my throat. This is a new video, closer to the building. This one shows the flames on the first floor. Shows him emerging sweaty and covered in soot, his face a mask of concentration. "You could've been killed."

He wraps a strong arm around my shoulders and pulls me to his chest. "Glad you're okay, cupcake."

I chuckle at the nickname. He hasn't called me that since high school when he stole my mini-cupcakes to explain how the team's new offense worked to one of the freshmen. Funny that he started using it again when I moved in.

We sit on the couch as coverage cuts to last weekend's press conference where Jake stoically sits next to Coach Santos and answers questions.

"Jake, can you tell us about the female you rescued? Was that your girlfriend?" a reporter asks.

My heart pounds in my throat as I wait for his response. This is the first time I'm seeing his post-game interview.

"Charlotte is a friend of mine from high school. We had English together. She sometimes kicks my butt in chess, but I'll deny she's better than I am."

Everyone laughs, and I chuckle.

"Was that her dog?"

"Duke is the dog Charlotte is fostering from Second Chances Animal Rescue in Charming. They do amazing work. In fact, they need help keeping their doors open. If you're looking for a great organization, they could use the donations. I'm hoping to volunteer there in the off-season."

I turn to look at him. "Really? You want to volunteer?"

"Of course. I wouldn't just bullshit to look good."

His expression is so sincere, I want to kiss him. Especially when he asks if we can make up that photoshoot that he bailed on.

"As a matter of fact, I just got my hands on a new camera, so yes, we can definitely do that shoot."

Duke trots over and sits between our legs. I reach down and scratch behind his ear as I explain how Roxy talked to the athletic director for me.

"I plan to tell him if he's not happy with my shots from the next game, he can find someone else."

"He's gonna love your work." Jake gives me a proud smile. "That's awesome." But then he gets that furrow between his brows. "Just be careful on the sidelines. I've seen more than one cameraperson get mowed over."

Highlights from his game against Kansas start playing, and I whistle. "Look at you, studmuffin. Forty-five-yard carry on that touchdown." I hold up my hand and we high-five each other.

He has that cocky grin I love. "Kinda feel like I'm getting my mojo back, which is a huge fucking relief. You have no idea how much my last two seasons at NTU sucked. Unless you Googled me. Maybe you do know."

I shake my head. "Sorry, I didn't follow football when I moved down here."

Leaning forward, he drops his head into his hands. His voice gets quiet. "Did you know Dakota was sleeping with Troy?"

"Shut up." My eyes bug out. *Troy Snyder?* "As in your old quarterback? Weren't you guys best buds?"

He nods. "Until I found him fucking your sister in my bed."

Yikes.

That had to hurt. But knowing Dakota, I'm not surprised. She goes after what she wants, damn the consequences.

If I had to guess, she probably wanted to place equal bets on the guys she thought would be drafted. Whoa, that's cynical.

"How long did that go on?"

His jaw goes tight. "Almost the whole time we were at NTU, based on their texts. I unapologetically went through her phone when she swore it was 'only one time.'" He tells me he grabbed her phone, locked himself in the bathroom, and went through their messages.

"That was quick thinking."

"She was always on her damn phone. It used to bother me. She'd be smiling at the screen but swore she was talking to one of her girlfriends. Basically our whole relationship was a lie. I feel like the biggest dumbass for trusting her."

"I'm so sorry. I had no idea. I would've told you if I knew." Now that I think back to our freshman year, she *was* super secretive with her phone. I assumed she was sexting Jake and being coy about it.

He clears his throat. "I've been meaning to tell you... All that shit with Dakota pretending we were having sex all the time, that was just her playing games. I remember how she did that just before you took off. I was literally in the other room, telling her to cut her crap, while she was moaning like we were going at it. And shit, then there was that video call. I'm so sorry. You didn't need to see all that."

My whole face flames. "We don't have to talk about this." I stand, but he grabs my hand and gently tugs until I sit again.

"Let me put it this way. Before you left, she and I hadn't had sex in months. Probably because she was sneaking off and fucking Troy any chance she had."

I fold my lips. "Not my business."

"No, I kinda think it is. I don't know what game Dakota was playing, but she was trying to fuck with you too for some reason."

Because she knew how I felt in high school, and she wanted me to understand that Jake belonged to her. Even if she didn't want him.

Only Jake doesn't know how long I've loved him, and I have no plans to tell him. I'll die of humiliation if I tell him I crushed on him hard for years. That's too pathetic. I'd rather get a bikini wax and dip myself in lemon juice than spell it out to him.

I pull on a thread hanging off the hem of my jean shorts. "You know how dogs pee on every street corner to declare ownership to other animals and mark their territory?"

He laughs, his dimples popping. "Am I the dog in this scenario or the street corner?"

"Sorry to say, but the street corner."

The humor in his face evaporates. "I'm starting to think I was more her property than boyfriend too."

Don't ask. Don't. "Do you still have feelings for her?"

"Not at all." He gets a sheepish expression. "This is going to sound terrible, but I never loved her. I wanted to. I tried to love her. She was the mother of my child, and I *should've* loved her. But I always felt she was putting on an act. It was tough to get behind that wall, you know?"

I nod, so relieved I can barely speak.

He sighs. "I kept trying to envision my life with her and always came up empty. I don't think it was meant to be."

After a moment, I motion to the TV. "Want to watch the first episode of *The Hot House* together on Thursday? Keep each other from flinging ourselves off the balcony?"

His laughter makes me smile. "I'll buy the booze. We might need it."

～

THE TEXTS COME in rapid fire two nights later.

You swear you're okay?

I've been crying since I saw that video.

Why didn't you call me? I would've come down to Charming!

One-handed, I try to respond to Maggie, who's been blowing up my phone.

As much as I hate that she's worried, my heart is full. It feels good to know there are people who care about me. Maggie's balancing a hectic life in Chicago with her twins and husband, who's in the NFL, but I have no doubt she'd haul ass down here if I asked her to.

I promise I'm okay!

"Hold the light a little higher." Jake bends over the engine of my car, his flexing arms doing magical things to my insides.

"Sorry." I jam my phone in my pocket and pray I can afford the monthly payments. It's refurbished, an older model to replace the one I lost in the fire. "I really appreciate you helping me."

"It's no problem."

My old landlord, Mr. Larson, offered to tow my car wherever I wanted, so we moved it to Jake's apartment complex because Jake thinks he or his brothers can fix it. I'm guessing Larson's being extra nice because he didn't have functioning fire alarms.

Roxy just told me the city is leveling huge fines at our former landlord for major code violations, not just for our craptastic building, but for the two others he owns. I'm just glad his other tenants will be safe.

"We don't have to do this tonight," I say as I switch the flashlight to my other hand. Jake wanted to take a look at my old Ford before he bugs his brothers.

"I don't mind. It used to bother me in high school when my brothers made me do all the oil changes in their shop over the summer, but now?" He grunts and twists something with pliers. "I actually miss it. Working on cars is kinda zen. Takes my mind off things." Meaning my sister's show that premieres tomorrow.

I yawn. "Does Buffy mind staying late?"

"She said we're cool as long as she could switch shifts with you next week."

"That's not a problem." I barely get the words out when he pauses to lift his t-shirt and wipe the sweat off his face, putting his washboard abs on display. His jeans hang low on his trim hips and hug his muscular rear.

And he's—wow. So, so sexy.

It hits me again. How Jake risked his life to save mine. He literally jumped into a burning building and carried me out.

The image of him stripping off his shirt to use it as a sling to carry Duke replays in my mind.

Jake clears his throat, a playful grin on his face. "Need the light on the engine, cupcake. Not on me."

Oh God.

I nod and shine the huge flashlight toward the car and hope he can't see my face burn. Embarrassed, I scramble to think of something to say. "Wanna play chess this weekend? I'm rusty, so you have a decent shot of winning."

He chuckles as he leans over the engine. "Are you saying the only reason I might win is because you haven't played in a while?"

"Maybe."

"If you help me make flashcards when we get home, you got yourself a deal, but get ready to get your cute little ass whipped. I've upped my chess skills."

It's my turn to laugh. "We'll see about that."

When he starts my car half an hour later, I let out an undignified squeal and jump up and down. "How'd you do that?"

"I have my ways." A cocky grin spreads on his face before he waves his fingers in front of me and winks. "Got magical hands."

My whole body heats. What I wouldn't give to feel those hands pressed to my skin.

Stop torturing yourself, Charlotte! Behave!

After we lock up and trek across the parking lot to his apartment, I catch a whiff of motor oil and Jake's natural masculine scent. Like a weirdo, I lean closer to sniff him again. *Mm. Sexy.*

Jesus, I have a problem.

He tosses an arm over my shoulder and gives me a noogie, and I elbow him in the gut. Even though I act annoyed, I'm also smiling.

Because this feels just like old times.

16

JAKE

WE'VE BARELY SET up the chessboard when the hard knock at the door makes Charlotte flinch.

"You expecting anyone?" I ask her. She's sitting on the couch, looking like she might hurl. The show, which I've started calling *The Hell House*, starts in a few minutes, and we're both nervous wrecks. I'd been hoping a game of chess might distract us.

"No."

When I swing open the door, I find Billy, Roxy, and Cam, who's carrying several boxes of pizzas.

"Thought we'd join your little watch party," Billy says as he hands me a six-pack and waltzes in as though I invited him.

At my obvious look of surprise, Roxy seems embarrassed. "Sorry. I thought Billy asked if we could stop by."

Resigned to having an audience for this, I hold out my arm. "Come in."

At least Charlie looks happy to see Roxy. The girls hug and huddle on the couch, whispering back and forth.

"This okay?" Cam asks as he shoves a slice of pizza in his mouth. "Us stopping by? Billy said you'd want company."

I don't know why Billy has turned into my shadow, but I

guess it's cool to have some friends here tonight. Not that I would've described Billy and Cam as more than teammates before this.

Billy plops down on the couch and rubs his hands down his jeans. "So what are we in for? With a name like *The Hot House*, will there be some girl-on-girl kissing?"

Roxy smacks him in the chest. "Why do you always have to be such a pig?"

"What? I'm only responding to the marketing. I'm an innocent bystander here."

As a teaser for the show plays, I sit on the other side of Charlie. The celebrities flash on the screen in skimpy bikinis, and when Dakota's hauntingly beautiful face stares back at me, I remind myself of the times she bitched me out. The times she swore at me. The times she dumped me with responsibilities while she ran off to party. All while posting what appeared to be a picture-perfect life online. The disconnect gave me whiplash.

No, I never loved Dakota. I was in love with the *idea* of Dakota, but not the woman herself. By the time I realized she was just a shallow shell, it was too late. I was in too deep, and there was no easy way to get out of that relationship without hurting Asher.

I suppose Dakota did me a favor because cheating is a hard line for me, and she gave me an out.

Something wraps around my pinky, and I look down to see Charlie's hand nestled against mine. I squeeze her finger and pray Dakota has the decency to keep us out of whatever drama she's planning to dredge up on this show.

At least it's late, so Asher is asleep. I'd hate for him to catch sight of his mother. He has her photo and still asks about her from time to time. I wasn't sure if I should just pretend she never existed since she never bothers to see him. He's still young, and she left so long ago. But that seemed wrong. It's not like Dakota died. She just took off and never looked back, and I'm pissed as hell about it for Asher. Now that I think about it, she rarely spent any time with Ash willingly unless it was to take pics for her social media.

"Dude, these chicks are hot," Billy says as he downs another slice. "I'd totally fuck that blonde."

This time, it's my turn to reach over and smack him on the back of his head. "That's my kid's mother, douchebag. Watch your mouth."

"No shit?" Billy looks at Charlotte. "That's your sister? Dakota Darling? Oh, damn, y'all were on that show, right? *Little Darlings*?"

Charlie rolls her eyes. She hates when people bring that up. "Took you long enough to figure it out."

I chuckle at her sass and stretch my arm behind her back. "It'll be okay," I whisper in her ear. "Whatever happens tonight."

Charlie rests her head against my shoulder, and my mind wanders to that look she gave me when I was working on her car last night. I flirted with her, which I've never really consciously done before, and she seemed embarrassed.

Nice job, asshole.

Probably shouldn't joke around with her like that. It's obvious she doesn't harbor feelings for me anymore, and I made things weird.

She groans. "I don't know if I can watch this. What if she's horrible? Or what if she pretends she's perfect? I'm not sure which version is worse."

I know exactly what she means. Dakota has a way of playing innocent when she's anything but.

When the narration for the show starts, my stomach knots painfully.

"On this season of *The Hot House*, we've brought in fifteen drop-dead-gorgeous celebrities who are working to make a comeback. Some have been sidelined by personal tragedies, others have had children, and some are dealing with substance abuse.

"We'll see behind the scenes as they hit the pavement and audition for upcoming shows or modeling opportunities.

"We'll also get a front-row seat to their therapy sessions.

"Because while these beautiful people have talent, they're also dealing with personal demons.

"Join us on this season of *The Hot House*, where viewers will help us pick the next big stars."

The intro ends with the tagline. "*The Hot House:* Hot star or hot mess? You decide."

"Fuck." I turn to Charlotte, and her expression must reflect mine. "I can't imagine any scenario where I get out of this unscathed."

"Maybe we should hide out in Mexico until the season is over."

I nod. "*Vámonos.*" Let's go.

Billy snorts. "Think it'll really be that bad?"

"Do you know anything about reality shows?" Charlie asks, turning toward him. "You're followed by cameras twenty-four seven. You're told to ramp up your emotions and the drama to make the show interesting. You're encouraged to argue and fight and do stupid things for ratings. And the worst part is the Frankenbites."

"What's that?"

"You sign a contract that basically gives the editors license to do whatever they want with the footage. Think of Frankenstein and the way the scientist used different bodies to create the monster. So let's say nothing interesting happens on the show this week when they're taping. The editors might then use parts of different conversations and piece them together or take a conversation out of order until the resulting narrative is scandalous and nothing like what was originally intended or said."

So even if Dakota doesn't say something horrible about me or her sister, the editor could make it seem like she did?

Great.

The Hot House is being shot at some swanky penthouse in West Hollywood. All of the celebrities are gathered in the living room as the host, some model named Evangeline, explains the rules of the show.

"One of you will get a contract for an upcoming movie. One will get a modeling contract. And the one who makes the most personal improvement will win a quarter million dollars *and* a contract with a top agency."

The contestants clap politely, but they're apparently too cool to act excited.

"And with so many sexy singles, don't be surprised if the nights here get a little steamy." Some of the contestants eye-fuck one another, which seems par for the course.

If I have to look on the bright side here, it's the relief I have to not be harboring any feelings for Dakota. Absolutely none besides being pissed she doesn't ever attempt to see Asher. But if she hooks up with some wannabe celebrity, I won't be crying into my Wheaties. I'm not sure if she's still involved with Troy, but I'm guessing she dumped him to go on this show.

There's some psychiatrist who will do one-on-one and group sessions to work through everyone's issues, a shrink named Dr. Fields.

They do a quick recap of everyone's careers, and when they get to Dakota, I hold my breath as I watch a montage of her big reality show moments. Mostly quick clips from that private school show, *Winchester Prep High*. Then it switches gears to *Little Darlings*. Shots of her as a sick kid in a hospital bed tug at my heart, but it's the video of Charlotte all alone and crying that wrecks me.

"How can they use footage of you without your consent?" I ask her.

Charlie's eyes are wide, her face pale. "I was a minor at the time. My mother signed off on everything when I was a kid. I have no control over how it's used now."

I tug her to me and glance at Cam, Billy, and Roxy, who are riveted to the screen.

Damn. This will probably be a huge hit if our friends can't take their eyes off it.

The TV flashes pics from Dakota's social media and notes she's an influencer with millions of followers. But it's the photos of Asher as a baby and pics with me and Troy that set me on edge.

Her voice narrates the montage: "I've come a long way— from nearly dying as a child to having more than my fair share of success. I have a beautiful baby, I've dated some beautiful men, and I have a beautiful life, but I'm ready for more."

My jaw is so tight, it feels like it might crack. Sure, she has a beautiful baby... who she basically abandoned.

It hits me for the first time. How Asher could be at risk for whatever made Dakota sick when she was younger. Doctors could never figure out why she was so ill.

I close my eyes, praying my son doesn't have to go through anything like that.

Dakota's voice gets emotional. "I've done a lot I'm not proud of, and I'm hoping to work through my demons and be a better person."

She sounds so sincere. I'd bet everything in my bank account it's all bullshit.

By the time the episode ends, I'm sweating.

"That wasn't so bad," Billy says.

Yet.

I'm right to feel uneasy because the voiceover goes on to say, "This season on *The Hot House*..." as shots of the contestants start up again. It's the video of Dakota wiping away tears as she talks to the psychiatrist that has me worried.

Not that I've done anything wrong. My conscience is clear. I never treated her badly or did anything that can't stand up under scrutiny. My mother would take a frying pan to my head if I ever mistreated a woman.

But Dakota has a way of spinning things that always makes her look good, regardless of the consequences.

Like she can read my mind, Charlie groans. "If my sister brings me or Jake up at all, I promise you she'll twist things to make us look bad."

Exhausted, I sink back on the couch and tilt my head back. "How many episodes again?"

"Ten." Charlie sounds just as crestfallen as I feel.

Roxy hugs her. "Maybe no one will watch and you have nothing to worry about."

It's possible. Unlikely, but possible.

Still, I'm bracing myself for the worst.

17

CHARLOTTE

CHARMING streets pass by in a blur.

As Jake drives me to the park, I can't stop thinking about last week's episode. Kota's even more beautiful now, if that's possible. No wonder I always felt invisible next to her.

Seeing those images from *Little Darlings* made my heart hurt. At the age I was then, you don't understand death, but we'd just lost a pet. Our cat got hit by a car, and I found his broken body in the alley behind our house. If Roscoe's lifeless eyes were anything to go by, I didn't want my sister to end up like that.

Watching Kota wail from her hospital bed while that guy recorded from his spot in the corner haunted me for years. I didn't like the way the man watched our every move. Even as a kid, I never welcomed that kind of scrutiny. The rest of my family seemed to thrive when they were the center of attention, while all I wanted to do was crawl into bed with Kota to make sure she kept breathing.

When Kota got better and sat up in her bed to spontaneously sing "Tomorrow" from that musical *Annie*, fans went crazy. Her hospital room was packed to the ceiling with gifts and balloons from well-wishers. According to my mother, that episode almost broke the internet. My sister was trending everywhere, on every social media platform.

I know Kota would never believe me, but I was happy for her success. I always wanted the best for her.

Jake parks, and we grab our gear. I shake my head to clear my thoughts. *The past is the past. There's nothing I can do to change it.*

"It's your one day off," I tell him as I tie my roller skates. "Wouldn't you rather be—"

"Nope. We're doing this." Jake holds out his large, calloused hand. I place mine in his as I bite my bottom lip to keep from smiling too wide.

He has no idea how much I need this. How much he centers me.

Now that I've shaken off the Kota funk I was in, excitement courses through my body at the thought of me and Jake spending the afternoon together.

We're holding hands. I take a few calming breaths so my heart doesn't gallop out of my chest.

Miss Louisa got her wires crossed and showed up to watch Asher this morning even though Jake didn't need her. She patted his cheek and told him to get some time for himself. I love her, and I'm super bummed this is her last week in town.

I'm finally feeling well enough to exercise. My wheeze is gone, and my doctor says I'm in the clear to be more active.

When we're done with my skating practice today, we promised Asher we'd take him out for burgers. I think Jake and I are both trying really hard to go about life as normal, even though *The Hot House* feels like a ticking time bomb.

Slowly, I stand and wobble. "See? I can do this."

Feeling brave, I let go of his hand, push off, and almost fall on my face.

Strong arms wrap around my waist and keep me from breaking something.

"Maybe this isn't a good idea," Jake says. He waits for me to stop wobbling before he lets go.

"I'm not a wuss. I can do this."

He looks dubious. "Why don't I pull you, and you can try to stay upright? Just to start off so you can find your balance?"

Wow. He really doesn't think I'm cut out for skating, but maybe letting him pull me isn't such a bad idea. "Lead the way."

With my small hand in his huge paw, he walks ahead along the sidewalk, and I follow behind. At first, I'm only trying to stay upright, but after a few minutes, I have the hang of it.

He glances back at me, his expression so serious. He's probably surprised I'm still on my feet. His thick, messy hair falls in his eyes, and I catch a whiff of that ocean-scented body wash he's always used.

Why does Jake have to be such a thirst trap? I seriously have no defenses against this man.

Trailing behind my roommate gives me a chance to covertly check him out. He's wearing worn jeans that mold to his tight ass and thighs and an old t-shirt that shows off his broad, muscular shoulders.

I love that he doesn't care about clothes. That always drove my sister crazy. Kota would bring home expensive brands and try to dress him up like he was her personal Ken doll. He hated that.

When he turns, I catch sight of his strong jaw that's covered in bristles since he didn't shave this morning.

He's been pretty quiet since our *Hot House* watch party the other night. "Are you freaking out about Kota?"

Stopping, he turns back to me. "How can you tell?"

"You've been brooding since we watched the show."

He scoffs. "I don't brood."

I push off on one skate and pull up next to him. "You're brooding now." I wave a finger around his handsome face. "You have that pouty thing going on even though you scored a touchdown yesterday." He looked fierce out on the field. I babysat Asher, and he and I had a blast watching his daddy play on TV.

He smirks. "Careful, cupcake. I'm the only thing standing between you and the concrete."

I yank my hand free. "I'm a big girl. I can do this on my own, you know." Feeling more confident, I skate faster. The wind blowing through my hair is exhilarating, which is when I get the bright idea to turn around and try to skate backwards like the guy I saw on a YouTube video last night.

Only the wheel in my left skate gets caught in a crack in the concrete. My arms pinwheel, and I let out a girly squeal of horror.

I'm pretty sure I'm going down hard.

Jake catches me at the last second, only my momentum sends me straight into his chest. Clinging to him, I close my eyes and try to catch my breath.

He sets me upright as I pant. A moment later, his thumb grazes my cheek. "You okay?"

It's my turn to pout. I gaze up at him and whisper, "I don't think I should take the roller-skating job."

"Won't you be busy shooting football anyway?"

"Potentially, yes, but that doesn't pay anything. It's just an opportunity to build my portfolio, maybe get some shots in the newspaper. But that won't pay the bills, not if I'm trying to save so I can buy my own equipment again. It's not like I'll be able to borrow cameras from the athletic director after I graduate. How will I get the funds to get my own apartment if I don't take this job?"

I melt under the attention of those big brown eyes. "Charlotte, you don't need to move out anytime soon." His deep voice, low and rumbly, makes me want to rub up against him like a needy cat. "My scholarships cover the rent and utilities. And it's not like I'm gonna let you go hungry. I can always snag extra to-go boxes from the cafeteria."

This is humiliating. "I'm not mooching off you, Jake." It's bad enough my family abandoned him and Asher. "I'm not a charity case. I can pay my own way."

His eyes go soft. "I'm not saying you're charity. Just... you helped me and Ash so much freshman year. Think of this as me returning the favor."

When he says it like that, he's hard to resist. I agree, but deep down I know I need to make my own way.

"Hang on. I'll get us back to my car." He holds out his arm, and I cling to his huge, sculpted bicep as we make our way around the park.

"I'm bummed this job won't work out. I like how tall I am with skates. Without them, I'm..."

"Fun-sized. Like a mini-Snickers candy bar."

I chuckle.

He's quiet for a moment. "So, um, you still going on a date with Kyle Green?"

"Thursday night." I turn my face up to look at him. Does this bother him at all? That I'm going out with another guy? Roxy set it up the other evening, and I didn't want to chicken out, but if Jake gave me any indication at all that he cared about me like that, I'd bail in a heartbeat.

But he doesn't.

"Cool. Just wanted to make sure so I didn't accidentally schedule you to babysit."

Inside, I deflate like a popped balloon. "What about you? Any hot dates set up?" *Please say no.*

"Nah. Kinda have my hands full right now. Besides, when would I have time to go out?"

Thank the good Lord for that.

He nudges me. "Have you been practicing your flirting skills?"

I snort. "What skills? Roxy told me to blink more so I don't look like a serial killer." Apparently, the only time I blink is if I'm taking a photo.

"Oh, shit." He laughs so hard, he has to stop and bend over.

"Please don't tell me you think I look like a serial killer too," I say. He won't stop laughing. "Great. I'm destined to die a virgin," I mumble.

His laughter fades and that crinkle forms between his brows as he straightens to his full height. "Wait. What? Did you say you're a virgin?"

Damn. He heard me.

The astonished look on his face really bugs me. "Yes, okay. I'm a virgin, but guess what? It's my senior year, and I'm tired of saving it for 'some special guy' who doesn't fucking exist. This is my year to lose it. Maybe it'll be with that hotshot baseball player I'm going out with this week. Who knows? Or maybe he'll be the lucky guy." I point to some rando walking by us, who startles as my hand waves near his face. "Sorry. I... sorry."

Jesus, I sound hysterical, and when I catch a glimpse of the amusement on Jake's face, I lose it all over again.

"If you laugh again, I'm punching you in the nut sack."

He holds out his hands while mirth dances in his eyes. "Calm down, cupcake. No nut punches necessary. I'm not laughing at you." The asshole chuckles. "I'm merely laughing in your general vicinity."

"Shut up."

After hooking an arm around my shoulders, he starts walking again. I roll alongside him with my arm around his waist and try to keep my balance.

He clears his throat. "What's wrong with waiting for someone special?"

"Jake, in case you haven't noticed, I'm almost twenty-two. I've never had a boyfriend, I never go on dates, and I've never had sex. That's all pretty sad in my book. Look, I was freakishly shy in high school and could never admit when I liked someone." I want to yell, *You're the someone, dummy!* And Billy doesn't count because he was 'practice.' "Now that I'm not a total wallflower anymore, trailing behind my gorgeous celebrity sister like I'm invisible, I'd like to do the deed. Get it over already. Isn't our generation all about the hookup culture? Well, I'm ready. Bring on the sex."

I've watched porn. I've learned some moves. I nod and tell myself I'm not terrified.

Stopping, Jake turns me to face him. "What are you talking about? You've never been invisible."

Says the guy who's never reciprocated my love.

"Let's forget this conversation, okay? It's humiliating."

That large hand tips my chin up. "You never have to be embarrassed with me. You already know all of my dirty laundry." He gives me one of those sweet smiles that made me fall in love with him when I was fourteen.

He's so close. With the way the sun is shining, his dark brown eyes turn the shade of whiskey.

What would happen if I leaned forward, pushed up on my toes, and kissed him? Admitted that I've been crushing on him for years? Admitted that my feelings for him never went away? Because he obviously thinks I got over him since I moved here.

If he kissed me back, it would be amazing. I'm pretty sure fireworks would go off behind us like it's the Fourth of July while a full symphony orchestra serenaded us.

But if he didn't?

Or if he only returned the kiss because he felt bad for me?

I'd feel so pathetic, I'd want to crawl in a hole and die.

I take a deep breath and regain some sense. It's not worth it. I won't put myself out there because Jake is the only person preventing me from being homeless. I'd be an idiot to jeopardize that. I don't even have any family anymore. I have Jake and Roxy, and I need to cherish these relationships. Not make a pass at my roommate.

I pretend like my heart isn't trying to burrow out of my body and resume our trek back to his car, where we exchange the roller skates for sneakers.

On our way home, we stop off at the grocery store. We need to pick up a few things for the week before we take Asher out for burgers. I'm bent over the rotisserie chickens, trying to find a good one for Duke, when a group of girls stroll up to Jake and start fawning all over him.

"You were so great yesterday!" Giggle.

"Why didn't you come to the party last night?" Giggle.

"Will you sign my cleavage?" Giggle.

My gag reflex kicks in. Would it be rude if I puked on them? I roll my eyes and head for the checkout.

Jake calls out behind me, "Charlie, wait."

When he catches up, I joke, "Next time I'll tell them you're getting over a raging case of chlamydia. That'll thin the heard."

"Jesus Christ, Charlotte."

"Don't worry. I'll make sure to note you're on medication."

Chuckling, he hooks an arm around my neck and rubs his knuckles into the top of my head. "Turnabout is fair play. What if I tell Kyle that you drool in your sleep? Or that you never shower?" He snaps his fingers. "I've got it. I'll tell him the photoshoots for the calendar are really an excuse to stalk the hot guys on the baseball team."

I freeze and turn to glare at him. "Jake, I'm already dealing with a serious serial killer vibe. Please don't blow this for me."

His voice lowers to a whisper. "I'm kidding, cupcake. I'd never do anything to derail you."

"Promise? Because I'm already anxious about that date, but I can't keep bailing on things like this. It's time I take life by the horns and make it my bitch."

He laughs. "Okay, ball-buster. I promise not to tell Kyle anything gross about you, but I might need a favor in return."

"Anything."

As we wait in the checkout line, he jams his hands in his pockets. "My mom is worried I'm becoming a recluse, so I promised I'd go to the bonfire and homecoming dance and whatever. You know, live the stereotypical college life for one weekend before I go back to the grind. She even offered to help with the extra babysitting costs. The only catch is all of the guys have dates."

His words hang between us.

"And... you need me to... babysit?" While he goes out with Yvette or Buffy or Matilda? Oh my God, does that mean he'll bring one of them home? I'm not sure I can handle hearing Jake hook up with someone.

Those big brown eyes meet mine. "Uh, no." He swallows. "Actually, I was wondering if you'd be my date."

I open my mouth, but nothing comes out. *Hold up. Is he asking me out?*

He rubs the back of his neck. "I mean, since you're making an effort in the dating department, I thought we could kill two birds with one stone. But fair warning, it's a two-day event. You'll probably be sick of me by the time it's over."

Would it be wrong to leap into his arms and kiss him?

I feel my face getting hot. "I'd be honored to be your date." Smiling, I look down at my shoes.

"Charlotte."

Turning my face up to his, I'm caught off guard by his serious expression. "Yes?"

"The honor would be all mine."

I'm so elated I almost miss the magazine on the stand that says "Dakota, the *Hot House* Darling: An in-depth look at this hottie's love life."

18

JAKE

GRUNTING, I crank the treadmill. Sweat drips off my brow and down my bare chest as I push myself harder.

Weights clank in a backdrop beat to the rock music on the stereo. I should be thinking about this weekend's game, but my thoughts keep straying to my outing last Sunday afternoon with Charlie.

To the way her eyes danced when she got determined to skate.

To the adorable way she clung to me when she needed help.

To her cute little ass in those cutoffs.

I close my eyes, hating how conflicted I feel. No one ever believes me when I say that Charlotte and I have always been *just* friends.

Only that somehow feels wrong now. I'm not sure what's changed on my end. Maybe it's because we're living together and I see her every day? Maybe it's because dragging her out of that fire scared the fuck out of me? Or maybe it's because she feels like my best friend again, and lately I've been wondering what it would be like if we were... more?

And when I thought she was going to wipe out? My heart was in my throat as I sprinted to catch her.

When I remember how she looked at me in the park, my whole body heats.

Fuck. I shouldn't be thinking about Charlie like this.

Because going there with her right now seems like a really bad idea. I promised myself I wouldn't get involved with anyone this year. There's too much on the line.

Except I do need a date.

Since Coach Santos took over as head coach here last year, he's been building up our homecoming festivities, adding the bonfire, a parade—all kinds of spirit week activities—and he wants the football team to show up for a few events.

I figured Charlie and I would have fun and I wouldn't have to deal with asking someone who might get the wrong idea about what the invitation meant. I'd fully intended to emphasize that we'd be going as friends.

But then Charlie and I got talking about her going out with Kyle, and fuck. I don't know. I didn't want to deliberately put myself in the friend zone.

He's picking her up tonight. She asked me if she should cancel. However much I wanted to tell her to bail, I'd be a suck-ass friend if I did. She's never gone on dates, and if anyone deserves to be treated like a princess, it's Charlotte.

Plus, that will incentivize me to keep my relationship with her completely platonic. It's the smart thing to do. Especially with the scrutiny I might face from Dakota's show. The last thing I need splashed on gossip magazines before the draft is how I jumped from one Darling sister to the other.

When Charlie pointed out that magazine at the grocery store, I wanted to shit my pants. It was a retrospective of all the guys Dakota has dated. Conveniently, she fudged the dates for when she got with Troy so they didn't overlap with me. At least the sports reporters who cover my games haven't asked about that yet.

I rub my throbbing temple. Fuck, I'm tired every time I think about it.

My brothers will give me endless shit if they find out I'm taking Charlie to homecoming. One, they hate her family and they'll say I'm an idiot for trusting another Darling. Two, they've teased me mercilessly about her for years. And three, they think we've been secretly hooking up since high school regardless of how many times I've denied it.

Out of the corner of my eye, I spot Roxy and our quarter-back. Cheerleaders aren't supposed to be back here, but since Coach is Roxy's dad, she basically does what she wants. And right now, that means yelling at our QB. Ezra Thomas is getting his ass chewed out.

When she spots me, she snaps her mouth shut. Turning back to him, she pokes him in the chest, hisses something I can't make out, and storms off.

He makes his way into the weight room and drops down onto the bench next to me.

"You okay, man?" I swipe my forehead with a towel.

"Remind me never to tangle with Roxy Santos again."

I could've told him that. Why would anyone mess with the coach's daughter? That has stupidity written all over it.

"You two dating or something?"

"Or something," he says with a smirk.

Yeah, that's not gonna end well.

Thomas looks like he wants to tell me more, but I make an excuse to move to the other side of the weight room. The less I know about Roxy's love life, the better. So when Coach goes ballistic because one of his players messed with his daughter, I can claim ignorance.

That night, when I get home, I feel at peace with this idea of

Charlotte going out with Kyle. She'll have a fun night, get wined and dined, and come home to me. We'll watch old sitcoms and eat pizza. Maybe play some chess.

It'll be fine. I'm totally cool with it.

Until she waltzes out of the bedroom in a sexy-as-fuck black dress that makes my heart stop.

19

CHARLOTTE

"You look great, babe," Roxy says as she adds the finishing touch to my smoky eye.

"So great!" Buffy squeals.

I might've been a little judgmental about Buffy. She's actually really nice. I mean, she definitely wants to bone Jake, but she isn't snarky with me like Yvette and Matilda. And if Jake wants her, well, there's nothing I can do about that.

"Thanks for letting me borrow another outfit," I tell Roxy.

Roxy is bustier than I am, but the wraparound dress is stretchy, and I was able to tie it super tight so the front was snug.

"I'm glad someone's going to wear it. I bought it for homecoming, but my date decided to be a dick, so he can fuck right off."

Ezra is a dog. He can definitely fuck off, but I don't say anything because Buffy isn't privy to what's going on with Roxy.

Roxy snaps her fingers. "Wait. Did you take your birth control?"

My face heats as I let out a nervous laugh. Despite my big talk, I'm not sure I could go from being a virgin to having sex on the first date, but it's good to be prepared. "Yes, Mom."

To be honest, Rox is a hundred times more considerate than my actual mother.

We step out of my bedroom just as Jake comes home. Duke hops up and down excitedly, and Jake reaches down to pet him.

When he stands upright, I give him a wide smile, but he freezes when he sees me. Then his jaw goes tight.

Self-consciously, I pat down the dress. "What? You don't like my outfit?"

His eyes travel down my body and back up again before he turns away. "You look great. Have fun on your date. Is Asher asleep?"

That's it? That's all he's going to say?

Buffy trots up to him to give him a rundown of her afternoon with Ash.

Roxy and I look at each other as they head into the kitchen.

All the excitement I'd had about tonight circles the drain. "Do I look bad, Rox?" I whisper. Honestly, I really liked having a reason to get dressed up. Kyle seems nice and all and I'm sure he's a sweet guy, but I thought having a practice date before homecoming seemed like a good idea. Especially after I'd asked Jake if he wanted me to cancel, and he told me I should go.

Which makes me think our homecoming "date" in two weeks is really a "hang out with Charlotte 'cause she's my buddy" kind of thing.

Maybe it's even a pity date.

Ugh, shoot me now.

"No." She glares at Jake. "He's probably just jealous."

Doubtful. The man has women throwing themselves at him at every turn.

Maybe he's upset about tonight's episode.

"Jake." I wait until he faces me. "Are you okay watching *The Hot House* by yourself? I feel bad I'm ditching you." I'd watch it with him, but I don't think it's healthy for me to obsess over shit Kota might or might not say. I cut ties with her for a reason and don't want to give her any more power over me. So I might watch a few episodes, but I'm not going to rearrange my life to catch every single one.

"Oh! He won't be by himself. I'm watching it with him!" Buffy says with a happy squeal.

He smiles at her, and my stomach sinks. "Great."

The knock at the door has my heart racing, but not in a good way. I suddenly don't want to go out, but Roxy opens the door and Kyle gives me a wave.

I don't want any more weirdness with Jake, so I grab my purse and head out.

It's the longest two hours of my life. Dinner is nice, but our conversation is painfully stilted. I suppose it says something that I'm enormously relieved when it's over.

As soon as I'm home, I kick off my heels with a sigh of relief.

"You're back early." Jake's studying notecards at the kitchen table.

"I tried blinking more to stave off 'stalker vibes,' but at one point Kyle asked if I had something in my eye."

Jake chuckles. "He's an idiot."

"How was the show? Anything terrible happen?"

"Two people hooked up. One chick nailed an audition. Dakota cried fake tears over someone's bad poem from their group therapy session—I'm guessing so viewers vote for her this week. Other than that, nothing major."

"That's a relief." I pick up my shoes and head back to the bedroom, but he calls my name.

"You okay, cupcake? Kyle didn't do anything he shouldn't, did he?"

Is it my imagination or did he growl out that last part?

"He was a perfect gentleman."

"Then why do you look so disgruntled?"

I think about that. "Aside from us not having anything in common? Or any chemistry?" Over my shoulder, I say, "Maybe I'm not looking for a gentleman."

With that parting comment, I go to bed.

Is it wrong to want someone who's ravenous for me? And fine, I don't really want to bang someone on the first date, but Kyle and I had zero chemistry, and that bummed me out.

Will I ever find someone who does it for me besides my big, clueless roommate?

"WE'LL BE BACK IN AN HOUR." Yvette takes Asher by the hand, but he scoots away and runs to me.

"Aww, buddy." I squat on the ground and hug him. "Have fun at the park with Miss Yvette. Be a good boy."

He points to himself and proudly nods. "I'm a good boy!"

"And who goes potty in the bathroom like a *big* boy?" Ash had been having accidents, but he's back on track now.

"ME!" he shouts with a huge smile.

I high-five him and ignore Yvette's eye roll.

She's giving off some high-level bitch vibes today, so I usher Asher to her. When they're gone, I sigh. If I hustle, maybe I can get out of here before they return. I love spending time with Asher, but I feel like Yvette is plotting to poison me.

After I brush my hair, I strip out of my clothes, about to jump into the shower, when I realize I left my stack of clean clothes on a stool in the kitchen.

I glance down at myself. I'm just wearing undies, but no one's here. Jake never comes home in the middle of the day and Yvette and Asher just left, so I don't bother covering up.

With the shower running, I run out to the kitchen. And then

I smell the coffee I made earlier and forgot to drink, so I reach for a mug in the cabinet and pour myself a cup.

Behind me, someone coughs dramatically.

I gasp and turn around to find Jake, Cam, and Billy sitting on the couch with sandwiches spread out on the coffee table. They're frozen, eyes glued to me.

And then I realize I'm almost naked. It's like a bad high school nightmare.

"What the hell!" I start to run, only I forget I'm holding a hot cup of coffee and it splashes all over me. "Damn it."

I don't bother trying to dry it. Instead, I march back to the bathroom and slam the door shut.

I shut off the water, wrap myself in a towel, and plop down on the side of the tub. Why is my life like a bad rom-com? Only instead of winning the guy, I come off like a serial killer and burn myself? I dab the towel over my chest where it's red from the coffee.

A minute later, someone knocks. "You okay, Charlotte?"

Jake.

"Go away."

"Sorry we scared you. I called out that I was home, but I don't think you heard me over the shower."

I hang my head. I have the worst luck of anyone I know.

When I don't say anything, he lowers his voice. "I brought you some Subway. Roast beef and Swiss with that oil stuff you like."

Why is he so damn nice? Why does he always remember my favorite foods? Why can't he be a dick?

"Thanks. I'll be out in a few."

After regaining my composure, I decide I can't hide in the bathroom all day. Besides, my clothes are still in the kitchen.

With a towel securely wrapped around me, I unlock the door and tiptoe down the hall. The guys stop eating to look up at me.

"I think I should have to see y'all naked too now. Payback, you know?"

Billy stands and whips his shirt off before the words are out of my mouth. I'm laughing when he reaches for the button on his jeans, but Jake yanks him back down to the couch.

"You're not getting naked," Jake barks.

"Well, I've already seen you in the buff, so I guess you're exempt, but I'm not opposed to seeing Billy and Cam," I tease.

Billy and Cam turn to look at Jake, who shrugs. "It was a video call gone wrong. Long story."

There was *something* long all right.

And thick too.

My neck gets hot just thinking about it. "Thanks for the sandwich. I'll eat it later."

"Did you burn yourself with the coffee, Charlotte?" Jake asks.

"I'm okay."

"Hey, Chuck." Billy swallows a huge bite of his hoagie. "I heard you're shooting the game this weekend." When I nod, he continues. "Think you could get a good action shot of me? My grandmother's been on my ass to send her a photo of me playing football."

"Sure. But full disclosure, I've never shot football before, so I might suck. If I can't get a good pic of you, though, we could set one up where you're in your uniform. The guys can pretend they're tackling you."

He snorts. "That totally works. Thanks. And I'm sure you're gonna kick ass this weekend."

"She always kicks ass," Jake adds, making me smile.

I grab my stack of clothes and head back down the hall.

As crazy as he makes me sometimes, I have to admit Jake's a great guy. He'll make a lucky girl really happy someday.

I just wish that girl was me.

20

JAKE

Float chamber. Choke valve. Throttle valve. Piston valve...

As I drive the guys back to the stadium, I mentally review all the parts of a carburetor. It's something my older brother David drilled into my head when I was younger because he assumed I'd work for him someday.

And as much as I hate the idea of toiling in his garage, I find the exercise takes my mind off Charlotte's perfect, bouncy tits.

Her tiny waist.

And that flimsy strip of silk between her slender thighs.

Billy taps on the window. "So we're not gonna talk about it?"

My hands tighten on the steering wheel. "Nope."

"Really? Because I just wanna say I always knew underneath her prim little exterior, Chuck was a stone-cold fox. Talk about spank bank material."

"Shut the fuck up, asshole. We're not talking about Charlotte." When he doesn't say anything, I look over to find him smirking. "What?"

"Just wondering when you're gonna admit you have a thing for her."

My knee-jerk reaction is to deny it. I've always denied it. But after everything she and I have been through lately, I'm not sure I can anymore.

"She went on a date last night." With Kyle fucking Green.

"And you let her?" Billy gives me a look of disgust.

"What was I supposed to do? Tie her up?" It's not fair that I've had my share of experiences over the years and no one has even taken her out on a date.

She's always been at the beck and call of her family. Now that she's on her own and more adventurous, I don't want to sway her one way or the other. If she wants to date other men, she should.

And I'd felt fine with her going out—until I saw how drop-dead gorgeous she looked in that black dress and wanted to drag her back into my bedroom and fuck her until she cried out my name.

Billy's eyes light up. "Didn't realize you were into ropes, but sure, let's go with a little light BDSM. Chuck might enjoy giving up control."

In the back seat, Cam laughs.

I glare at Billy. "Charlotte and I have a complicated history. She's my ex's *little sister*."

He scratches his head. "Yeah, but weren't you two friends first?"

Instantly, I'm on guard. "How do you know this?"

"Relax, dude. Charlie told me." He points a finger in my face. "And I can see by your reaction that you want to know what else she said."

I pull into the stadium and throw my car into park. "Look, I'm not going to deny I have feelings for her, but my last relationship—with her sister, coincidentally—imploded spectacularly, and I'm not sure I'm ready for anything serious. The thing about Charlotte is despite her..." I pause, not wanting to share her plans to lose her virginity because that's none of his fucking business. "Despite her casual dating plans, she is serious relationship material. And I really don't wanna fuck her up or fuck up our friendship. She's important to me."

Billy jumps out of the car. "Then I guess you'll get to watch when she eventually moves on with another guy, huh?" He struts off like he hasn't just tilted my world on its axis.

Dread forms in my chest as I think about last night. I all but pushed Charlotte out the door with Kyle. She seemed glad to be home, but what happens next time? What happens when she does meet someone? Eventually, she will. She's a beautiful, sweet woman. Any man would be lucky to date her.

I think about calling one of my brothers to get advice, but Charlotte is a sensitive topic, and David and Eli are not sensitive guys. I can't handle them saying crass things about her right now.

Cam reaches forward and pats me on the shoulder. "Billy lives to give people crap. I'm sure you'll figure out what to do about Charlie."

I look down at my lap. "I asked her to homecoming, but I don't know if that was the smartest move. I don't want to give her the wrong impression about what I can give her. And even if we do date, her sister will lose her shit when she finds out."

"Why tell her?"

The words hang in the air, and I still.

That's a damn good question.

And it makes me wonder. Dakota's in California. Is it possible she won't give a shit what Charlotte and I do?

∽

ON THE WAY home from practice, my phone rings. I put the call on speaker as I drive.

"*¿Como está mi hijo favorito?*" My mom's sweet voice fills the car.

I chuckle because my mom calls each of her sons her favorite. "Hi, *mamá.*"

"Did you get a date for the dance?"

"I did."

"And? Is she pretty?"

I really don't want to discuss Charlotte with my mother, but I have to give her something. "*Ella es hermosa.*" Swear to God, I have no idea how she and I have been friends all this time and I never really appreciated how stunning she is.

"Well, are you going to tell me her name or do I have to drag it out of you?"

I consider lying, but what's the point? I'd rather get this out of the way now. "It's Charlotte, Ma."

The line goes quiet. And then, "You mean, *your* Charlotte? From high school?"

"I don't know that I'd call her *my* Charlotte, but yes."

"The same one who, how do you kids say it, ghosted you?"

I cringe. "She had her reasons. Anyway, she's a senior now at Lone Star State too. We've talked it out. We're good. Especially now that Dakota is out of the picture."

My mom gasps. "*Esa es la chica del fuego.*"

I've been wondering how long it would take for her to piece it together, that Charlotte was the girl I dragged out of the fire.

Weirdly, the focus of the reports was on me jumping into the building and not the unconscious woman. The fire department didn't release her name early on, which I suppose is good since Charlotte hates being in the spotlight.

A few reporters called my mom after that video went viral, but she was so freaked out that I'd deliberately run into a flaming building, she really didn't pay attention to much more than the fact that I'd made it out alive.

She goes quiet again. *"Mijo. Ten cuidado."* Be careful.

"Ma, I was upset when she took off. She told me she left me a note, and I think Dakota found it and trashed it." The more I think about it, the more that seems the most likely scenario. Charlie never lies to me, while Dakota's specialty is deceit. "Anyway, I'm not gonna get hurt or anything. You don't need to worry."

"Jacob, I mean be careful that *you* don't hurt *her*."

My head jerks back. "What does that mean? Why would I hurt her?"

She lets out a long, drawn-out sigh. "You've always been the most clueless of my boys. *Mijo*, Charlotte has always liked you. Ever since you were a freshman in high school, that girl followed you around with stars in her eyes. That's why your brothers always teased you. And when you started dating Dakota, I'm surprised poor Charlotte didn't crumble into dust and blow away."

It takes me several moments for me to process what my mother says, and then I pull over onto the shoulder because I feel like I've just been hit with a two-by-four.

I clear my throat. "She said she left NTU because she had feelings for me. I thought it was just in college because we spent a lot of time together. She was always over babysitting Asher."

"In high school, she baked you cupcakes, went to your games, made you posters for spirit week, helped you with homework. She even hung out with you when you went through your guitar phase. I love you, but we both know you can't play the guitar."

"Is it weird that she always did more for me than Dakota ever did?"

"That's because when you love someone, you'll bend over backward to make them happy. Dakota didn't love you, baby. We both know that."

Whoa.

Whoa.

Love? Does Charlotte *love* me?

My mom continues her rant about Dakota. "I know the last few years have been tough, but I'm glad you're not messed up with her anymore. *Le falta un domingo.*" She's missing a Sunday. That's my mom's nice way of saying Dakota's not playing with a full deck.

I tilt my head back and stare at the ceiling. "I don't know what to do about Charlotte."

"If you don't have feelings for her, don't lead that poor girl on." She pauses. "But if you do, you still have to be careful. She's not someone you can have a fling with."

No shit. Wasn't I just telling the guys this very thing?

It's my turn to sigh. "That's a lot of pressure. What if I fuck up?"

"You were always a good boy, and you've grown into a good man. Trust your instincts."

That's just it. Ever since I broke up with Dakota, I don't fucking trust my instincts anymore. Hell, I barely trust my teammates now, and that was always a given. Your teammates always have your back. That was something deeply ingrained in me. Something I would've sworn on until I found Troy in bed with Dakota.

"Before I forget, let me tell you why I called," my mom says. "I have some vacation time coming up, and I was wondering if I could get Asher for a few days. Maybe over homecoming week so you can enjoy the dance and bonfire without having to worry about babysitting."

I'd have the whole apartment, alone, with Charlotte. Just thinking about it makes my blood run hot. "You're so good to me, *mamá.*"

She laughs. "I love you too, *mijo.*"

～

THAT NIGHT, I can't sleep. I can't stop replaying the moment Charlie pranced out of the bathroom wearing those little panties. I can't stop seeing the way her tits bounced. I can't stop thinking about how her hair draped over her slender shoulders and how I'd love nothing more than to rake my fingers through it before I fist it tight and drag her rosebud mouth to mine.

I'm fucked.

So much for staying focused on football.

When I do doze off, I dream about crossing the hall and slipping into Charlotte's bed. How she'd fold back the blankets and pat the mattress. How she'd open her arms to me.

I wake with a start. Asher is splayed out across the bed like a starfish. Quietly, I head for the bathroom, lock the door, and blast the shower.

After I strip, I jump in and take my cock in my fist and give in to the fantasy.

First, I'd nibble Charlotte's gorgeous tits, pinch those perfect pink nipples. Suck them, bite them. Make her squirm.

Then I'd slide down her body and lick her sweet pussy until her legs quaked.

And when she swore she couldn't come again, I'd slide into her wet heat until she arched her back and pulsed around me.

Groaning, I lean my forehead against the tile as I come.

I never let myself think about Charlotte like this. Not since we were freshmen in high school. Once I thought she'd firmly friend-zoned me, I felt like she was off limits.

But now that I've gone down the rabbit hole, I'm not sure I can put a lid on this any longer.

I can only hope I don't screw up our friendship.

21

CHARLOTTE

THE ATHLETIC DIRECTOR, Mr. Armstrong, unlocks the cabinet and waves a hand at the shelves. "Take what you need. Be sure to always sign out the equipment with my assistant. I already have a copy of your school ID, so you're good to go anytime you want to shoot."

Getting a new ID was a whole ordeal. When you're broke, everything is tough. I'd babysit Asher for free because I love him to pieces and he's my nephew, but Jake's been paying me, and I finally have enough to replace a few more things that were lost in the fire.

Wait. What did Mr. Armstrong say?

My mouth drops open. "I can borrow anything?" There are three top-of-the-line SLRs, several telephoto lenses, camera bags, a tray of memory cards—everything I could possibly need.

He chuckles. "The boosters went a little overboard, didn't they? But this is one of the perks of working for a Division 1 school with a marquee team."

God bless the boosters. "Thank you for this opportunity. I promise I'll take good care of everything. Are there particular images you want besides action shots of the game?"

"Anything that shows Bronco spirit. So cheerleaders, fans, and mascots are all great. Next weekend, if you want to also get some of the tailgating in the parking lot before the game, that might be fun for my newsletter."

That all sounds doable. I start to relax. "No problem."

"Check in with me on Monday. We'll go through the images and talk more."

"Yes, sir."

"If this works for us, maybe you'll consider shooting baseball in the spring?" He gives me a hopeful look.

Laughing, I nod. "I'm totally open to it."

When he's gone, I reverently run my hands over the beautiful sleek camera bodies. I could never afford anything this nice, but it gives me something to aim for.

Once I pack a camera bag, I heft it over my shoulder and head out for the field.

A guard stops me. "Credentials, please."

I proudly point to my newly laminated badge hanging on the lanyard around my neck, and he waves me through. I feel so official.

Stepping out onto the field is surreal. The staff is setting up for the tunnel run, so I head to the sideline and unpack my gear. The stadium is quickly filling, a buzz of excitement in the air.

I get two cameras strapped around my neck, one with a telephoto lens, and one with a shorter lens to shoot anything close up. When I spot our cheerleaders, I wave at Roxy. She looks so darn cute in her cheer outfit. She gives me a saucy wink before she does a backflip. I start shooting the squad, hoping to get some good ones for the AD, maybe even a few Roxy can give her parents.

I get down on my knees to photograph Mr. Pearson and his goat Essie, who's a local celebrity. They're both decked out in Bronco colors.

Which reminds me.

I scan the arena, looking for Merle, but there are too many people.

When I told Jake what a huge fan Merle was of the team, Jake got him a pair of tickets for this game. I've been so busy that I haven't been able to volunteer at the shelter since the fire, but Merle said he understands and that as long as I'm rehabbing Duke, working on the calendar, and making more flyers, he's happy. Plus, since Jake mentioned the shelter at the press conference, Merle says he's had plenty of help, which is a relief.

The announcer introduces UT, and the crowd goes crazy. Since we're close to Austin, there are tons of Longhorn fans here. It's a charged, wild atmosphere. It feels like anything could happen this afternoon, which makes me anxious for Jake. This is a big game, and he was broody this morning. I wondered if he was rattled about my sister's show, but he says no one has really bothered him about it yet, which is a relief.

When it's our turn to get introduced, the crowd goes from loud to ear-blisteringly insane.

I get as close to the edge of the field as possible before I start to shoot. It's so loud, I can't even hear the whirring of my shutter that's pressed to my face.

As "Paradise City" by Guns N' Roses blares, the guys race out the tunnel and through this huge blow-up archway. Smoke machines make them seem almost mythical, like they're Greek gods charging onto a battlefield. The crowd chants the lyrics and hops up and down to the beat while waving Bronco towels.

I've always enjoyed football games. Maybe it's because I grew up going to them so I could cheer on Jake, but being on the field is surreal. The energy is incredible. I can see why the guys love this. Why they sweat and slave all year.

I can't hold back the smile on my face when I see Jake. He's so stoic. So focused. I love how committed he is to this team.

Aiming through my viewfinder, I make sure to get several shots of him. It's easy to spot Billy because he's already horsing around and lifting his arms to the crowd.

As the team heads for the sidelines, Jake spots me and seems to make a point to walk by me. I hold out my pinky. He snags it back and then hooks his other arm around me and hugs me to him. I'm dwarfed by his size—he's even bigger with all of his gear—but he feels so good wrapped around me, I sigh.

"Good luck today, though you don't need it."

"Thanks, cupcake." He winks. "I like seeing you out here."

He jogs off, and I stand there with a dopey smile. I have it so bad for that man.

Some guy with a pad of paper nudges me. "Is Jake Ramirez your boyfriend?"

I spot the word 'reporter' on his lanyard and almost choke. "He's my best friend. That's all."

It's probably not smart to talk to Jake at the games. He needs to focus, and I have work to do as well.

The dude seems like he wants to ask me more questions, so I haul my equipment downfield as quickly as possible. Capturing the coin toss gives me an excuse to escape.

We win possession, and the Broncos take the field.

I double-check the aperture and shutter speed on the camera with the long lens. Football is fast, and it would suck if my photos were blurry. Sports photography requires good light, a fast shutter speed, and a small aperture to give you depth-of-field. Unless you want the background blurry, and then you need a large aperture, which means a smaller f-stop. That opens the lens and allows in more light.

The one benefit to my old manual SLR that died in the fire is I know how to manage the settings on these cameras. I don't have to rely on auto mode.

While I've never shot sports before, now that I've had some

time to consider how to shoot it and studied several tutorials online, I feel ready.

I force myself to watch everything through the viewfinder as I shoot the game. My camera whirs as I capture image after image. Having a top-of-the-line camera with a drive that takes almost instantaneous pics, one right after the other, is pretty cool.

On the first drive, Ezra's pass is deflected, but on the second down, he finds Jake.

Jake cradles the ball and cuts right, barely escaping two Longhorns. Someone else lunges for his legs, but he picks up speed. Everyone seems to drop away as he takes it downfield and right into the end zone.

The crowd loses its mind. Jake's handsome mug flashes on the jumbotron, and I snag a pic. I feel like I'm going to burst with pride for him.

These guys make the game look easy. No one sees all of the hours they put in at the weight room. Running drills. Studying plays. Watching film. At the scrimmages and meetings. All while juggling school and homework. And in Jake's case, while also being a father. He's so good with Asher and loves him so much. He deserves this moment where all the Bronco fans in the stadium scream his name.

UT manages to score on the next possession, and it's a close game, but we pull it out in the end. Jake nabs two touchdowns and also executes a beautiful lateral pass that results in his teammate scoring.

I capture everything. The looks of elation on the Broncos' faces. The fans celebrating. Mr. Pearson's little granddaughter getting a victory trip on the goat.

When it's over, I'm so exhausted, I can barely stand. I can't imagine how tired the players must be.

There's no way I can find Jake in the crowd that rushes the

field, so I head for the exit. When I get home, I have a text from him.

You're my lucky charm, cupcake. Hope you can come to all my games!

I collapse on my bed with a smile on my face.

THE NEXT AFTERNOON, I'm curled up on the couch with Duke, scrolling through all the images I uploaded onto the laptop I borrowed from the sports department. I owe Roxy big time for hooking me up. Now I'll be able to finish the calendar for Second Chances at home instead of always needing to be on campus.

I pause on a shot of Jake laughing with Billy on the sidelines. Jake's sweaty and his hair is sticking up in ten different directions and there's a streak of dirt on his face, but he's never looked more handsome.

The only drawback to digital is I won't get to develop this image in the darkroom. Although I probably shouldn't spend hours staring at this man.

Jake carries Asher over from the kitchen, and they drop down next to me. "You gonna let us see the photos?"

I tap my chin. "Hmm. I don't know. Whatcha gonna give me?"

He chuckles. "How about a Blizzard? I promised Ash we'd get some ice cream."

Asher grabs his dad's face. "Two scoops Wocky Woad."

"*One* scoop of Rocky Road." He tickles Ash until the kid squeals. "*After* you eat lunch."

"I might be persuaded," I tease.

After I scroll to my favorite image, I swivel the laptop so he can see the screen. It's a shot of Jake on that drive to his first touchdown. I panned with him, so the background blurs and shows his motion. He's in focus, determination written all over his face. The muscles in his arms and legs are taut as he sprints.

"Holy shi—" He stops himself, looks at Asher, and reconsiders what he wants to say. "Holy crap, Charlotte. This is incredible. Think I could get a copy for my mom?"

"Of course. I'll save the best ones for you on a drive." I'll admit I took a chance on panning. I hadn't really shot anything like that since my Photojournalism I class, and doing an exercise for a course is different than an on-location assignment.

Jake waits until Asher is focused on petting Duke and mouths, "This is cool as fuck. Thank you."

I'm floating on a cloud of pride all night.

The next day at our meeting, AD Armstrong is just as enthusiastic. "Charlotte, these photos turned out better than I could've imagined."

It feels so good to be praised for my work. All Dakota ever did was bitch at me for not getting her best angle or making her nose look too big or not making her boobs bigger. Or complain that I made her skin too shiny or her forehead too wide.

The AD picks three shots for his weekly newsletter, two to post on the Bronco football website, and a few to send to the media.

"Before I forget..." He hands me a card. "Call this kid when we're done. He's the sports editor at the *Bronco Times*. He'll definitely be interested in this collection for the special edition they're doing for homecoming."

Once we're done discussing captions, he leans forward in his chair and temples his fingers. "Now that I've seen your work in action, I have a proposition. If you can cover all the home games, I might be able to get you paid."

And when my shots get featured across the interior spread of the school newspaper a few days later, it seals the deal—I'm officially in love with being a sports photographer.

22

JAKE

I BARELY HAVE the front door open before my two older brothers come barreling through and tackle my ass to the ground.

"You dicks." I groan and shove them off me.

Although I'm annoyed, a part of me feels like I'm finally part of their club. David and Elijah are a decade older than I am, and when I was a kid, I was definitely the weird middle child. I'm eight years older than my younger brother, who was only five when our dad decided he'd fuck off and divorce our sweet mother. Sure, he came around for a few more years, but then he pretty much forgot all about us.

"Where's Colby?" I grit out as Eli tries to put me in a chokehold.

"He's got some eighth grade dance."

"*¡Muchachos, pórtanse!*" My mom claps her hands as if that's ever been an effective tactic to get us to behave.

Charlotte hides her smile behind Asher's head as she bounces him in her arms. Next to us, Duke jumps and barks.

I've been a little worried about this reunion. My mom is cool, but I'll kill my brothers if they're assholes to Charlie.

Elijah hops up off the ground and holds out his hand. I'm

tempted to drag him back down again, but I'd rather not get injured doing something stupid. I let him pull me up.

"*Mamá*, remember all the times you put him in charge?" I point to Eli. "You really think that was such a good idea? He's the reason you came home from that potluck dinner at church and found your coffee table in pieces."

Eli mumbles, "Snitches get stitches, little brother."

David looks like he's going to crack a joke when he notices Charlie. She gives him a shy wave. "Hi. Long time no see."

He gives her a curt nod and takes Asher out of her arms.

I frown. "Okay, bro, don't be rude. Y'all know Charlotte."

She moves closer to me, and I smile because she looks so fucking adorable in that Bronco t-shirt with my number on her back, grease strips on her face, and knee-high socks. Her hair is up in a high ponytail. I've been trying to play it cool all week, but I'm pretty stoked she's going to the bonfire with me tonight.

My mom shoots David a look that warns him he'd better behave and gives Charlie a hug. "So good to see you, *mija*. How have you been?"

They chat for a minute while I gather Asher's stuff and then we all walk to my mom's car so I can load up her old Honda. It pains me to see her drive this piece of crap. The floorboards are rusted and have small holes, and if you lean forward in the passenger seat, you can see straight through to the road.

I hope someday I can get her her dream car, a refurbished 1976 Gran Torino, painted red with a vector white stripe like that show our grandfather used to watch, *Starsky and Hutch*.

It's always bittersweet to part from my son. I clear my throat. "Asher ate a late lunch, but he might need a snack before you get home."

My mom waves off my concern and peppers Ash in kisses. "I'd never let my boy go hungry."

"Come here, kid." I hold my arms open, and Asher leans into

me as my mom holds him. "You promise you'll be a good boy and listen to your *abuela*?"

"Okay, Daddy. I pwomise."

"Love you, buddy." I kiss his forehead and load him into the car seat.

I know it's important for him to have some time to bond with my family, but I'm bummed I can't join them. My brothers are supposed to take him fishing this weekend.

"Please make him wear a life vest. I know y'all will be on a pier and not a boat, but he doesn't know how to swim." Just one of the many things I haven't had time to do with him yet. I have an endless mental list of plans that will have to wait. It's frustrating.

Eli slaps my back. "We're assholes, not idiots. We'll take good care of him."

They're taking him to a small lake by our house where we grew up going.

Like she can tell I'm depressed I can't go fishing with my brothers and son, Charlotte hooks her pinky in mine and turns to my family. "Be sure to take lots of photos for Jake."

My mom nods. "What a good idea. We'll be sure to do that. You two have fun at the bonfire tonight." She kisses my cheek and hugs Charlie again.

I watch them drive away.

"You okay?" Charlotte asks softly.

"Just drowning in parental guilt. Wishing I could do more with Asher."

Her eyes go soft. "He's in good hands. No one loves him like your mom and brothers. And things will get a little easier after the season."

"You're right." I smile at her until I remember how David behaved. "Were my brothers dicks to you?"

"Not dicks, no. A little standoffish, but I understand. They have good reasons to hate my family."

"It's not you. You know that, right?" I lower my head until she looks at me.

"Don't worry about it. I'm a big girl."

"I'm serious, Charlotte. They're not mad at you. They're frustrated with the situation." My brothers freaked when Dakota ditched me with Asher after she gushed about wanting to have him in the first place.

As irritated at her as I am, I'd endure her bullshit all over again to have my son.

"Come on. Let's get to the bonfire." Charlie drags me to my car.

We roll down the windows as we head out to the field behind the stadium. The sun is barely starting to set and there's already a crowd. It's a cool evening and everyone is in good spirits.

"Don't want to lose you, cupcake. If we get separated and you can't reach me for some reason, I'll wait for you at that taco stand." I point to where the food trucks are set up.

We meet up with the rest of the football team. Coach and the AD are chatting off to the side.

Charlotte tugs on my jersey. "Do you mind if I take some pics tonight?" she yells over the stereo system, which is blasting our classic rock warmup playlist.

"'Course not. Do your thing."

She gives me one of those lingering smiles that makes me wonder if my mom is right. If Charlotte has had feelings for me since high school.

I watch her walk away. She's wearing some cutoffs that make her ass look amazing and her slender legs long.

"Just friends, huh?" Billy elbows me hard. "Best rethink that."

"Why are you always pestering me?"

He holds a hand over his heart. "You wound me, bro. I'm *trying* to be a good person. Which means I'm not making a move on your girl like I want to."

I don't even bother arguing that she's not my girl.

Because Charlotte feels like she's mine.

Fuck it. I'm done debating this.

I'm going after what I really want.

23

CHARLOTTE

WITH THE BONFIRE flames licking into the night sky, I focus my lens on the cheerleaders in the foreground.

I ignore the sharp sting of the pebbles digging into my knees as I shoot Roxy getting tossed up into the air. She seems to defy gravity as she and her fellow cheerleaders twist and tumble in tandem. With her hair flying and skirt flaring, she spins as though she's as light as the embers floating off the bonfire.

After Coach Santos introduces the team and warns everyone to be safe tonight, the music kicks back on, and my attention drifts to the football players off to the side. Jake's eyes immediately meet mine, and I smile. He crooks a finger, calling me over, and my heart kicks into high gear.

"You getting some good pics?" he asks when I reach him.

"You tell me." I scroll through the shots on my camera as he peers over my shoulder. The wind shifts, and I catch his scent, the ocean breeze of his body wash and his sexy cologne.

His lips meet my ear. "You're so fucking talented, cupcake." Shivers run up and down my arms. "Are you cold?"

He strips out of his letterman jacket and drapes it over my shoulders. I close my eyes, freaking out a little on the inside. Jake has no idea how many times I fantasized about a moment like this in high school. The letterman is probably a stupid tradition, but the football players always had their girlfriends wear their jackets, and my weak teenage heart wanted that so badly.

He's just being nice, Charlotte. Don't make more of this like you always do.

"Thanks." His scent surrounds me, and I wish I could bottle up this moment. The chilly breeze. The warmth of the fire. Jake's jacket keeping me warm.

He leans close again. "Can I ask a favor?"

"Of course."

"Some of my teammates and their girlfriends were hoping to take a group photo. Would you mind shooting that?"

"Not at all."

I slide my arms through his jacket as Jake steps away to talk to one of the guys. A minute later, several huge football players hoist their girlfriends onto their shoulders.

"Aww, this is so cute." I direct them to move closer, and then I have to step back and squat to get everyone in one shot.

After I take a few, Jake tells the guys to hold up and then turns to me. "Can you ask Roxy to take a pic? Basically the same shot you just took, just with one more couple?"

I tilt my head, confused, but he's already called her over.

He makes me hand over the camera to Roxy before he drags me over to the group. "Hang tight."

That's the only warning he gives me before he lifts me onto his shoulder. Like, I'm literally sitting on his left shoulder.

"Jake!" I laugh as I wobble, but then he reaches up a hand, and I cling to him for dear life.

He yells, "'Kay, Roxy. Go for it." He looks up at me and grins. "Smile for the camera, cupcake."

She takes several shots. I'm smiling so hard, my cheeks hurt, and I forget to worry about whether or not I'm blinking.

When we're done and he slides me down to the ground, I'm out of breath. I almost feel like Jake is claiming me somehow, but that's crazy, right? He wanted to be in the photo, and I'm his good friend, so he had me join him.

Roxy returns the camera and leans into me to whisper, "What was that about? Are you two doing the deed?"

"No. We're just friends." God, I feel like a broken record.

Her eyebrow lifts. "Because the looks he's giving you tonight..."

Jake's giving me looks?

I turn to find him talking to Cam, but his eyes are glued on me. Every molecule in my body heats.

"Holy hot sexual tension, Batman." Roxy bumps me with her hip. "I want all the deets tomorrow!"

"There won't be any deets." Will there be deets?

When Jake stalks toward me with that look in his eyes, I want to melt into a puddle at his feet.

He turns to Roxy. "Thanks for the pic."

"Anytime, Ramirez."

The crowd's getting wild as the fire starts to wane. "Want to get out of here? Since it's still early, I was thinking we could pick up some snacks and go stargazing."

My heart stutters in my chest. "O-okay."

I swallow, thinking back to our freshman year in high school and the last time we did this. Only back then, we were with a bunch of his friends. I was so nervous, I didn't know what to do with myself, and I think I gave off some serial killer vibes that night because he never asked me to do that again.

As covertly as possible, I shove up the sleeves of his jacket to wipe my sweaty palms on my shorts. I'm so anxious, my body can't decide if I'm hot or cold.

I keep waiting for him to mention whatever teammates we're meeting up with, but he's quiet as we make our way to his car. A wild group of guys start a spontaneous mosh pit around us, and I almost get trampled, but Jake shoves someone out of the way, takes my hand in his, and leads me out of the crowd.

As we walk, I laugh at how the tips of my fingers barely stick out of his jacket. It's huge on me.

"What's so funny?" he asks.

"Your jacket is enormous."

He tugs me closer and whispers, "I like you wearing my letterman."

Oh my God. *What does this mean?*

WE HOP in his car and stop off at the mini-mart by our apartment. The whole time, I'm buzzing with excitement and trying to calm down.

"You know the drill."

Smiling, I feel like Jake's talking in code, and I'm the only person who understands. Dakota always ditched us to party with her friends, and Jake and I would watch Asher. Once he went to sleep, we'd veg out with snacks and watch movies.

I hunt up and down the aisles for our favorites—Doritos, Twinkies, Ding Dongs, beef jerky, and Extra-Spicy Chex Mix.

We meet by the register where he has some fruity wine cooler for me and beer for himself.

"Just like old times." He winks, and my heart skips in my chest.

"Careful, stud. You have a game tomorrow."

He nods. "I solemnly swear to only have one beer and a handful of junk food. We'll save the rest for next time."

Next time?!

Inside, I'm doing cartwheels. In my head, they're graceful

and smooth. Like how Roxy would do them instead of my twitchy, circus clown movements.

We take off down a dark road until he pulls over through a path that opens up to a field.

"How'd you find this place?" I ask as I unload the food from the trunk.

He grabs a blanket and the drinks and shrugs. "One of my first nights here, I needed to think. My mom was still helping us get settled, so she watched Asher. I went driving and found myself in this field. Look up."

We step out from behind the trees into a clearing, and my breath catches at the sight of so many stars. An infinitesimal number blink down at us. The crisp air is thick with the scent of cedar and damp earth and a hint of mesquite from the bonfire, and for a moment, I feel like I'm standing on the edge of the universe.

"This is incredible."

"I knew you'd love it." The smile he gives me hits me as intensely as the sight of the brilliant sky.

He lays out the blanket and pats the ground next to him. I sit and hand him my drink. I don't have to explain anything. Those large hands squeeze the top, and a second later, the cap is gone, no bottle opener needed.

I hand him his beer, and we switch drinks. After he opens his, he holds out the bottle neck, and I clink it with mine.

"Cheers," we say at the same time and laugh.

We sit in silence and stare up at the sky.

"A shooting star!" I point at the bright streak cutting across the inky night.

He bumps his shoulder into mine. "What'd you wish for?"

"How'd you know I made a wish?"

He gives me a look, and I chuckle. "Okay, yeah. I made one. I wished for you to have a great game tomorrow."

His dark eyes burn into me. "You know what I love about you?"

At the word 'love,' all of my insides quiver. "Wh-what?"

"I love how much you care about the people in your life." He reaches out and cradles my face. His rough palm sends chills all over my body. "It's taken me a long time to realize something, cupcake."

I swallow. "What's that?"

He drags his thumb against my bottom lip. "You're the one I should've dated in high school." My eyes immediately flood, and his eyebrows furrow. "I'm an idiot, Charlotte. I never appreciated what was right in front of me this whole time. Can you forgive me for…"

He doesn't finish the sentence, but I know what he's trying to say. I don't want to bring up my sister either.

I nod and choke out, "It's okay."

His jaw tightens, and he shakes his head. "It's not okay. It's pretty fucking far from being okay, but I'd love to try to make it up to you. If you'll let me. If you'll give me a chance."

I'm so shocked, I can barely breathe, but once his words sink in, I melt like a piece of chocolate in the hot sun.

His thumbs take slow swipes across my cheeks to dry my tears.

The moment is so surreal, I'm positive I'm going to wake up in my bed and tonight will have been a dream. "Are you… are you sure?"

Our eyes connect, and the heat there almost incinerates me. "I've never been more sure about anything in my life."

I arch up because if I don't kiss him right this moment, I might die, but he leans away. "Is this your first kiss, Charlotte?"

"Ugh, no." My shoulders slump. "I think you saw my first kiss in the park that day."

His jaw goes tight. "With Babcock?"

"Unfortunately, yes."

He's quiet a moment, and I'm afraid he's upset, but the next thing I know, his hand burrows into my hair, and he gently pulls me to his hard chest. "Then let's make sure my kiss replaces his."

When his lips meet mine, those fireworks I've always dreamed about go off. Bright burning light fills me with heat and want and soul-searing lust.

It's slow and dreamy and makes me forget I haven't a clue how to do this.

It's everything a first kiss should be.

He licks my bottom lip. "Open for me, Charlotte."

Our mouths meet again and his tongue slides in, making my whole body pulse. He tastes like toothpaste and malty beer, and beneath that, I smell his skin, his crisp cologne, and body wash.

I groan and scramble up into his lap where his broad chest presses against mine. He grabs my thighs and tugs me around, so I'm straddling him.

The evidence of how much he wants me is thick and hard beneath me.

I dig my hands into his hair and drag his mouth back to mine. Now that I've had a taste, I don't want to come up for breath again. It's crazy—I've never done this before, but my body instinctively knows what to do. My mouth knows how to move with his. My hips know how to grind against his. My heart knows how to beat in tandem with his.

We're parts of a moving puzzle that have finally found their interlocking pieces.

His large palms wrap around my ass and squeeze as he rocks me against him, sending shockwaves through my core.

"Oh God." I rest my forehead against his shoulder and squirm against him. "Do that again."

He chuckles and thrusts up, and I shiver.

"Are you wet for me, cupcake?" That deep voice in my ear

makes goosebumps break out along my skin. He drags his nose against my neck, placing open-mouthed kisses under my jaw. "If I reach into your panties, will you soak my fingers?"

I nod frantically. "Yes." Maybe I should be embarrassed by how wet I am right now, but here under this blanket of stars in the darkness, I feel stripped bare in the best way.

"Hmm. Maybe I need to check."

He flips us around until I'm on my back and he's hovering over me with a wolfish grin. I've never seen him like this. Never seen him almost feral.

Excitement and nervousness hitches my breath as he kisses down my body. When he starts to lift my shirt, I stiffen.

All of a sudden, I'm struck by the stark differences between me and my sister. She has huge boobs she plumps with sexy lingerie. She waxes off any hair that dares to blemish her pubic region. She does a million squats a week to give her a round bottom.

I don't do any of that.

"Hey. What's wrong?"

How do I say this? I cover my face with my hand and mumble, "I'm not what you're used to."

Silence greets me.

"What's that supposed to mean?" Shit. Now he sounds angry.

I push him off me. "Look, I know I'm not a troll, but I'm not some bodacious blonde like Yvette or..." I don't say Kota's name. I'm sure he hears her name, though, because he flinches.

Turmoil wraps around me like a suffocating blanket until he reaches over and lifts me back onto his lap.

"Jake, I—"

"Shut up." He wraps his strong arms around me and kisses my forehead. "I'm only gonna say this once, so I want you to listen. Charlotte Darling, there is no one else here tonight. Just you and me. I know we have a shit ton of baggage. I know we've fucked this up a million ways, but I want this. I want you." He grabs my chin so I have to look him in the eye. "Do you want the truth?"

I swallow past the thick knot in my throat. "Always."

"When I first met you freshman year, when you were lying there on Mr. Romano's desk, terrified to play Juliet, do you know what I thought?" He doesn't wait for my response as he kisses me. "I thought you were the most beautiful girl I'd ever seen, and I wanted to ask you out."

My eyes flood again. "But then I gave you my serial killer vibe and you reconsidered?"

He chuckles and rubs his nose against mine. "I didn't think you were into me, so I wanted to respect that."

I sniffle. "So if I had just spoken up, flirted back instead of being an emotionally stunted weirdo, we would've...?"

"You're not emotionally stunted. You were young. We were both inexperienced, and in my case, just plain dumb."

We both start smiling. I rake my fingers through his hair and kiss him slowly before I whisper, "I really liked you in high school. I've always liked you." My heart pounds with the confession, and I brave a glance at him.

His eyes go soft in that dreamy way I love. "Not realizing that is my biggest regret."

"And this thing between us... Is this more than just one night?" I try to keep my voice steady because I'm terrified of what he might say, but I've been around football players long enough to know not to assume anything.

His head jerks back. "Of course it's more than one night. In fact, the next time Billy hits on you in that playful way he thinks is so funny, tell him to fuck off. Tell him you're mine."

You're mine.

A huge smile lifts my lips. "Yours, huh?"

"You're wearing my jacket. That's my name on your back. Pretty sure everyone should know what that means."

I'm speechless. Jake's never been a possessive guy, but the way he growls out these words makes me shiver.

"I like being yours."

"Best thing I've heard all night, Charlie," he whispers before he grazes his lips against mine.

I KEEP GLANCING at Charlotte as I drive down the dark road. Her hands fidget in her lap and her knee is bouncing a mile a minute. Is she wondering what will happen when we get home too?

Reaching over, I lace my fingers through hers, and the smile she gives me makes my heart beat harder.

I always thought that was crap fairy tales taught kids. Because how could a woman's expression give me a physical reaction? In what world does a simple smile make the organ in my chest contract more intensely?

Speaking of physical reactions, I'm still rock hard from making out in the woods, but I didn't want to push things too far. Charlie probably needs me to take things slow. Get her comfortable. Help her trust me. After years of fucking things up, I want to do this at her speed.

She's been saving her virginity for someone special, and I want to be worthy of that gift.

For now, I want to get her home and see what happens.

What starts out as a few raindrops on my windshield turns into a torrential downpour as we reach our neighborhood.

"This weather is crazy," I mutter, slowing my car to take the last turn onto our street.

Of course, there are no spots, so I double-park in front of my apartment. "Why don't you head in? That way you don't get wet, and then I'll go park."

She gives me a look. "Don't be silly. I won't melt from a little water."

It's my turn to smile. I love how low maintenance she is. Night and day from her sister.

I wasn't lying when I told her she's the only woman I was thinking about tonight. I know why she worries I'm comparing her to Dakota, but I'd take Charlotte any day over some buxom blonde who doesn't give a shit about me.

Charlotte's hotter. She just doesn't know it.

But I plan to worship her gorgeous body until she understands.

The only place to park is on the other side of our apartment complex. After I pull in and turn off the car, I laugh at how hard it's raining. "Was it not clear just ten minutes ago? Let's leave your camera gear in the trunk. I'll get it out first thing in the morning."

She slips off my jacket and folds it, putting it down next to her. "I don't want to ruin your brand-new letterman."

"But you'll get drenched."

She shrugs. "That's okay." After unlocking her door, she turns to look at me over her shoulder with an adorable twinkle in her eyes. "I'll race you."

I chuckle. "And if I win?" Don't mean to brag, but I did break track records in high school. I'd consider throwing our race, though, if it makes my cupcake happy.

Her lips twist as she considers the possibilities. "Then I'll let you pick where I sleep tonight."

That rod in my jeans throbs. I clear my throat and nod.

"But what if *I* win?" she says playfully.

I do my best not to laugh. After all, maybe she has covert sprinting skills, and I'm about to get my ass kicked. "Then I'll let you pick where I place my goodnight kiss."

She blushes adorably. "And my options for that kiss...?"

"Anywhere on your body." I'm so fucking turned on, and the possibilities for that kiss aren't helping.

"Deal."

We get out and close our doors, and I look at her over the top of the car after I lock up. We've been standing here for two seconds and we're already sopping wet.

"Ready?" I have to raise my voice so she can hear me over the downpour.

I'm about to take off when she yells my name. I turn to look at her just as she lifts her Bronco jersey and bra and flashes me her beautiful tits.

Tits that quickly become dripping wet.

I swallow, stunned that my sweet Charlotte is so playful. And ridiculously fucking hot. She laughs and races off, her blonde ponytail swinging behind her, and I stand there like a dumbass, too hard to function.

When some blood flow finally reaches the big head on my shoulders, I take off after her. She's fumbling with her keys, trying to open the door, when I reach her and hoist her over my shoulder and spank her. Nothing too hard, but she squeals and laughs as I bite her closest ass cheek.

"Who knew you'd play dirty?" I ask, wondering how dirty she'll want it when I finally get her naked in my bed.

Once we're in, I kick the door closed and slowly let her slide down my body. "You're a naughty girl, cupcake."

We're both panting against each other. Water drips off her eyelashes and down her pale cheeks. One of the lamps is on in the living room, but the rest of our apartment is dark and quiet.

Duke barely lifts his head from where he's curled up on my couch.

She nibbles her plump bottom lip. "You've already seen me nearly naked, so..."

I swallow. "Maybe we should get out of these wet clothes."

She grabs my t-shirt and drags me down the hall toward the bathroom, pausing to fling off her wet jersey.

We stand in the dark hallway, our chests heaving. "Your turn," she says shyly.

Oh, fuck yeah.

I flip on the light in the bathroom because I'm dying to get a better look at my sweet girl. I watch a raindrop drip down her cleavage. Her beautiful pink nipples stand at attention through her damp, sheer bra.

I strip off my shirt and heat beneath her attention as she studies my shoulders, chest, and abs. Yeah, I fucking work out, and I've never been more grateful than this moment when she looks like she wants to lick me from head to toe.

Hopefully, we'll get to the licking soon.

"Take off your bra, Charlotte," I say. She tilts her head down, like she's embarrassed. Fuck that. "Eyes on me, baby."

She smiles, her cheeks tinting pink as she flicks open the clasp between her tits. It springs apart, and I'm treated to two high, round beauties.

I lean forward and nibble on her earlobe. "Want to keep going? We can stop anytime you want."

She shivers. "I was thinking I'd take a shower."

I nod, disappointed that we're stopping, but I'll wait as long as it takes for her to feel comfortable with me.

After I kiss her forehead, I head toward my bedroom to change and maybe jerk off because I'll never sleep with this erection if I don't, but she calls out my name.

"I think you misunderstood," she says quietly. "I... I was

wondering if you'd like to maybe... maybe take a shower with me."

Was this sexy little vixen always hiding in my prim, beautiful Charlotte? Jesus, I'm a fool.

I stalk toward her and lift her into my arms. "Hell, yes, I wanna shower with you."

Her tits press against me, and I groan. She feels so good.

Charlie giggles as I nibble on her neck and carry her into the bathroom and kick the door shut. I place her on the vanity, step between her legs, and take her face in my hands. When our lips meet, she opens for me, and I slide my tongue slowly against hers.

She squirms, and I smile to myself. She probably needs a release as badly as I do. There's no way I'm gonna pressure her to have sex tonight, no matter how naked we get. But maybe we can do other things. This is her first time, after all, and I want all of her firsts to be special.

I rub her arms and shoulders. Let my fingers trail down her slender waist. I graze the side of her breast, and she moans.

When I can't resist any longer, I circle one of her sweet buds. She leans back and looks down at my hand, which makes me throb harder in my jeans. Fuck, yes, I want her to watch.

I gently pinch her before I lean down and lick her puckered nipple. She squirms again, and I take her in my mouth and run my tongue around her. Suck. Nibble. Tug.

"Jake." She jams her hand in my hair and holds me to her.

"That feel good, baby?"

"So good."

After giving the same treatment to her other breast, I move back and look down at her. She's flushed and panting. Her tits heave.

Fuck me, I've never even considered taking pics or videos

during sex, but I suddenly see the appeal. I wish I could burn this image in my brain.

And then I remember that moment in the field when she froze, and it gives me an idea. "Stand up, cupcake."

She slides off the counter, and I spin her around so she's facing the mirror. I take her hair out of the ponytail, and it fans down her back.

"When you look at yourself, I don't think you see the stunning woman everyone else sees. And that's a crime."

Her eyes meet mine in the reflection.

"No, don't look at me. Look at yourself. Look at how you glow. You're fucking gorgeous, Charlotte."

I'm a beast, a hulking figure behind her. Dark from the sun, scarred from football, and huge as I hover over her. She's pale like the moon and petite with flawless, smooth skin. A fairy princess. So tiny, I could probably wrap my hands around her waist. But somehow, when I see us together, we make sense.

We've *always* made sense, and I was too dumb to realize it.

While I watch her in the mirror, I graze my lips down her neck as I swirl her nipples with my fingers. She arches her back and lets out a breathy moan.

I flick open her jean shorts and slowly slip my hand into her panties. I give her time to say no, to change her mind, but her eyes only get more desperate as her chest heaves.

Sliding my fingers past her mound, I groan when I feel how wet she is.

"Spread your legs."

She instantly obeys, and fuck, I'm so turned on by how quickly she moves. How she obviously wants to please me.

I circle her clit, and she gasps.

"Do you ever touch yourself, baby?"

She nods, frantic now.

"Can you come like this?"

"Y-yes."

I slide my thick middle finger through her folds and she grinds against my hand. Reaching lower, I find her entrance and gently press into her. Damn. She's tight around my finger. *Really* tight. Even if I wanted to, I'm not sure we should fuck tonight.

It takes a moment, but she starts to relax. Then she shoves down her shorts and panties and reaches back to hold onto my shoulders, which stretches her beautiful body like she's an exquisite work of art. Some goddess on a stand in a museum. Aphrodite, crafted by Zeus himself.

But instead of marble, she's flesh and blood. Instead of some haughty immortal, she's the most down-to-earth girl I know.

Mesmerized, we both watch my finger slide in and out of her tight hole.

"Look at how sexy you are. Fuck, you turn me on, Charlotte." I grind my cock against her back. "Feel that? That's all for you. I've had a nonstop erection since I saw you naked in the kitchen that day."

She swallows and turns her head to look up at me. "Take off your jeans. I want to touch you too."

Needing a minute so I don't explode all over her, I close my eyes and rest my chin on her head and take a few breaths. When I'm in control, I pop open my jeans and yank them down, along with my boxer briefs.

When my cock springs free and she sees what I'm packing, her eyes widen comically.

She points to the mirror. "That's... no. That's not gonna fit."

Smirking, I kiss her temple. "You've already seen me naked, baby. This can't be a surprise."

Whirling around, she says, "That was a video call. You were big, yes, but not *this* big. Objects in the mirror are larger than they appear and all that."

I chuckle as I reach over and crank on the shower. "How

about this? Let's just take things slow. Make each other feel good. There are no expectations on my part. We can stop anytime."

My heart hammers at the thought she might turn me down. "Really?"

Pulling her to me, I kiss her until the tension in her ebbs away. "Of course. Your speed. Always."

She takes a deep breath and steps into the shower and tilts her head as her eyes trail up and down my body. A slow smile lifts her lips. "What are you waiting for? Get in here."

25

CHARLOTTE

STANDING under the blissfully hot water, I wait for Jake to follow me into the shower.

For the record, this is me being brave.

It's strange, but under Jake's heated gaze, it's surprisingly easy to take this leap. I've never been particularly proud of my body. It was hard growing up with my mother always comparing me to Kota. I was too skinny or my boobs were too small. My ass too flat. My hair not as thick. Nothing about me was ever right.

All of those criticisms screaming in the back of my mind shut down when Jake stalks toward me looking like I'm a juicy steak he wants to devour one bite at a time.

He's such a beautiful man. His damp hair is tousled and dangles over the sharp planes of his tanned cheekbones. He drags a hand through it, and all of the muscles in his arms and shoulders contract. It's a chain reaction the way his abs follow suit, tightening.

I swallow at the way his cock jerks against his stomach.

Yeah, he's big. Like, porn-worthy large.

Holy hell, Jake's built like a machine.

When he reaches for me, I step into the cradle of his arms

and rub up against him the way I've always wanted to. My nipples tingle as they scrape against his chest.

His hard length presses against my belly like a sundial eager to reach the sky.

Hot water rushes over us as he leans down to kiss me. He backs me against the cold tile and then adjusts the showerhead so it hits me straight on.

For a second, he stands there and stares at me, tracking a slow path over my breasts. Down my stomach. To the juncture of my thighs where he pauses before he resumes the path down my legs.

"Goddamn perfection," he grunts before he reaches for me again.

His mouth is hungry when he kisses me, his tongue sensually sliding against mine.

Gathering every last bit of courage, I reach down and wrap my hand around his length. At least I try to. My fingers don't reach all the way. I give it a gentle squeeze, and he shudders.

"Tell me what to do." Of course I've seen people give hand jobs in porn, but nothing really prepares you to come face-to-face with a behemoth.

His large, rough hand wraps around mine. "Like this."

Together we run our palms up and down his cock, and he shows me how to curl around the head before sliding back down to the base.

After I get the hang of it, he lets go and resumes his exploration of my body. He kisses my neck. Lowers his head to pluck my nipples. Nibbles on them until I'm throbbing between my legs. I'm swollen and wet and excited for the next step.

"Do you need to come, cupcake?"

I nod, so turned on, my usual verbal filter dissipates. "I want your fingers inside me again."

He groans. "Gladly."

Judging by the size of his hands, you'd think he'd be rough or too hard, but no. He carefully reaches between my legs and spreads my wetness around my clit so softly, I moan. That finger slowly spears me before he does this magical movement that makes my whole body go tight.

"*Espérate.*" He clears his throat. "Not yet, baby. If you think you might want to have sex at some point, I should try to stretch you out a little. Because it'll be a tight fit."

He doesn't need to remind me that he's packing.

But the idea of him doing anything to me down there cranks the throb between my legs to a full-on techno beat. I don't know what stretching me out means exactly, but I'm definitely intrigued. "Okay. Yeah."

He kisses me and looks into my eyes. "I'm just going to add a second finger. Let me know if it's too much." I spread my legs wider, and he grins. "Watch."

A shiver streaks through me. I'm definitely into this watching business.

We both look down where he slowly squeezes a second finger into me. He's right—it's a tight fit. I'm panting and writhing on his hand when he's fully in there, but he does that magical thing again, some twisty movement, and my whole body lights up. He works his fingers in and out of me, and the sight of it almost makes me come.

"Yes, whatever you're doing, yes," I pant as I lean back into the tile.

"See if you like this," he says as he drops to his knees and licks my clit.

Holy Lord in heaven, this feels good.

"Jake! Yes. Oh God, yes!"

That's all it takes for me to fly apart.

I dig my hand into his hair as I pulse against his mouth. Squeezing my eyes shut, I let myself go. And it is sublime. Heat sears through me, sizzling a path through every vessel and nerve until it's almost too much.

"Fuck, I can feel you squeeze my fingers." He continues to lick until I push him away with a laugh. Smirking, he slowly removes his hand before he sticks those two fingers in his mouth. "Delicious."

My bones feel like they've melted. Holy crap, no wonder people lose their minds over sex. I get it now, and we haven't even gone all the way.

"Want to help me finish this off?" he asks as he wraps a hand around his erection.

"You have no idea." When I drop to my knees, I see the surprise in his eyes. "Show me." Again, I have no clue.

He moves to block the showerhead, so the water doesn't hit me directly. "Just watch your teeth."

No teeth. Got it.

I wrap my hand around his swollen flesh and bring it to my face where I rub it against my lips. It's a total porn move, but that looks sexy in those videos, so why not try it? I like how soft he is. How he's steel wrapped in velvet. I glance up and the look of intensity in Jake's eyes has me eager to make him fly apart too.

Tentatively, I lick across his slit, and a pained groan leaves him.

"Is this okay?" I ask.

"Fuck, yes. Don't stop."

He takes a fistful of my hair, and I can barely keep from smiling. I love this version of Jake. Where he curses and grunts and looks like he wants to fuck me into oblivion.

I lick the pearly white fluid off him. He's salty and sweet, and I immediately want more. I run my tongue around his head, and his dick swells in my hand.

His attention is riveted to my mouth.

Here goes nothing.

Making sure to fold my lips over my teeth so I don't nick him, I take him in my mouth and suck, loving when he lets out a loud moan.

"Use your hands too."

I nod and run them up to where I've made his head wet and spread that over his length. When I take him back in my mouth, I squeeze him with my hand before I resume that path up and down his cock. It takes a second to find a rhythm, but a minute later, he's cursing and swelling in my mouth. His hand in my hair tightens, almost to the point of pain, but I kinda like it.

I don't think Jake even realizes how he's urging me up and down his cock with that fistful of hair. I'm at his mercy, and I love it.

With a groan, he pulls out and reaches down to jerk off. At my confused look, he rasps, "I'm gonna come. Didn't want you to choke."

Who said he couldn't choke me?

I smack his hand away, wrap my palm around him, and send him back into my mouth where I suck and lick until he fills me too fast to swallow it all.

When I can't take any more, I pull him out, and ropes of thick cum paint my lips and neck and breasts. It's the hottest thing I've ever seen in my life.

I lick him clean, lick my lips. Paint my nipple with his cum. Rub it between my fingers. I know that sounds weird, but I'm completely fascinated. I've waited a long time to do anything sexual, and now that we've popped this cork, I don't wanna stop.

"Fuck, Charlotte. That..." He yanks me up and into his arms, where he kisses me until we're both out of breath.

Steam rises around us, and I smile when he grabs my body wash, squirts some in his hands, and rubs them up and down my arms and shoulders. He pays particular attention to my breasts, and by the time he's carefully washed between my legs, he's stiff against his stomach again.

I return the favor, stepping up on my toes to wash his shoulders and arms, and yes, I take my time washing his cock that seems eager for my touch.

"You're insatiable," I joke.

"You have no idea. But just ignore that. It'll go down. Eventually." He chuckles.

My mouth and jaw are a little sore from that blow job, otherwise I'd offer another one. Instead, I lean up to kiss him while I jerk him off with my hand. "Let's see if this does the trick."

26

JAKE

EXHAUSTED but also really fucking sated, I strip off my damp t-shirt and jeans before I flop on my bed. "Took Duke twenty minutes of sniffing every weed and mound of dirt for three blocks. Why do dogs always have to find the perfect place to drop a deuce?"

I reach for Charlotte and curl around her. I slide my thigh between her smooth legs. Wrap an arm around her waist. Nuzzle against her neck. My little spoon fits perfectly.

This is a first for me. I'm not a snuggler. Sure, I hug my kid and cuddle him, but I've always liked having my space when it comes to women.

But the last thing I want right now is to let go of the beautiful girl in my arms.

"I would've taken him out." Her voice is raspy.

Probably from all that screaming, I think with satisfaction. She gave me two orgasms, so of course I made sure she got there a second time.

She was gearing up to take Duke for a walk, but there was no way I was gonna let her go back out into the rain. Come on now. What kind of asshole does she take me for?

"I like you in my bed," I mumble against the top of her head. Maybe a little too much, judging by my erection.

"Again?" she asks with a chuckle.

"Ignore it. My dick's just being greedy. I should save some of that energy for tomorrow's game. Are you shooting it?"

She nods with a yawn. "Yeah. Is that okay?"

It kills me that she feels she has to ask. She used to bend over backwards whenever her family snapped their fingers. "Baby, you never need my permission to handle your business. Plus, I really love having you at my games."

I glance down in time to catch her grin.

That smile carries me the entire next day. I can't stop thinking about our night together. It replays in my mind over and over again. I should be concentrating on this afternoon's game. Instead, I keep seeing Charlie. Lying out beneath all those stars. Laughing in the rain. Naked and down on her knees in the shower.

"You're in a good mood, Ramirez," Thomas says next to me as he pulls on the Bronco game jersey over his pads.

"Yup." I know he wants me to elaborate, but it'll be a cold day in hell before I divulge my personal stuff with my teammates again. Billy and Cam wormed their way into my life because of Charlotte and Roxy, but I have no plans to expand that circle. I ignored my instinct when it told me Troy was shady and instead did what I always did—tried to bond with my teammates. To my detriment.

My instinct tells me Ezra Thomas isn't the good guy Coach thinks he is.

Not sure why, but Thomas rubs me the wrong way. Maybe it's because my last QB fucked my girlfriend behind my back.

Or maybe it's because Ezra's a cocky little shit.

"Must be that hot girlfriend of yours. What's her name?"

My jaw tightens. "Charlotte."

He smacks me hard on the back. "Too bad she doesn't have a sister."

Yeah. No comment.

At least he hasn't snooped into my past. Maybe I shouldn't be so hard on him.

I ask him about the bonfire, and he prattles on and on about his night. At least it gets his focus off me.

Getting into a beef with my QB is the last thing I need, so I force a smile while he tells me about some chick he hooked up with afterward.

I don't know if I'm feeling energized from being with Charlotte, having her on the sidelines, or if I'm just clicking with my team, but I have one of the best games of my college career. It's worth every second I had to hold my tongue with Ezra in the locker room.

As soon as the game's over, one of the team's press coordinators corrals me to the side to be interviewed.

A tall brunette with a media lanyard smiles at me as she talks into the mic. "Jake, you had twenty-nine carries, three touchdowns, and an impressive two hundred and thirty rushing yards. You were unstoppable out there. What was going through your mind this afternoon?" She angles the mic toward me.

"I just want to give my best every game, and the stars aligned today. Coach got us pumped up with a bonfire last night, and my teammates played their hearts out. I'm grateful I got to be a part of it."

"This is your fourth game with over a hundred rushing yards. ESPN is calling you one of the rising stars of college football."

Out of the corner of my eye, I spot Charlie and smile. "Honestly, I feel like I'm just getting started. The Broncos have set me up for success, and I plan to take advantage of that."

The press conference afterward isn't quite as easy to maneuver. Especially when a reporter asks about my son.

I'm debating how to answer when Coach puts his hand on my shoulder and responds. "Jacob Ramirez is a top-notch athlete who's juggling DI football while raising a son as a single father. Many of you already know this. However, I've instructed him to keep comments to football to maintain his privacy. I hope you'll respect that."

I love this man. Kinda wish he was my father.

The reporter completely ignores Coach. "Jake, what about your ex, Dakota Darling? Is she in your son's life at all? And do you have any comment about her new show? Are you nervous about this week's episode of *The Hot House*? They're supposed to be digging into her past with her exes."

Before Coach can intercede, I lean forward. "I have no comment about her show, but I wish her the best."

Coach nods like he's happy with my answer. I've been prepping that response since I heard about that damn show.

There's no way I'll address whether Dakota is involved with Asher because that's opening up a can of worms.

It isn't until I'm in the locker room and taking a shower that I begin to process what that guy said about how the show will talk about her past relationships.

And then I say a prayer Dakota doesn't fuck up my life.

But tonight isn't about my ex. It's about my beautiful, sweet girlfriend Charlotte and taking her to the homecoming dance like I should've done in high school.

27

CHARLOTTE

NERVOUSLY, I pat down my dress. It's another slinky number out of Roxy's closet. I'm not used to putting this much skin on display, but she swore it would make me feel sexy. She's not wrong.

"Damn, girl." Billy yanks me into a bear hug, and I laugh. "Your boy is gonna go all caveman when he sees you."

Feeling my face heat, I laugh awkwardly.

I don't know that I'd call Jake *my boy*.

After the game, Roxy and I booked it back to my place so we could get ready. The guys always have to deal with the media before they hit the showers, so I told Jake I'd meet him at the homecoming dance, which is being held in the ballroom of a swanky new hotel.

After Billy lets me go, Roxy hooks her arm into mine. "Told ya you'd look hot in that."

"Thanks for playing fairy godmother, Rox. I love this outfit." The hot pink halter dress ties behind my neck and leaves my back exposed. That's the one benefit to having a modest chest. I don't need a bra, but I am wearing nude-colored pasties on my nipples in case I take photos because the flash might make this fabric see-through.

Not only did Roxy let me borrow another outfit, she also did my makeup. We're talking lashes and lip liner and base that she patted carefully on my face with a sponge and made my skin look flawless. I've never been one for making too much of a fuss when it comes to makeup, but I have to admit I had fun getting ready with Roxy tonight and love the final result.

I'm anxiously eyeing the entrance. I don't know why I'm nervous. Actually, I'm a strange mix of nerves and excitement. I freaking live with the man, but at the thought of seeing him again after what we did last night...

Of course, I saw him at the stadium where he had the game of his life. I'm so stinking proud of him, and I'm dying to show him some of the pics I took.

He gave me a quick hug before the media person dashed him off to the press conference, but not before he whispered, "Can't wait to see you tonight."

That voice.

I shiver.

My toes curl in my shoes when I remember how it felt to wake up to a very naked and very hard Jake this morning. He said he has a strict 'no sex' policy on game days, which I completely respect, but I couldn't help but tug down the sheet and give him a little peek of what he was missing.

Totally out of character for me, I know, but there's something about being with him that makes me confident in a way I never have been before. For the first time, I feel really good in my skin. I'm not Dakota's little sister or a wallflower afraid of my shadow. It's crazy because we didn't even go all the way last night, but it felt like some kind of weird personal milestone. I got naked with a man, had two freaking orgasms, and slept wrapped in his embrace.

You know that scene in *Titanic* where Jack jumps up on the bow of the ship and screams he's king of the world? Totally in touch with that right now.

Speaking of heartthrobs, the ballroom door opens, and there he is.

Everything around us fades away. I only see Jake.

He's wearing a sleek black suit and looks so handsome, my insides flutter.

He spots me right away and gives me that devilish smile as he stalks toward me. Leaning down, he kisses me on the cheek and whispers, "You look fucking gorgeous."

"Thanks. You're pretty sexy yourself."

His eyebrow lifts. "You think I'm sexy?"

"Shut up. You know you're a studmuffin."

He grins in that playful way that makes my heart beat faster and hands me a box. When I open the lid, I gasp.

"You got me a corsage. It's beautiful!" They're pink roses with baby's breath. "And it matches my outfit."

I bring them to my nose and smell the delicate fragrance. "Thank you. I love it."

He grins. "Full confession, Roxy told me what color you were wearing."

After he takes the corsage out of the box and slides it on my wrist, his smile widens.

Next thing I know, I'm in his arms and his lips are on mine.

I hang on for dear life and revel in this moment.

When we come up for air, I look around. Yeah, several people are watching us, and Billy, that idiot, starts slow-clapping. His teammates join in, and I burrow my face into Jake's chest as he laughs.

But then he grabs my chin and tilts my face to meet his. "No hiding."

I swallow and nod. He's right. I'm done hiding. "Great game today. Congrats."

His thumb grazes my lower lip. "Before I get distracted, we're supposed to take official homecoming photos."

Groaning, I shake my head. "You know I always blink."

"You didn't at the bonfire."

"How do you know that? You haven't even seen those photos yet." I mean, he's right, but that had to be a fluke.

"I had a good feeling about it." He winks. "Come on. My mom made me promise, so you can't chicken out."

He drags me to a giant archway of balloons where a photographer is taking formal portraits and taps the guy on the shoulder. I don't hear what Jake murmurs to him, but he has a mischievous look in his eyes when he's done.

"Just relax and have fun. I have a plan," Jake tells me when he stands behind me and places his hands on my waist.

Have fun. Yeah. I can do that.

Except now I'm nervous. After a few shots, the guy shouts, "Honey, you're blinking."

Jake holds up a hand. "I got this. Do it again."

And then he dips me dramatically. I'm laughing as the flash goes off. Giggling as Jake presses his lips to my neck. Cackling when he tickles my ribs. Gasping for breath when he pulls me in for a kiss so hot, his teammates start hooting and hollering again.

Wow. I could get used to this.

When we're done taking photos, Jake laces his fingers through mine and heads for the dance floor. The music is fast, and we're hopping around like fools, but I'm having so much fun that I'm not thinking about how I might look. Billy laughs as he does "the sprinkler" around some girl while Cam does the robot on the other side. Roxy is ignoring Ezra and dancing with Diesel Smith, one of the huge linemen.

I'm out of breath by the time the lights dim a bit and a slow song starts.

Jake pulls me to him, and I drape my arms over his broad shoulders. I tilt my head back to look at him. "You're quite dashing in this suit."

"You're quite breathtaking in that dress."

I give him a shy smile. "Thanks for inviting me to homecoming. I'm having a blast."

He rubs his nose against mine. "It's to make up for the one I didn't take you to in high school." My eyes suddenly sting, and I blink them back and look away. "Aww, cupcake. I didn't mean to upset you. I was hoping to make tonight special."

Sniffling, I nod. "It is special. It's just..."

I wanted to go to homecoming with Jake so badly senior year. I almost asked him to go with me, but then his parents got into a huge fight, and he decided he wasn't attending the dance.

Instead, he went to a party, got rip-roaring drunk, and hooked up with Kota.

"I've made a lot of mistakes, Charlotte," he says quietly. "I'm sorry for all the ways I've hurt you. I plan to make it up to you."

I debate the words I've been mulling over since he kissed me in the field last night. I can barely spit it out. "What happens when Kota finds out?" Because she will eventually, and I'm afraid she'll want to light me and Jake on fire when she does.

He sighs. "I guess I'm hoping she doesn't care. She's moved on, right? Theoretically, she's off living her best life on that reality show and living her dream. Why should she give a shit what we do?"

I give him a look, and he laughs. "Jake, come on."

"I'm serious. She and I broke up a long time ago." He looks into my eyes for a moment. "And for the record, nothing I had with her is like what you and I have. You're everything, Charlie."

Smiling, I lean up on my tiptoes and kiss him. I know he's

not just feeding me lines. When Kota wasn't bragging about his sexual prowess, she'd complain that Jake never did anything romantic with her. Never held her hand. Was never into public displays of affection. Never included her on his social media. Was too obsessed with football.

And yet with me, he's been nothing but sweet and thoughtful. As important as this season is to his career, I don't feel like an afterthought to him.

He runs his thumb against my jaw. "Here's what we're *not* doing. We're not gonna hide this. I hope Dakota has grown up and is too busy with her own shit to care about us, but in the event I'm wrong, then too fucking bad. She can suck it up. Plus, we're in Texas and she's in California. How's she gonna know? What's she gonna do? She's sequestered at her posh LA mansion right now anyway. You and I can't live the rest of our lives based on what-ifs."

He's right.

I nod, hoping this doesn't backfire, but I'm tired of living in my sister's shadow. Tired of catering to her every whim. It's time I do what I want.

Jake kisses me, and all thoughts of my crazy sister melt away.

Speaking of doing what I want...

28

JAKE

"Is this even legal?" I ask out loud as I park about ten feet from a sheer drop. The guys wanted to hang out at the quarry, and I was about to bail and take Charlotte home because I'd much rather chill with her, but her eyes lit up in that adorable way that makes her nose wrinkle.

"I got food, bitches!" Ezra yells as he pops open his trunk. Everyone goes diving for the boxes of waffles.

"Hold tight," I tell Charlotte before I sprint to nab our snacks before some asshole steals them.

Once I've secured our bacon and waffles, I grab a blanket from our trunk.

Charlie is shivering, but she's smiling. After reminding her that I didn't take her to homecoming in high school because I was too busy being a dumbass, I wanted to make it up to her. Make her forget the past.

Couples spread out across the short field next to the quarry. I pick a quiet place back by the trees and toss open the blanket.

After we eat, I sprawl out with Charlotte in my arms and yank the other half of the blanket over her. "You're cold. You sure you wanna stay?"

Her slender thigh slides over mine. "Maybe you should warm me up."

I can definitely get on board with this. Reaching down, I grab her ass. "You gonna let me see whatcha got under this hot-as-fuck dress?"

I've been half hard since I laid eyes on her at the dance, but when she giggles and grinds against my thigh, I go full-on steel bar.

"There's not much underneath."

Hell.

After making sure we're far enough from my teammates, I lean over to kiss her. We make out, slow and soft, until she squirms against me.

"Are you wet, cupcake?" I ask as I nibble her ear.

"Yeah. Looks like you have a problem too." She palms my erection, and I groan. Fuck, I love how bold she's getting.

By the time we get home, we're ripping each other's clothes off. Duke is snoozing on the couch and doesn't bother to greet us, which is perfect because that means I can walk him later.

I've got Charlotte's halter dress untied in the back, but when I get it down her chest, I pause at the stickers on her tits.

"What are these?" I rub a finger over one.

She laughs. "Pasties so I didn't have high beams in photos."

After she peels them off, I help her wiggle out of her dress. She's standing in a nude thong and heels, and her hair cascades down her slender shoulders.

The smell of her arousal makes me ravenous. I can't get out of my clothes fast enough. Off come the jacket and tie, and then she's helping me unbutton my shirt.

We somehow make it to my bedroom, where I kick off my shoes and pants and boxer briefs and strip her bare. As we topple onto the bed, I remind myself to go slow. I'm not sure if she'll want to go all the way tonight. Regardless, I plan to do this at her speed.

I settle in the cradle of her thighs and kiss her until her hips move frantically against mine. I make my way down her gorgeous body as I lick her neck. Suck on her perfect tits. Nibble down her stomach.

"Open for me. Let me see that sweet pussy." Her knees move up so they're by my ears, and I run my finger over her damp opening. My finger comes away glistening. Fuck, that's hot.

Leaning down, I lick around her swollen clit until she arches her back and digs her hand into my hair. "Jake."

"What do you need, baby?"

"Fingers. Put your fingers in me."

I smile against her damp skin. Charlie is a woman who looks after everyone in her life. I love that about her. But it's time she starts putting herself first. I want her to get used to telling me what she needs, when she needs it. We can start here—with orgasms. "Good girl."

Goosebumps break out on her legs when I slide one thick finger into her opening. Looking up, I groan at the sight before me. Her hair is in disarray and spread out on my bed. Her back is arched, and her nipples are hard little points. Her slender stomach contracts as her thighs tighten around me.

I know she'd go off like a roman candle if I licked her clit, but where's the fun in that? Instead, I slowly work in a second finger.

As I pump in and out of her, it's my turn to groan. "You're so fucking sexy, Charlotte. I could come from watching you fuck my hand."

She shudders, and I finally give in and lave her clit. First I use the flat of my tongue, long and slow movements from where my fingers sink into her to her swollen bud. And then I flick it back and forth as I work her harder with my hand.

"Yes! Jake! Yes!" Her knees pin my head down as she flies apart.

I work her over until she starts laughing and pushes me away. Obnoxiously satisfied with my results, I flop on the bed next to her and hug her to me.

Usually, after sex, I want space. Room to breathe.

Except Charlotte's different. I can't get enough of her. When I'm at practice, I'm thinking about her. When I'm in class, I'm wondering what she's doing. When we're in bed together, I want to wrap my arms around her.

No, I definitely don't need space from Charlotte.

Her sleepy face lifts up over me. A shy smile tugs at her lips as she whispers, "Your turn."

29

CHARLOTTE

BOBBING UP AND DOWN, I come off Jake's dick and gasp for breath. His hand tightens in my hair, and the look of intense concentration on his face as he watches me suck him off makes me crave him all over again.

I flick my tongue over his swollen crown and relish the loud groan that rumbles from his chest.

He hasn't made any attempt to do more than this tonight, and I love that he's not pushing my boundaries, but he needs to know I want more.

I crawl up onto his stomach, trapping his cock between our bodies. "Jake, can we... you know?"

Instinct has me grinding against him. His rock-hard erection sliding between my legs makes me shiver.

He swallows. "Are you sure? We don't have to do more if you're not ready."

Is he serious? I've wanted this. For. Years. "I'm ready." So, *so* ready.

Leaning over to the bedside table, he reaches in the top drawer and pulls out an unopened box of condoms.

I don't know why, but I'm elated it's not a half-used box.

Because the idea of him with someone else makes me feel savage.

"Magnums, hmm?" I tap my bottom lip and feign humor even though his monster-sized manhood is no joke.

A cocky grin tilts his lips. "What can I say? I've been blessed."

I roll my eyes with a laugh.

When he can't open it, I take it out of his hands and run my nail along the cellophane wrapper. I pop the box open. "Um, I'm on birth control. Do we need a condom too?"

"Just to be extra safe." He pauses. "But I've been tested for everything, and I'm in the clear."

I nod, and he tears one condom open and places the circular piece of latex in my palm. "Scoot back and put it on me. It's lubed, so that should make things easier."

I'll probably need all the help I can get.

I stare at his giant dick in one hand and the rubber in the other, suddenly way out of my depth 'cause shit just got real. Jake is enormous. I'm tiny. I'm sure there's a health class somewhere that explains how women's bodies stretch to fit a man, but I have to do *a lot* of expanding to make this work.

Misunderstanding my confusion, he takes my hand in his. "Like this." He rolls it down his length, and all thoughts of physical compatibility fly out of my head because that was hot. "Come here, Charlie."

He slides me forward until I'm sitting on his stomach, tangles his hand in my hair, and pulls my mouth down to his. He must know I'm anxious about this because at first all we do is kiss.

"Relax." He presses his palm to my cheek. "Say the word at any time and we stop."

"I don't want to disappoint you." I don't know where that came from, but I wish I could take it back.

His brows furrow and in between kisses, he says, "You could never disappoint me. I've had an amazing weekend with my girl. You think not going all the way tonight could tarnish that? We have all the time in the world. There's no rush."

My girl. The tension drains out of me when I hear those words. I trust him in a way I've never trusted anyone before.

I lean down and kiss him, more than a little aware of his hard cock now pressing against my rear. I'm about to ask how we do the next step when he rolls me onto my back and settles between my legs.

Oh, this is better. Because the idea of hopping on his giant dick feels like trying to leap on a merry-go-round when it's spinning too quickly. I definitely want to get on top at some point, but maybe not my first time.

"Let me know if I'm going too fast or if it hurts."

I nod and run my fingers through his thick hair. "I'm ready."

He smiles, and it strikes me in the chest. I love his smiles. I want to hoard them all.

He clears his throat. "Charlie, I just want you to know how much this means to me. This, with you, is everything, and I'm so fucking honored to be your first."

And hopefully my last, but I bottle that up. I don't want to freak him out.

His length nudges between my legs, and I open wider. It takes a few minutes for him to work his way into me.

At first it stings, but when I hiss, he stops and lets me get used to him. After I nod, he nudges a little deeper, and I start to pant. Everything throbs, but the pain ebbs away, and now I just want more.

"Fuck, you feel amazing," he grits out. His face is a mask of concentration and his arms strain as he cages me in. Closing his eyes, he groans as he bottoms out.

"Is it weird I don't have that barrier?" I ask on a gasp when I feel him pulse inside me. "I thought virgins were supposed to have a hymen or whatever."

"All I know is you're fucking perfect. Give me a second." He takes several breaths before he opens his eyes. "Sorry about that timeout. Needed to get my bearings so I didn't embarrass myself."

Having him here like this, on top of me, *inside of me*, is the most amazing thing I've ever felt. I lift my knees, and he slides deeper, and we both shudder.

I smile. "I'm gonna be sore tomorrow." Why I like this idea, I'm not sure.

His eyes go a little wild, and he grazes his teeth down my neck. "Someday we'll go without condoms, and I guarantee I'll be thinking about my cum dripping out of you the entire next day."

Pretty sure my eyes glaze over with lust at his dirty words.

He pulls out slowly, and I hate the loss of him. I wrap my arms and legs around him and yank him back to me. "Don't go."

A dark chuckle erupts from him. "Don't worry, cupcake. A zombie apocalypse couldn't drag me away from between your thighs."

He sinks into me again, and a high-pitched sound I've never made in my life suddenly explodes from my mouth. "Do that again."

At first, our rhythm is a little awkward, but then he kisses me as he reaches down between us to rub my clit. "Gonna need you to come again. Wanna feel that tight little pussy squeeze my cock."

I had no idea Jake was a dirty talker. His groaned words ramp me higher and higher until I'm a spring coiled tight.

Shifting, he changes his angle and nudges some part of my body I never knew existed, and I start chanting his name because it feels so good.

Before I know it, our bodies are slapping together, and we're a tangled web of limbs. On a shriek, I arch back and come. Everything between my legs flutters and squeezes Jake, who curses and surges deeper. He holds me tight as he pulses and empties into the condom.

"Holy shit." I laugh, panting and sweaty and out of breath. "That... I don't have words."

He lifts his head, looking a little dazed. "Fuck. That was heaven, cupcake. I've never... I've never felt anything like it."

His lips meet mine in a lazy, slow kiss. He starts to pull away, and I cling to him. "Where are you going?"

He chuckles. "Gotta take care of the condom. Hang tight." He slowly exits my body, and I groan at the loss.

My pussy suddenly has a giant Jake-sized parking spot that's empty.

When he returns from the bathroom, he has a warm, damp washcloth. "Spread your legs, baby."

Surprised, I do as he asks. I'm about to tell him to be gentle, but the worry evaporates when he carefully wipes me down, pausing to give me a mischievous smile before he presses a kiss to my belly.

"Gotta take care of my girl." He winks, and I sigh.

I'm blissfully happy when he curls his warm, naked body around me.

That elation lasts exactly five days.

Until my sister's next episode.

30

JAKE

"EARTH TO RAMIREZ." Ezra bounces the football off my helmet, that dick.

I glare at him, and he laughs as he holds up his hand. "Just checking in. You look spaced out."

Was I fantasizing about pounding my girlfriend into my mattress? Why, yes, I was. "Thinking about the game this weekend, asshole."

He rolls his eyes, and I try to focus on the new routes Coach wants us to practice, though my mind strays back to Charlotte.

We've been sneaking around after Asher goes to bed. I'm not exactly sure how to handle things with my son. It seems too early for Charlie to move permanently into my bedroom, though that's what I want.

But I realize my son won't understand what's going on. If, God forbid, my relationship with Charlotte goes south, I don't want him to get hurt. Well, there'd be no way around that, but him accepting her as my girlfriend squarely places her in a mother role, and he's been through too much with Dakota for me not to be cautious.

After practice, as I head to the locker room, Billy slaps my shoulder. "How are things with Chuck? You two looked cozy at homecoming last weekend."

I can't contain my smile. Even though it's still tough to open up to my teammates, I want to share this with someone. Despite all the shit Billy's given me since I joined the Broncos, he's a good guy, and I appreciate the effort he made to help me figure things out with my girl.

"It's going well. Charlotte is..." Honestly, I don't even have the words.

Her beautiful smile first thing in the morning makes my heart beat faster. Seeing her at the end of the day feels like coming home. Making her come all night gives me a high like no other. Does life get better than that?

He chuckles when he sees my expression. "That good, huh? I knew once you got your head outta your ass, things would work out for you two."

There's no way I'll ever share details about my sex life with Charlotte, but there is one thing I can talk about.

"You know what's really cool? The way she loves my son. The way Asher's always a priority in her life." I shake my head, ignoring the tightness in my throat. "It means a lot to me."

"Bro." Billy pounds his chest. "You're giving me the feels."

"Shut up."

He laughs. "I'm being serious. I mean, yeah, I'm also giving you shit, but Charlie's a great girl, and I'm glad you two are working things out." Pausing, he glances around. "Has there been any blowback from that show your ex is on?"

"I keep waiting for the other shoe to drop, but so far so good." It's possible I've been worried over nothing. I've gotten calls from reporters doing pieces on Dakota, and I give them the same line I did at the press conference. I wish her luck. That's it. Maybe if I stick to this approach, shit won't blow up in my face.

"Good to hear. Listen, Roxy's doing some big Thanksgiving

dinner in a few weeks at the Stallion Station and wants to invite you guys for dinner."

We have a game the following day, so most of us are hanging around campus. "Thanks, man. Let me check with Charlotte to make sure she doesn't have anything planned for us, and I'll get back to you. But that sounds like fun." I side-eye him. "Something going on with you and Roxy?"

He blows out a frustrated breath. "I wish. She friend-zoned me a long time ago. Said I was 'too wild.'"

"But isn't she..." I don't know the right word to use. Dating? Seeing? Fucking? I go with the most benign term I can think of. "Hanging around Ezra?"

Billy snorts. "Exactly. He's a bigger manwhore than I am. I'm guessing she'll figure it out eventually."

I'm so grateful I don't have to deal with that shit anymore. No more guessing games for me. My girl and I are straight. Feels fucking amazing.

I'm in such a good mood when I get home, I almost forget Dakota's show is on tonight.

"Maybe we should skip it," I murmur against Charlotte's neck after I get Asher to bed. Our chessboard is set up on the coffee table, but playing would require me to stop touching her.

We're sitting on the couch, and she's straddling my lap as she runs her fingers through my hair. I close my eyes and sigh, wishing we didn't have to worry about the stupid *Hell House*.

Charlotte kisses my temple and pushes me back. "Maybe I could help you forget?" She lifts her eyebrows suggestively and sinks to the ground. I love her new boldness. Though, to be honest, we haven't had full-on sex again because she's been sore. But it's been fun doing other things.

I'm ready to turn off the TV and enjoy some naked time with my girlfriend when Asher's voice calls out on the baby monitor.

"Damn. This was just getting good." I pull her up and kiss her forehead. "Hold that thought."

But when I return fifteen minutes later, Charlotte is ghostly pale as she watches Dakota's show.

"What's wrong?"

She swallows and lifts her eyes to mine. They're filled with tears, which she quickly wipes away.

When she doesn't say anything, I know it's bad.

I sit next to her and grab the remote to rewind. I'm recording all the episodes in case something major happens so I can prepare Coach for the fallout.

After a moment, I stop on the scene of Dakota talking to the therapist, Dr. Fields. "This part?"

"Yes." Charlotte starts to get up, but I grab her hand. "Babe, stay. We have to be able to talk about whatever went down."

Reluctantly, she settles next to me as the therapist smiles sympathetically at her sister. "How are you feeling, Dakota? I want to keep tabs on this and make sure you're not overextending yourself."

"I'm doing great. This experience has been energizing." She gives him one of her winning smiles. It's so convincing, I almost forget she's a bald-faced liar.

"The only reason I ask is due to your health issues as a child. Doctors never identified why you got so sick, correct?"

"That's true, and if I'm being honest, sometimes that scares me, but I do regular checkups, work out daily, and eat organic. And I'm happy to say I've been given a clean bill of health."

"That's great news. Now let's switch gears." He tilts his head. "You've mentioned having some difficult relationships. I hope we can get you on the road to healing from past traumas so you can have healthy relationships with men moving forward. Let's start with Jake Ramirez. He's your baby's father. How did you two meet? Can you explain the circumstances?"

Oh, fuck. No wonder Charlotte's upset.

"I can watch this later." Grabbing the remote, I'm about to click it off, but Charlotte stops me.

"You're right. We can't hide from this. As much as I wish we could, my sister will always demand to be the center of attention. Let's just get this over with."

I'm not surprised by her angry tone, but I am caught off guard by the cold look in her eyes directed at me.

Dakota smiles wistfully as she plays with a long lock of blonde hair. "I met Jake at a football party. It was homecoming weekend, and I was a new transfer. My show *Winchester Prep High* had just been cancelled, and I was upset. I wanted to blow off some steam, and when I got invited to a football party, I thought, why not? Jake hit on me immediately. Like, the minute I walked in the door, there he was. This beautiful guy who was super charismatic. He tugged me down onto his lap, told me it was my lucky night, and in many ways it was."

Oh, hell, no. "Charlotte, that's not how things happened."

It's probably not a good sign that she won't look at me.

Dr. Fields hands Dakota a box of tissues, and she wipes her eyes. "I'm sorry I'm getting emotional."

"That's okay. Take your time."

She looks down at her lap. "Our night together was explosive. Like, the hottest sex of my life. We were young, seniors in high school, but my God, Jake had skills."

I feel my ears go hot. This is fucked up. Most guys I know would love to have their sexual prowess bragged about by an ex, but that's not me. I'm a private person, even more so since dating Dakota, and she fucking knows this.

The entire time she talks, the shrink takes notes. "Now, I just want to note that you were both eighteen at the time."

Actually, I was seventeen, and Dakota was almost nineteen because she got held back a year when she was young, but she always lies about it even though seventeen is the age of consent in Texas. Guess she didn't like the optics of dating a younger guy.

She nods. "Unfortunately, the condom broke that night. In some ways I wasn't surprised because of his size..." *Christ.* What the hell is wrong with her? Why would she say that on national television? "I took the morning-after pill, but it didn't work. Nine months later I had my son, Asher, who's the light of my life."

Sure. The light of her life she hasn't seen in two years.

Dr. Fields nods. "If I understand correctly, Jake got custody of him."

She sniffles and wipes her eyes again, but her chin wobbles. "I can't discuss the details due to an NDA, but I had some personal problems I was working through and thought that was best at the time. It's a decision I regret every day."

I roll my eyes. *Está loca.* She's crazy. She made *me* sign an NDA, not the other way around.

"Why do you think things between you and Jake didn't work out?" the therapist asks.

Her chin wobbles again and her voice cracks. "If I had to guess, I'd say it's because there was always a third person in our relationship."

I'm shocked she's going to admit to sleeping with Troy almost our entire time at NTU—more than half of our relationship—but I'd love for that to come to light. Maybe then people will realize what I was dealing with while I played there.

"Can you tell me who that was?" Dr. Fields asks.

She nods as tears stream down her face. "This is really messed up, but it was my sister."

What. The. Fuck.

31

CHARLOTTE

I'M TUCKED in the far corner of the computer lab where I hope I'll be left alone. I don't know if I'm being paranoid, but I could've sworn people were staring at me all day. It was something I'd gotten used to at NTU because Kota was always posting things, and sometimes I'd end up in her footage or pics. I've loved having some privacy at Lone Star State, and I hope this is all in my head.

I'm still seething from last night's episode. Kota has the nerve to blame me? The episode ended with her telling the entire world that *I'm* the reason she and Jake broke up. No mention of her sleeping with his teammate or partying hard every weekend or treating Jake like crap.

The season isn't even over yet. How much more will she unload?

My mom must be loving this stupid show. If I had to guess, she thinks I deserve whatever public humiliation Dakota levels at me. Because without me, one of them had to step up and actually take care of Asher. Which, according to Jake, they blew off once he broke up with my sister.

What's that saying? Birds of a feather? My mom and Kota are both spoiled brats.

It's probably no surprise they're super tight.

They were always whispering, always keeping things from me. Always hoarding secrets I wasn't privy to. Always making me feel like a third wheel in my own freaking family.

God, I hate cliffhangers. Even more so now when I'm the one being hung out to dry.

My phone buzzes for the third time, but I ignore it and focus on the images on the computer screen.

"You gonna get that?" Billy asks as he plops down in the cubicle next to me.

"Nope." A part of me feels guilty for avoiding Jake, but I need some time to think. We live together, so I'll see him tonight.

After I show Billy the shots from last weekend's game, I drag everything I think his grandma might want onto a drive, which I pop out and give to him. "Here you go."

"Thanks. Those images are pretty dope."

"Hope your granny likes them."

He dips his head until our eyes connect. "You okay? Last night's episode was rough."

My stomach tightens. "I'm used to Kota doing this kind of crap."

Why I couldn't see how she would twist things around when we were younger makes me feel like a complete idiot. It's so clear to me now.

Billy clears his throat. "You know Jake doesn't have any feelings for her, right? They were a hookup gone wrong."

My eyes flood and the words rush out of me. "He and I had *three years* before he met Dakota. It took him *one night* to sleep with her." I shake my head. "I know I can't hold the past against him. We weren't together then, but it still hurts to hear the details."

Yes, Jake swore up and down things weren't like what Kota described, and while I believe him, I also know he was taken enough with my sister at the time to sleep with her. At the end of the day, that's all that matters.

Billy scratches his bristly jaw. "I have a theory about this. Did you know I used to play quarterback in high school?"

I have no idea where he's going with this. "Don't you play defense now?"

"Yeah, but being QB is in my blood 'cause that's the position my father played. And yes, I'm a huge disappointment to him. Anyway, the reason I brought this up is because a lot of times, a quarterback will test the waters on the first down. He'll see what the defense brings to the table. He's not really gunning for a touchdown yet. He's warming up and getting a feel for the other team, but on the second down, he's serious. He's looking for the big play." Billy points at me. "You're the big play. You're the second down."

I blink, still trying to make sense of his analogy. "You're saying that Jake wasn't serious about Dakota, but he is with me?"

He snaps his fingers. "Precisely."

I wish I could take this to heart, but Billy wasn't there. He didn't see how committed Jake was to my sister. Sure, things weren't ideal. He was under a lot of pressure. They'd just had Asher and his football schedule was intense, but I never got the impression that he wasn't trying his best to make it work.

Billy reaches over the desk and picks up a copy of *The Bronco Times*. "Is this your pic on the front page?"

I nod, and the first smile I've had all day finally emerges. I'm damn proud of that photo.

He whistles. "Pretty hot stuff."

It's an action shot of Jake stretched out as he reaches for the football in the end zone. The ball, which he pulls in for a touchdown, grazes his fingertips. I'd gotten lucky and positioned myself in a good spot. I've been watching where the other sports photographers shoot from and how they move around the field and trying to emulate that, which helped me snag that image.

While Billy starts talking about a party he went to, I click over to the calendar spread for the shelter. It's all done except for the one slot I'd been hoping Jake would fill. Only a photoshoot with him is the last thing I feel like scheduling this week.

Not that I think last night's episode is the end for us. I don't. I'm just upset because I thought I was done having to deal with the past. It hurt enough living through it the first time. The last thing I want to do is watch it replayed for the world to see. I'd been hoping I could skip *The Hot House* altogether, but maybe that's naive because it leaves me with a huge blind spot.

"Can I get a copy of the calendar too?" Billy asks as I email a PDF proof to Merle with an explanation that I'll get the final image placed by the weekend.

"I'm getting two complimentary copies for all the models. I just spoke to the printer the other day. I should have these ready by the first week of December."

The best part is the school offered to pay for the printing since I'm featuring Bronco athletes, so all the proceeds can go to Second Chances.

As soon as Billy takes off, my phone buzzes again, and I see Jake's name on the caller ID. With a sigh, I answer.

"Hey, you okay?" he asks. "Been trying to reach you. I have twenty minutes before I need to head to practice."

"I'm fine."

He's quiet for a second. "I don't know much about women, but my brothers always say that when a girl says she's fine, she's not."

I nibble my bottom lip. "There's some truth to that. I'm just... I'm having a hard time. It's nothing you need to worry about, though."

"Charlotte, we're a team. I'm still pissed about the episode last night, but we're stronger if we weather this together. Talk to me."

He has a point.

I glance around to make sure no one is close enough to overhear my conversation. "I don't want to relive the past, Jake. If the roles were reversed, would you want to hear how I jumped into bed with another man ten minutes after we met when I'd friend-zoned you for years?"

He curses under his breath. "Of course not, cupcake. I'm so sorry. I know I can't apologize enough for that. And for the record, I never deliberately friend-zoned you. Everything she said last night was full of half-truths."

I get it. I do. "Can we discuss something else? Have you touched base with Coach Santos yet?"

"We're supposed to talk after practice."

"Hopefully he'll have some good advice."

"Will you be home tonight when I get back?"

"Yes." Even though I want to run and hide, I can't stay in the computer lab for the rest of my life.

His voice gets husky. "Maybe I can help you forget that you've had a bad week."

Reluctantly, I smile. I know it's silly to be upset at him for something that happened years ago. "Got any ideas how to do that?"

He chuckles. "I have a hundred and one things I want to do to you naked."

Even though I should probably keep my guard up, I can't. Not with Jake. Not when he makes me feel this alive.

Heat rises to my cheeks as I consider the possibilities. "Then you'd better hurry home so we can start on that list."

32

JAKE

AFTER A QUICK SHOWER, I change and book it to Coach's office. I've been jotting down notes all day about what I want to say to the press. I may have initially said I didn't want to comment about my personal life, but now that Dakota has dragged Charlie into this, I don't think I have a choice.

"Jake, close the door and have a seat." Coach motions to the woman sitting across from his desk. "This is Evelyn Prescott. She's the school's media liaison. You may have seen her at our press conferences. I asked her to join us and share her thoughts about how we should handle any collateral damage from your ex-girlfriend's reality show."

Evelyn, who's dressed in a sleek suit, turns to me with a kind smile. "I'm sure we all caught last night's episode. And I have to ask, are you still dating Dakota's sister?"

Fucking Dakota. Even my own team believes her. "It's not like that, ma'am. Yes, I'm currently dating Charlotte, but I was never with her while we were at North Texas. In fact, I only started seeing her in the last few weeks." I turn to Coach. "She's the girl who's been shooting our games for the AD."

He lifts his eyebrows. "The one from the fire? The one you saved?"

I nod. "I guess you could say that's how we got together. But I want to clarify that Charlotte and I were friends for three years before I met Dakota." Here comes the awkward part. I clear my throat. "And being young and dumb, I didn't realize Dakota was Charlotte's sister when we, uh... hooked up... at that party in high school."

Coach rubs the bridge of his nose. "You kids and your parties are gonna be the death of me."

I'd laugh at his look of exasperation, but I wish I could kick my own ass for what went down that night.

Evelyn jots notes in her journal and turns to me. "I was talking to Coach Santos before you joined us, and we both agree the best approach is to continue redirecting the media to focus on football. You're entitled to your privacy, and unless something truly explosive comes to light on that show, Coach and I think you shouldn't comment on your personal life."

Chingao. That's not what I want to hear.

Coach nods. "Since we're undefeated and getting close to the playoffs, we'll have NFL scouts here until the end of the season. You don't want them to think you're distracted or have your own agenda. Think of this as your way to keep the team focused."

We've had two scouts here for the last few days. All the guys have been on their best behavior on and off the field in the event one of them might overhear our conversations.

But the idea of not clearing up Dakota's suggestion that Charlotte somehow interfered in our relationship doesn't sit right.

"Sir, with all due respect, if we were just talking about me, I would be on board with this approach. But Dakota dragged Charlotte into this, and I don't think it's right people might think she's a home-wrecker. In fact, she transferred to Lone Star State to get away from me. Because she had feelings for me. And I had no idea she was here when I accepted your offer to play football for you."

Evelyn holds out her hand. "All the more reason to not comment about the things Dakota is suggesting. Because, frankly, transferring schools looks bad. Charlotte left NTU because she was interested in you. That actually supports what Dakota said, that Charlotte was a third wheel who interfered."

Goddamn it. I'm not explaining this right.

I rake my fingers through my hair and tug at the ends. "It's not fair to Charlotte. She's innocent in all of this. She went no-contact for two years. I had no idea when she left NTU that she had any kind of romantic feelings for me at all."

Evelyn nods. "I hear what you're saying. I do, and there will be a time and place to release a statement about this once the season is over. But if you start now, you're opening yourself up to criticism at a crucial time of the season. It could be detrimental to you and your team and everyone's focus, which should be on making the playoffs and not on some silly reality show. Because the moment you open this door, you can't close it again. Think of it this way. If you comment and Dakota responds publicly, you're going to turn our program into a circus instead of a team that's focused on making the playoffs."

I groan, hating that she's making a lot of sense.

Evelyn gives me a patient smile. "Part of why she's dredging up this sob story is for ratings so viewers continue to vote for her, and if you give in and react defensively, you're playing right into her hands."

Shit, she's right.

Coach nods. "I know this is tough, Jake, but do it for me. Do it for the team. That's why you came here, right? To play football? Well, it's time to prove it." He pauses. Clears his throat. "I know Charlotte is important to you, but I really think you two should cool it for a while. No reason to give the media more fodder than necessary."

What the fuck?

Stunned, I sit there, mute. Coach gets called out to talk to one of our physical therapists. Evelyn excuses herself.

And I wonder what the hell I'm gonna do.

~

I'D LOVE nothing more than to take a long drive until I get my head on straight, but I haven't seen Asher all day. My stomach is in knots, though, as I debate what to tell Charlotte.

I can handle holding off on making a statement. Maybe. But the thought of separating from my girl for any amount of time is downright painful.

Until I figure out what to do, there's no way I'm telling her about Coach's suggestion to cool off our relationship. It'll crush her. Especially since she's also having to deal with those baseless accusations from her sister.

When I get home, Asher's wearing PJs and sitting on the couch with Charlie, who's reading him a book. Duke is curled at their feet.

"Hey, kiddo." I drop all my shit by the door and stalk to my son. I drop to my haunches as he flings himself in my arms.

I never want to be one of those men who's too cool or busy to show my kid affection. My dad wasn't big on hugs, but my mom never missed an opportunity to show me and my brothers she loved us.

I ask Ash a couple of questions about his day, and he rambles on about playing in the sand and making mud pies.

"What time did Yvette leave?" I ask Charlie, who's staring at the dark TV screen.

"An hour ago." She looks down at her lap and tugs a loose string from her shorts.

"Did everything go okay with her?" I stand with Asher in my arms, worried by how quiet Charlotte is being.

She turns her red-rimmed eyes to me. "Yvette said she wasn't surprised you picked my sister instead of me because Kota is the better-looking sister."

What the hell? "Why would she say something like that?"

Her harsh laugh is something I've never heard before. "Uh, maybe because it's true. Empirically, Kota is the more attractive of the two of us. She's taller. Her boobs are bigger. Her nose is perfectly straight, and her teeth are perfectly white. Her hair looks like something out of a shampoo commercial—perfectly sleek and smooth. She's the life of every party." She waves her hand. "You know, all the reasons you *actually* picked her."

Fuck.

Guess I deserved that.

"You know that's not true, right? You're absolutely more beautiful than Dakota."

She gives me a smile that doesn't reach her eyes. "Sure. Listen, I'm going to bed. Asher already brushed his teeth."

It's not even eight o'clock yet, but I have the feeling she wants to escape me right now, which sucks.

Yeah, I'm definitely not mentioning what Coach said.

Except now she's thrown down the gauntlet. There's no way I can let her go to sleep thinking I find my ex more attractive than her. It's simply not true.

After I get Asher to sleep, I gently knock on her door. When I don't hear anything, I crack it open. I don't want to wake her, but I can't leave so many things unsaid between us.

My mom always tells me and my brothers not to go to sleep mad at your significant other. I think it's a lesson she learned from shit going south with my father.

Charlotte's room is quiet, and I'm about to sneak back out when I hear her sniffle.

Fuck it. I'm not letting her run away from me. Not this time.

I close the door behind me, set the baby monitor on the bedside table, and slide in behind her. Of course, my ass hangs off the edge because the mattress is so narrow. "Scoot over."

"I'm on the edge," she whispers. "I'm about to fall off."

For some reason, I feel like we're talking about more than just the bed. *Me too, baby. Let's do this together.*

There's one way to fix this.

"This is like that scene at the end of *Titanic*," I grumble before I scoop her on top of me so she straddles my stomach.

"Jake, I don't think—"

"Shut up, and come here." I hug her to my chest until she relaxes. "I'm not letting you go this time, cupcake. I know you're scared and freaked out and want to hide from me until you get a handle on everything, but like I told you on the phone, we're a team, and we'll figure this out together. No more running. Not from me."

She nods and clings to my shirt. Her shoulders shake as her tears drip along my neck.

It kills me she's so upset.

"Don't cry, baby. Everything will be okay. We have each other now. You don't have to deal with the fallout from your sister's shows by yourself anymore."

Charlie's family never gave her any support. She's always had to do everything by herself. That ends now.

I run my hand over her back and shoulders. Through her hair. Down her neck. She smells so good, I want to drown in her scent.

"Did you know I noticed you the first day of our freshman year of high school?" I murmur in her ear. "I walked into Mr. Romano's class, and when I saw you sitting in the back corner, there was a stream of light shining in through the window. Swear to God, I froze. You looked like an angel with all that blonde hair and your shy smile." I kiss her forehead. "You and I were meant to be, but I was just too young and stupid to know it at the time."

She sniffles again. "You're not just saying that?"

"Fuck no. I meant it when I said you absolutely caught my attention back then. One hundred percent. You're beautiful, Charlie." And if it takes me the rest of my life to prove this to her, so be it.

Charlotte doesn't understand that she's the full package. Sure, my ex looks nice on the outside, but once you got past that shiny exterior, there was no substance to the woman. She reminds me of those facades at Universal Studios where they make the movies. All these pretty storefronts with no actual building attached. Just empty space.

Charlie sits up, and her tear-streaked face shoots an arrow straight through my chest. "What did Coach say today?"

Definitely can't tell her everything that happened in that meeting. At least not right now when she's so upset.

I reach up and dry her soft cheeks with my thumbs as I cradle her face. "That we should hold off on commenting about *The Hot House* until the end of the season because he doesn't want the team to get distracted."

"That makes sense."

"It pisses me off. I hate that you're getting dragged through the mud."

The resigned look on her face kills me. "I'm used to it."

I swallow. "Listen, I can still release a statement. It might piss off Coach, and that will suck, but I can't stomach the idea of people getting the wrong impression of you."

She shakes her head and leans down, clinging to me like a koala bear. "Thank you. It means the world to me that you're willing to make that sacrifice, but I don't want you to jeopardize the good thing you have here. Coach Santos has gone out on a limb for you. Finish the season. We'll make the best of it. Like you said, we can do this together."

I hold her to me as it hits me like a fucking bolt of lightning. The realization makes my heart pound. "Charlotte, I need you to know something." I take a deep breath. "I love you."

At first, she's quiet. "You do?"

I turn my head to look her in the eye and brush her hair out of her beautiful face. "Of course. You're the most incredible woman I know. Beautiful inside and out. You have the biggest heart of anyone I know." I graze my lips against hers. "I love you. I think I've always loved you in one way or another. But this, where we're at now, I've never felt this way about anyone else. Just you."

Her eyes well again, but the smile on her lips as she says those sweet words back is one I'll never forget. "I love you, too, Jake."

She trails her fingers through my hair as she kisses me, and for the first time in my life, my future is clear. I love my family. Football. My team. But the woman in my arms gives everything else meaning. If I can wife her up someday, I'll die a happy man.

When we kiss, our tongues move against each other in a slow, sensual slide that has me instantly rock hard, which Charlotte figures out when she scoots down.

Her eyes widen with a giggle.

I grab her ass and squeeze. "You do this to me. Every time, woman."

It's the reason I had her sit on my stomach. I didn't want my body's reaction to her being so close to distract us from what needed to be said.

Shyly, she tilts her head, and her mass of blonde hair falls over her shoulder. "I'm not sore anymore."

A low growl rumbles in my chest. She makes me feel like an animal. It takes control to not rip her clothes off and sink deep into her body.

My eyes hood as I look her over, my attention zoning in on the way her nipples come to hard points against the thin cotton of her white tank top.

With a grin, I take one in my mouth, biting down just enough to make her gasp. I flatten the fabric around her chest and lick and suck her into my mouth. By the time I get to the second one, she's grinding down on my eager erection.

I graze my thumb across her plump bottom lip. "Take off your clothes, cupcake." She strips off her top before she stands up over me and slowly scoots down her panties. Damn, she puts on a good show.

For a moment, I just take her in. Her long, slender legs. That shadowed heaven between her thighs. Her beautiful breasts.

I stroke up her smooth calf and tug her down until she's on her knees, straddling my chest. "Lean forward. Grab the wall."

Mentally, I make a note to get us a strong headboard in the future. One that Charlotte can hang on to when she's riding my face.

"But Jake, if I lean forward..." Her eyes go wide.

A dirty grin spreads on my lips. "If you lean forward, you'll be in the perfect position for me to give you a special kiss." I wink at her. "Think of this as knocking out something else on your bucket list."

I don't need the lights on to know my girl is doing a full-body blush.

When she doesn't say anything, I lift my chin. "Baby, we haven't done the deed since last weekend. Let me warm you up. Let me make you feel good." She nods slowly and leans over me to place her hands on the wall. "Good girl."

Fuck, she's so hot like this. Draped over me with her thighs spread open over my face and completely at my mercy.

I run my nose along her inner thigh, and goosebumps break out on her skin. She's freshly showered and smells so fucking good. Taking her ass in both hands, I tug her down to me and groan when I lick her. She's already wet.

But then she says my name.

Pausing, I look up at her and she nibbles her bottom lip. "Could I... could I return the favor?"

She wants to give me a blow job? Hell yes.

I'm about to tell her she can head south when I'm done here, but when I start to nod, she lifts herself off the bed and turns around, only she's still straddling my shoulders.

Seeing how most of my blood flow has converged at my dick, bypassing my brain, it takes a second for me to figure out we're sixty-nining.

"Fuck yes." I shove down my shorts and groan when she leans over my body, putting her hot little ass and wet pussy in my face.

With a growl, I grab her hips and dive back in, licking along her wet slit and flattening my tongue to give her clit some attention. But with this new position, I can't help but wonder if maybe she'd enjoy some back door action.

When she grabs my dick and gives my head a lick, it's hard to concentrate, though. Especially when I glance down her body and watch her work me with her hand as she bobs on my cock. But I want to make this good for her.

I work one finger and then two into her tight pussy before I give in to temptation and lick her asshole. She squeals, and I chuckle. "Does that feel good, baby? Or do you like this better?"

With my thumb, I gather some of her wetness and circle her back entrance slowly before I push in gently.

She flutters on my fingers and loses her momentum on my

cock, pausing just to hold me in her mouth, which still feels pretty fucking good.

I'm loving the incoherent sounds she's making, so I keep going. "Babe, you look so hot fucking my fingers."

I can barely think straight when she takes me down the back of her throat.

Fuck. I'm not gonna last like this. With my other hand, I reach around and circle her clit as I watch my thumb move slowly in and out of her asshole. I'm wondering if this is too much for her when she starts riding my hand, drenching my fingers.

I remove my thumb and replace it with my tongue. I give her a few licks and that's all it takes for her to come. Her thighs quake for a second before she collapses on top of me.

Somehow I manage to hold off.

Leaning up, I bite her ass cheek. "That feel good, baby?"

"I can't speak. I'm dead."

Chuckling, I run my hand up and down her thigh.

With a moan, she sits up and turns around, so she's straddling my stomach again. "You made me come so hard," she says shyly.

I tug her down to me and she kisses me. I'm ravenous for her. "Can I grab a condom?"

Don't want to assume anything. She's still new to all of this.

"Yes. Hurry."

Grinning at her disheveled state, I slide out of bed. I wash my hands in the bathroom and grab a foil package. I'm already rolling it on when I reach her.

She opens her legs, but I shake my head. "Get on top." I get into bed and slide her on my chest. "Ride me, cupcake. Work off all that stress."

She takes my bottom lip between her teeth and tugs gently.

"Pretty sure it all leached out of me when you licked me to oblivion."

I reach up and tangle my fingers in her hair and pull her down to kiss her. As our tongues tangle, I line up with her opening, loving how she moans when I start to push.

But then she puts her hand on me and sits up. "I thought this was my turn to fuck you?" The playful look in her eyes slays me. My little vixen bites her lip as she reaches behind her and grabs my cock as she pushes back.

Between her hand and the tight squeeze to fit in her pussy, my eyes almost cross.

By the time she's fully seated, we're both panting. I grab her thighs and help her rise up.

It's almost too good. I close my eyes and try to hold off, but she feels like heaven wrapped around me like this.

"Don't you want to watch?" she whispers.

I have to hold my breath as my cock pulses, and I do my best to think about football routes so I don't blow. "Always."

Then my woman leans back to brace herself on my thighs as she slides her legs forward. Resting her ankles on my shoulders, she puts her pretty pussy on full display as she rides my cock.

"Jesus. Watching you stretch around me is hot as fuck." I reach between her legs. Graze my thumb where her body's stretched out around me and swallowing my length. I use her wetness to gently flick her swollen clit. "Can you come again?" I grit out.

"Maybe. If you keep rubbing me."

That sounds like a challenge. One I'm eager to take.

As I run my thumb over her, I watch her gorgeous tits bounce as she bottoms out and slides back. Her pace quickens as her breathy moans get louder, and finally, I can't take it any longer. I gently pinch her clit, and that sets her off.

She feels so damn good, fluttering around my cock. My hips

arch off the bed as I come, and that gets me a shriek. She pulls herself forward and bounces frantically, all the while quaking around my dick. It's fucking incredible.

When she collapses on top of me again, we're both sweaty and out of breath.

I wrap my arms around her. Run my hand up and down her back. "Love you, baby. I'm so glad you're mine." I honestly don't have words for how amazing that was. Seriously the hottest sex of my life.

I know it wasn't just the physical act that made it special. It's how she trusts me. How I trust her. It elevates everything.

She squeezes me tight and burrows her face against my neck. "Love you too, Jake. I've... I've always loved you."

That whispered confession does something to my chest. Fuck Coach's suggestion to take a break. Because Charlotte Darling is mine, and there's no way I'm letting her go.

Not even for a little while.

33

CHARLOTTE

"Don't you look like the cat who got the cream," Roxy teases as she joins me in the computer lab.

Oh, yeah. I got creamed.

But I don't say anything, just smile wider.

Jake loves me! I'm fighting the urge to twirl around the room.

His confession last Friday night has had me walking on air for the last several days. I've been hopped up on adrenaline ever since.

"I have a good pic of you from Saturday's game. Hang on." I scroll through the shots from last weekend until I find the one I'm looking for.

Roxy's flying high, doing the splits, over her spotter. The muscles in her arms and legs are taut as she extends, and she has this amazing smile. It was worth the Charley horse I got for crouching on the ground and nearly getting kicked in the face when one of the other cheerleaders went tumbling past.

"Holy shit." Roxy's mouth drops open. "That's the best action photo anyone has ever taken of me."

"If you can hang out a few minutes, I'll print it for you." I send it to our giant color printer.

As we're waiting for the image, she gets a text. When she reads it, she growls. "That asshole."

Let me guess. "Ezra?"

"Why do I put up with his bullshit? He's so hot and cold. This is totally confidential, but he's thinking about entering the draft this year as a junior. One minute he begs me to change my plans and promise I'll follow him if he's drafted, and the next he leaves me on read the entire weekend. He literally never calls me when he goes home. It's like I don't exist then."

The guys aren't allowed to have their phones out at practice, but the minute it's over, Jake always responds if I've messaged him. As I think back on our relationship, the only time he ever got cagey was our senior year of high school when he got mixed up with Dakota.

Roxy angrily punches the letters on her cell to respond. "He never used to be this way. When I first met him, before he made QB1, he was always polite and sweet. I think success has gone to his head."

"Sorry, Rox. That sucks." I debate how much advice I should dole out, but I always want honesty from my friends, so that's what I serve up. "Have you talked to him about how he makes you feel when he goes MIA?"

"He acts like I'm crazy. Like I'm making it all up in my head."

"So he gaslights you? Ugh. That's the worst." Sounds like he's taking notes from my sister's playbook. "Then why bother? You're one of the most beautiful girls on campus. You could have anyone. Why are you putting up with his crap?"

Her shoulders droop as she lets out a sigh. "I ask myself this all the time. We started as friends with benefits, which I'd never done before. I figured I'd try it out. Except seeing him with other girls made me want to rip out their extensions, so I tried to break things off with him, but he didn't want to. He promised we'd be exclusive. Only he said he couldn't 'one hundred percent commit to anything long term.' So we're not exactly dating. I guess it's more of a situationship."

"You don't sound like you're convinced he's being faithful."

"I'm so tempted to check his phone, but I don't want to be that girl, the one who's so jealous she has to check up on her boyfriend all the time. Except he's not my boyfriend. And *this* is why the whole thing makes me mental. Ultimately, I never know where I stand with him."

I'm quiet for a moment. "Your dad would lose it if he found out one of his players was treating you like that."

"Ezra must have a death wish. He's so lucky I haven't told Coach anything."

It's so cute that she calls her dad Coach sometimes.

As I grab the shot of her out of the printer, I ask the question I've been wondering for a while. "What about Billy? I know he used to joke about wanting to date me, but he obviously has a thing for you."

"As beautiful as that boy is with all his sexy tattoos and as much as I like him as a friend, my dad would kill me if I dated him. Everyone knows he and Cam used to tag-team their dates. Not that anyone complained. Those girls bragged about it like they'd just won the lottery. I don't think Cam and Billy do that anymore, but it was bandied about on that gossip blog last fall, and my dad read it. Plus, Billy is really cavalier at practice, almost disrespectful sometimes, and my dad *hates* that."

"I'm sorry, Rox. I actually think you and Billy would make a great couple. You'd be a good influence on him, but I know how much your dad's opinion matters to you."

After she takes off, I'm still thinking about what she said as I head to the darkroom. Hearing about someone else's dating drama makes me so grateful for my relationship with Jake.

My phone dings, and I open it.

Love you, cupcake.

That's all he says, but it puts a huge smile on my face. As much as we've been through, as hard as it's been to get to this point, I'm grateful for the challenges we've faced because we're stronger than ever.

Love you too. Always. I add the lick emoji and giggle. It's fun to tease him.

He responds with the devil emoji. **Food for thought, babe!**

I'll never get over being in love with this man. It's like we were written in the stars.

I break out the negatives from our photoshoot last Sunday. I took most of the images with a digital camera, but the school newspaper had an old manual Canon lying around that no one ever used, so I borrowed it for a few days.

After I check the negatives on the contact sheet, I slide one strip into the enlarger, flip off the overhead lights, and get out the photo paper, which I can see because the red safelight automatically pops on if the room is dark. Once I've done my test image with different amounts of light on the enlarger, I jot down notes on each one so I can remember how long I exposed the segment.

It takes a while to find the perfect setting, but that only builds my excitement for the final image. Because it's always worth the wait.

My life has often felt chaotic and frenzied, particularly with my family, but the darkroom is one place I have absolute control. Do I want to push the film when I'm developing it? Does this photo need more contrast? Should I print full framed or cropped? Does something need to be burned or dodged? It's all in my hands, and there's no feeling like printing the perfect image.

When I'm in the darkroom, I often lose track of time. That's especially the case today as I rock the exposed paper in the tray of developing solution and watch the image of Jake emerge.

From the blank paper, his dark eyes appear first. Then his disheveled hair. Finally, his smile. He's mid-laugh as Duke licks his face.

I've already placed the final calendar image of Jake posing with a puppy from Second Chances and sent the layout to the printer, but these black and white shots are just for me. Technically, they're for Jake since his birthday is coming up, and I want to give him something special.

The next one I print is of Jake and Asher, who's giggling because his dad is tickling him. I can still hear his infectious laughter. Duke gazes up at them, and I swear that dog is smiling. As I stare at the image, I realize I'm looking at my whole heart. Everything I love is right here.

Lastly, I print a selfie Jake and I took. I'm looking at the camera, completely unaware of the way he's staring at me.

Like he can't take his eyes off me.

I cover my mouth as a knot forms in my throat.

If I ever doubt how he feels about me, I just need to look at this photo.

This, what I have with Jake, is real.

Things might get crazy with all the shit I'm sure Dakota will unload on her dumb show, but I have to steel myself for those tough times and know what I'm fighting for.

It's in this photo.

I'm smiling all the way home.

34

JAKE

LEANING BACK ON THE COUCH, I groan. "I ate too much."

Charlotte smiles and snuggles up to me as I wrap my arm around her. "That's impossible." She pats my stomach. "Just watch. You'll be hungry again in an hour."

She's not wrong.

Over the last few weeks, things with Charlotte have been better than my wildest dreams. This girl just gets me. She's always gotten me. She gave me this incredible set of photos last night for my birthday. Knowing how much time it takes to make each print made her gift that much more special. I want to do something for her for the holidays. I'm not sure what, though. I'm hoping she'll come home with me to visit my family at Christmas.

While I obviously haven't "cooled things off" with Charlotte as Coach suggested, I haven't flaunted that in his face either. Except for when she shoots our games, our worlds don't really collide. We're both so busy on those afternoons, we barely see each other, and it's usually across the football field. We should be cool.

The one thing I did do, though, is pull Roxy aside and ask

her to not mention anything to her dad. I explained why, and she was livid on my behalf, so I know she's got our back. And I might've mentioned that I'd appreciate it if she didn't worry Charlotte with the details. She understood and agreed.

I feel a little guilty keeping this from my girlfriend, but there's no reason to stress her out any more than she already is. She's already on pins and needles from that fucking show.

Deep in thought, I kiss Asher's head. He's asleep on my lap after diving face first into a huge plate of turkey and stuffing.

Roxy collapses on the other side of Charlie. "Not gonna lie. I think I outdid myself."

"Your Thanksgiving feast was the bomb, Rox." Billy sits on the arm of the couch.

She leans against his side and yawns. "Thanks. Now I have to go home and pretend I have room for another dinner."

We're all recovering from the huge meal. Cam, Diesel, and the rest of the guys file out of the kitchen where Roxy put them to work doing dishes, and they join us in the living room at the Stallion Station.

Cam turns down the football game on the TV and looks at me. "I hate to rain on your parade, but did you want to watch tonight's episode of *The Hot House*?"

There goes my great day.

Billy winces. "They're kicking off two members, there's another hookup, someone wins an audition, and Dakota makes another bombshell confession."

I scratch my head. "How the hell do you know this?"

"Bro, they post teasers online every week."

As much as I'd love to chill with my friends and forget *The Hell House* exists, I don't want to head into tomorrow's game blind. It'll leave me vulnerable, especially with the press conference afterward. Coach might not want me to answer any questions, but that doesn't mean the media won't ask them. And I don't want to be caught off guard.

Fuck, I hope this doesn't blow my concentration tomorrow. We have two more games before the playoffs. Even though we're undefeated, competition is tough this season, and we need this win to hopefully clinch a playoff berth.

Not to mention we play North Texas University tomorrow. Kicking Troy's ass is gonna require my complete focus.

"What are the odds Dakota will get voted off?" I muse out loud.

Billy shakes his head. "Not likely. She's one of the most popular chicks on the show. Her fans are ravenous."

Charlotte sighs. "The Little Darlings are intense. They wear pink leather bracelets and have watch party meet-ups across the country every time she's on a show. They're like a swarming pack of mean girls."

"*Little Darlings.* Wasn't that the name of her show back in the day?" Billy asks.

"Yeah, but it became synonymous with my sister."

I blow out a breath and turn to my sweet girlfriend. "Sorry, cupcake. Would you mind if we watched it?"

"Of course not," she says quietly.

It sucks because I know the last thing she wants to do is sit here with all of these people and endure this crap. "Babe, we could catch it at home. We don't have to do this here."

She hooks her pinky in mine. "I'm fine. Really. As long as I can get another slice of Roxy's pecan pie, I'm good to go."

I kiss her forehead. "You know you're the best, right?" I whisper.

Billy points at us with a smirk. "I think I deserve some credit for you two happening." Circling two fingers in the air a little too suggestively for my comfort, he adds, "Love is in the air..." He scoops up Roxy, flops onto the couch, and sits back with her on his lap.

"Yeah, you'll be on our Christmas list," I deadpan.

Roxy pats his cheek like he's a misbehaving schoolboy and scoots off. "Please promise me y'all will put away the leftover pie."

Cam chuckles with a wink. "Darlin', there won't be any leftover pie."

She smiles and grabs her purse. "All righty. Later, gators. Love y'all."

Everyone yells out their thanks as she takes off. I glance down at Asher, wondering if the commotion will wake him, but he's in a solid food coma.

Billy watches her go, and after the front door shuts, I clear my throat. "Any progress with you and Roxy?" It's the worst-kept secret that Babcock has it bad for Coach's daughter.

He groans and flops back on the couch. "Not much, since Ezra's being such a cockblock."

That would be a problem. Not that Ezra is anywhere near deserving of Roxy Santos.

Our discussion of Billy's love life pauses as credits for *The Hell House* roll, and I say a prayer Dakota reins in her bullshit tonight.

My eyes glaze over for some of the stuff. Because who really cares which of these dumbasses wins an audition or how these divas apply makeup? I'm annoyed I need to sit through it once a week.

During group therapy, the contestants are challenged to make a declaration of what they want moving forward in their lives.

It cuts to Dakota in the confession booth. Her eyes are teary as she dabs the corners, which I'm sure is for sympathy. I never genuinely saw her cry when we were together. Not even when she had Asher. It was like her tear ducts were soldered shut.

Dakota's voice wavers. "I've done my best to block out the past. To block out the ways my sister and ex betrayed me, but honestly, it still hurts." Tears well in her eyes and her lower lip quivers. "Charlotte had a huge crush on Jake. She told me about it when we were younger, but I hoped by the time I dated him that she was over it since he obviously didn't reciprocate. But I was wrong. She wasn't over it, and she was so pathetic the way she'd follow him around like a stray puppy. All of our friends would comment about her being a little creeper about it.

"Who defended her?" She raises her hand. "Stupidly, I did. I trusted her, like I trusted him. I can't say definitively whether they hooked up while Jake and I were together, but I wouldn't be surprised if they did. I remember telling him how uncomfortable I was that they spent so much time together, and he blew me off. Said I was making a big deal out of nothing."

"What the fuck is wrong with her?" I rarely lose my cool, but this shit has to stop.

Charlotte isn't even looking at the screen. Her head is tilted down at her lap. I wrap an arm around her and try not to jostle Asher.

Dakota dabs her eyes again. "Moving forward, I'd like to come to peace with that so I can see my son again. To do this, I need to be able to openly communicate with my ex. I might be in Los Angeles for the foreseeable future, but he and I have to find a way to share custody. I might be an actress, but I'm a mom first."

Jesus Christ. Is she doing this for the ratings? I have difficulty believing she gives a shit about our kid.

Dramatically, she appears to be trying to get ahold of her emotions. "Jake, if you're watching, I'm sorry about whatever you think I did, but you hurt me too."

Does a sociopath get their feelings hurt? Doubtful.

I'm curious how she thinks *I* hurt *her*. She probably means that time I walked in on her and Troy and ruined their fuck fest.

By the time the show is over, I'm shaking with anger.

Where has Dakota been for the last two years? I've never gotten even one phone call or text from her asking about our son since she took off for LA. Who's changed his diapers and wiped up vomit and bathed and fed him? Me. Who rocks him to sleep when he's afraid during thunderstorms or sick? Me. Who knows all of his favorite toys, stories, and movies? Me.

Even before we broke up, she wrangled everyone she knew into watching Ash so she could run off and party.

Dakota wants to take Asher away from me? Over my dead fucking body.

35

CHARLOTTE

EVEN THOUGH IT'S almost December, the afternoon is bright and sunny but chilly. Basically perfect football weather.

As we wait for the team to get introduced, the Lone Star State band plays the *Rocky* theme while Bronco fans shadowbox. People are so excited for today's game against North Texas U, I can almost forget the crap my sister said last night on her show.

Shake it off, Charlotte. You can do this. Don't give Dakota any more power.

Biting my thumbnail, I scan the crowd. I think I get more nervous for Jake on game days than he does. We're so close to the playoffs, and I know how badly he wants to win the championship this year. Plus, this is his former team. Bragging rights are on the line. Hopefully, he can block out my sister's drama and focus.

I've taken photos all day, starting in the parking lot with the tailgating parties. The game hasn't even started yet, and my energy is lagging. I should've eaten more than a granola bar this morning, but now it's too late to do anything about it. Pretty sure staff photographers shouldn't be seen chowing down on the sidelines.

When I catch a whiff of someone's nachos, my stomach lurches. I've felt nauseous all day. Another reason I didn't eat more this morning. I think it's because I was so upset last night. I didn't want to worry Jake, so I took a long shower until I could get my emotions under control. I hate crying around him. I don't want him to think I'm some delicate little flower.

By the time the team charges out of the tunnel, I'm a nervous wreck. I know how badly Jake wants to have a great game. He says he needs amazing stats for the entire season to make up for his sophomore and junior years at NTU. I can't imagine how hard it was for him to play with Troy knowing he and Kota were hooking up.

But now, today, he has to play against his former best friend. I hold my hand against my stomach and pray I don't projectile vomit from nerves. NTU is undefeated right now too.

Fans scream, welcoming the hometown team to the stadium as Guns N' Roses blasts from the sound system. Someone unfurls a huge banner that says "Paradise City" and is decorated with bucking broncos. It took me a while to figure out why we use that song, but I get it now. How Charming is obsessed with football. It's such a great little town that really supports the university.

I don't spot Jake until he's on the line of scrimmage for the first possession, which we have. Behind me, some girl screams, "JAKE RAMIREZ! I FUCKING LOVE YOU! I WANNA HAVE YOUR BABIES!"

That would be cute, funny even, if he hadn't knocked up my sister. I resist the urge to turn around and shoot that person a dirty look. Not that she would notice me down on the field.

But my mood does a one-eighty when my cell buzzes with a text. I pull it out of my back pocket to see a message from the athletic director. **Please make sure I get those photos this**

evening before you leave. Several media outlets are requesting our images.

He means *my* images, but I don't let that upset me.

Inside, I'm squealing. I've never had an opportunity like this before. AD Armstrong said there's a chance my pics could get picked up by a wire service, which would mean my photos might land in national publications.

Because the Broncos are undefeated and we're almost at the end of the regular season, the press wants full access to my images. I'd get credited, of course, if any of them are printed in newspapers or sports magazines. But nailing great shots for the next two games is really important.

The best part, aside from the stipend I'm getting at the end of the season, is that the AD told me this morning I could travel with the team for their last game next weekend. And if we make it to the playoffs, I'll get full press credentials to attend! It's such an incredible opportunity, I almost fell over when he told me.

For the tenth time, I double-check my two cameras and lenses. I might sleep all of tomorrow after lugging around this equipment so long. I have to be careful with the neck straps because they can cut off circulation. I almost passed out at the last game because the lenses are so heavy, and when they're hanging off your neck, you don't realize you're light-headed until you stand up from a crouched position.

We win the coin flip and take possession.

I'm kneeling on the ground near the fifty-yard line when the ball snaps. I focus on Ezra, my shutter whirring as I take shot after shot. He might be a dick to Roxy, but he's a great quarterback. I can't just ignore him, as much as I'd like to.

He doesn't make much headway until the third down when he finds Jake along the forty-yard line.

The throw is a little high, but Jake leaps up for the catch

before he tucks it against his body and heads for Bronco territory.

Everyone's screaming as he strongarms his way out of the hold of one of the defenders, but two more guys are on his heels. I'm so caught up in the action, I almost forget to shoot.

Jake jukes one way, then the other, leaps over some dude lunging for his legs, and books it downfield. Another defender leaps at him and misses.

He's at the thirty-yard line.

Twenty.

Ten.

Touchdown! The jumbotron lights up as Jake holds up the ball in celebration.

Tossing out all professional decorum, I scream in delight, "Go Broncos!" The stadium goes wild.

By halftime, we're up twenty-one to seven. Jake's having an incredible game, having scored two of our three touchdowns, and we've sacked Troy twice, that troll.

I find myself by the tunnel as the guys head for the locker room. I've just tucked away my cameras so I can grab some water when Jake and I make eye contact as he trots by. I'm so caught up in the excitement of the game, I run up to him and leap up into his arms to kiss him.

"Great game! You're killing it."

"Thanks, cupcake." He laughs, kisses me again, before he pats my ass and rejoins the team.

I touch my lips, which pull up in a huge smile.

Life has never felt so good. Coming to Lone Star was the best decision I ever made. I'm busy thanking my lucky stars for Jake and our new school and all of the blessings we've had when I pause.

Did someone just call my name?

There it is again. It came from the stands.

I grab my camera bag and look up, still smiling.

Splash.

That's when I'm doused with a huge container of soda.

I flinch as the cold liquid and ice hits my face and shoulders, but the debris keeps coming. More soda and some food. A hot dog with mustard and relish smacks my shirt and slowly slides to the ground.

I gasp, afraid more crap will rain down on me. Someone must have tripped and accidentally dumped their food over the railing.

When I look up, though, there are two girls in the stands, glaring down at me. I have a hard time making out their faces because they're covered in face paint, but one yells, "Hey, skank! How does it feel to get Dakota's sloppy seconds?"

Horrified, I'm frozen stiff.

I don't see the soda can until it's too late.

36

JAKE

WHEN WE MAKE it back onto the field, there's a weird energy on the sidelines. I can't explain why, but I'm suddenly uneasy.

Coach is always telling us we can't get caught up in what goes on in the stadium, either here or on the road. At this level of competition, so much of our success is mental, and now isn't the time to get distracted.

I shake that shit off because we have a game to win. And let me just say that nothing feels better than kicking Troy's ass.

Billy grabs my shoulder. "You okay?"

"Yeah," I say slowly. "Why wouldn't I be?"

He blinks. Pauses. "I'll catch you after the game."

"Sure." I watch him head onto the field. Was that weird or am I imagining things?

I don't dwell on it because this game is too important to lose my concentration.

By the time our victory music plays at the end of the fourth quarter, we've decimated my former team. I head out on the field and greet a few old friends. Even though I had a great game, Evelyn doesn't want me talking to the press without her. Kinda sucks, but I get it, so I try to avoid the media.

When I turn around, Troy is waiting for me.

"Hey, man. I know you don't want to talk to me, and I get it." He's sweaty and rubbing his shoulder, probably from that last sack. He looks around and lowers his voice as he steps closer. "Just wanted to let you know she played me too."

I don't need to ask who *she* is.

A few months ago, I'd have had a hard time not tackling his ass to the ground, but now I don't care. *I have my cupcake and can eat her too.* I chuckle to myself. Life is good. Just need to deal with Dakota's drama for a few more weeks. I can gut it out.

"Whatever, dude. You made your bed." Technically it was my bed.

The truth is I don't give a shit about the past anymore, and that apathy feels fucking incredible.

I look for Charlotte, hoping to touch base with her before I head for the showers, but there are so many people on the field, it's like looking for a needle in the haystack.

When I reach the field house, I'm expecting some back slaps from Coach. Maybe an "atta boy" for kicking ass today. Possibly the game-day ball.

Instead, he barks my name when I get to the locker room.

"What's up, Coach?" I ask with a frown. For a dude who just got one step closer to nabbing a spot in the playoffs, he doesn't look pleased.

He leads me to the closest private room, which is where the trainers wrap us before a game. It's empty.

"Did I not make it clear that you needed to cool things off with your girlfriend?" he asks.

My head jolts back at the question. Where the hell did this come from?

He rolls his eyes. "Did you or did you not make out with Charlotte at halftime?"

"Make out? No, sir. I did not 'make out' with her." Jesus.

What's his problem? "I hugged her. Kissed her once. Maybe twice." I don't really remember. "She was on the sidelines and excited about how well we were doing. I apologize if it was an inappropriate time, but I didn't see the harm."

Coach holds out his hand, and Evelyn, who I didn't notice join us, hands him a phone.

"The AD asked a few students to record the team's entrance for some promo video he's doing. This kid also happened to record us leaving at halftime."

I start to sweat because this can't be good if Coach is this pissed. The fact that he's in the locker room right now instead of at the post-game press conference means whatever I'm about to see is bad.

Thinking back to that kiss with Charlotte, I realize it probably looked passionate because we were ramped up because of the game, but it wasn't porno-level crazy. It's not like I jammed my tongue down her throat.

My heart hammers as the video starts to play.

It's taken from the tunnel and shows the guys running off the field. I spot Charlotte tucking away her gear, but she's almost out of the shot. When she stands, her top half is cropped out. You can see my legs as I veer away from the team and head to her. I pick her up as she jumps in my arms. You see her dangle against me and then my hand lands on her ass.

This must catch the videographer's attention because he shifts to focus on us. I give Charlotte another peck and pat her butt when I put her down a minute later. I have an idiotic grin on my face when I catch up with the team.

My lips tilt up as I watch my gorgeous woman who looks so good in Bronco colors. Her goofy grin matches mine. She touches her lips like our kiss was special. Because it was. All of our kisses are.

Is this what has Coach in a tizzy? Because that wasn't terrible. Just looks like I'm hyped up from the game and stopped to kiss my girlfriend. What's the big deal?

As I stare at the screen, something makes Charlotte pause.

She looks up, still smiling and looking so beautiful my heart kicks up a notch.

But what happens next feels like I'm watching some terrible teen movie. Food rains down on her. Sodas and hot dogs get hurled at her from the stands above. It lands on her head and hits her in the face. Soaks her shirt. Hits her camera bag.

What the hell?

Some girl screams, "Hey, skank! How does it feel to get Dakota's sloppy seconds?"

"Oh, fuck." I shouldn't curse around Coach, but the words slip out.

I swallow hard as bile pushes up the back of my throat.

Then that bitch throws something small, and it hits Charlotte in the head. Hard. She wobbles one way, then the other before she falls over.

And doesn't get up.

Coach glares at me. "That poor girl's injury is on you."

37

JAKE

"COME ON, MOTHERFUCKER!" I smack my steering wheel, frustrated as hell the car in front of me isn't moving.

After Coach reamed me out for kissing Charlotte in a public venue during halftime, he finally told me to get my ass to the hospital because that's where the paramedics took her. He might be pissed at me, but I know he cares about Charlie because he asked me to text him an update as soon as I had one.

I didn't bother to change or shower. Just threw on some sneakers, grabbed my shit, and booked it to the parking lot, where I've been sitting for the last forty minutes in gridlock traffic.

Nobody could tell me how badly she was hurt.

I'm going out of my goddamn mind not knowing.

It takes another twenty to get to the main drag. I'm so used to hanging around the stadium after a game, I didn't realize how slow traffic crawls through town.

Then I see an accident ahead, which is blocking the main drag going both ways. No wonder.

At the next light, I try calling Charlie for the millionth time, but it goes straight to voicemail.

"Baby, I hope you're getting these messages. I'm on the way to the hospital. Hang tight. Traffic is a bitch, but I'll be there soon."

The words feel insignificant. I don't know what to say. I feel like shit she got hurt, and Coach seems to think it's my fault for not "getting some space" in my relationship with Charlotte like he suggested. What did he want me to do? Ignore her on the sidelines?

And yeah, I get that he means back off her in general, but that's not me. I'm not gonna fuck her over like that. Not after everything we've been through to get to this point.

Que Dios la cuide. In a panic I channel my mother's piety and say a prayer that Charlie's all right.

I spend the next hour inching through town. Literally could've jogged to the hospital faster than the time it takes me to drive there. I'm still a few minutes away. I try calling her again, but hang up when I get her voicemail.

Not gonna lie—I'm having flashbacks to our time at NTU when she ghosted me out of the blue.

Calm down, dude. Maybe she doesn't have a signal.

Except when I finally make it to the ER, she's not there.

"What do you mean she left already?" I ask the nurse at the information counter.

She scans the screen in front of her. "She checked herself out."

I hang my head with a groan. While I'm glad Charlotte was well enough to walk out of here on her own, I hate that she was probably alone and scared. The scent of bleach and antiseptic reminds me of the aftermath of her apartment fire, and my stomach tightens.

Panic makes me jittery as I drive home, which takes another hour even though I don't live that far away.

Buffy makes a face, one I don't understand, when I open the door. She's sitting on the couch in the living room with Asher.

He runs up to me, and I scoop him up. "Hey, bud. Missed you."

I kiss him on the head and set him down. I usually spend more time with him after a game, but I need to see Charlotte with my own two eyes and make sure she's okay.

"Is Charlie in her room?" I ask Buffy, who looks down the hall warily and nods.

Why is everyone being so damn weird today? Which reminds me of how strangely Billy acted this afternoon. Did he know what happened to Charlotte and didn't bother to tell me?

When I get to her room, I'm confused why all of her clothes are on her bed. "Babe, are you okay?"

She freezes before she slowly turns to face me. She has a bandage on her forehead and her swollen eyes are black and blue.

Oh, shit. "Are you okay? I just missed you at the hospital. Come here." I open my arms to her, but she shakes her head.

Her eyes tear up and she tries to wipe them. "Why didn't you tell me?" she asks, her voice shaking.

I drop my arms. "Tell you what?"

The heartbroken expression on her face tears me up. "Why didn't you tell me Coach Santos didn't want us together? That he wanted us to cool things off for the rest of the season?"

Who fucking told her this crap? Like I'd ever break up with her.

Frustrated, I run my hands through my hair. "Because it's none of his damn business."

Her eyes narrow. "And yet you told Roxy."

I blow out a breath. "I asked Roxy not to tell her dad that we were together. Thought she might let something slip since you two are close."

"You. Told. Roxy. But not me."

Shit. "I'm sorry, okay? Maybe that was wrong. I just figured you were already stressed out because of *The Hell House*, and I didn't want to add to that. But what would it have changed? It's not like we would've stopped dating."

Her nostrils flare. "Let's forget the part where you think I'm a delicate little flower who can't handle anything. Had I known Coach didn't want us seeing each other, I wouldn't have thrown myself in your arms at halftime."

I shrug. "Okay. Yeah, I can see that. But come on, cupcake. I don't think you're helpless. It's not like that. And I'm sorry if my actions got you hurt today."

She rolls her eyes at me. "Jake, fuck that girl, okay? I'm fine. I look like hell, but I'm gonna live."

There's my little fighter. "Can I have a hug? How'd you get home, anyway? Did Roxy give you a ride?"

Her eyes widen as she growls. "You don't get it, do you? This morning, AD Armstrong said I could travel with the team to your last game, and if the Broncos made the playoffs, I could cover those games too."

Holy shit. "That's awesome. I'm so proud of you."

I scoop her in a hug. She's stiff for some reason. Aww, hell. Maybe I'm hurting her. I set her down gently, and she shoves out of my arms.

"Yeah, it *was* awesome, Jake. Literally the highlight of my college career." I'm not sure why she's so pissed if that was all good news. "I was walking on clouds all day. Until I got beaned by that asshole at halftime. Do you know what happened when I got to the hospital? I got a call from the athletic director. He said he has to retract that invitation and I need to return the camera gear. Something about liability because my sister's show is so high profile and me getting caught in the crosshairs of her fans or whatever puts the school in a bad light. Because of all the negative press the team got before he came on board, he said he can't take any chances. So I'm out."

"Are you serious? That asshole. Look, let me talk to him on Monday. I'll—"

"No. I'm not asking you to fight my battles."

"Charlotte, we're a team, remember?"

Her eyes go flat as she whispers, "Then why didn't you tell me Coach Santos didn't want me around? Why didn't you confide in me? Why would you keep that a secret? I'm so fucking tired of secrets, Jake. My family never told me shit when I was growing up. I was always the odd one out while Dakota was in on everything. Everything!"

Okay, I'm out of my depth here. Clearly this isn't all about me talking to Roxy. And I'm really damn tired of Dakota's ghost lurking around every corner. Not that I'm upset with Charlotte for that. She's the innocent bystander in all of this.

Charlie turns around and starts tucking her clothes into a bag. "What are you doing?" I ask.

"Moving out."

I freeze. She's leaving? "Charlotte, no. Come on, baby. Don't do this."

I walk up behind her and gently wrap my arms around her shoulders and push my face against her neck. "In six months we're graduating. Are you really going to let these people win? Fuck that bitch at the stadium and fuck Armstrong. Fuck Santos too for all I care. You and I are bigger than all this crap, Charlie. Don't run away because you're upset."

She stills in my arms and hangs her head. "I've worked so hard for this, Jake." Her voice cracks, and I close my eyes, hating that she's hurting. "You have too. I'm not saying we break up, but I want... I want to take a step back. I need some space to think, and I can't do that here. Roxy said I could sleep on her couch."

"Babe, no." I scramble to think of a solution and turn her

around so I can see her face. "Look, stay here. We'll cool off until the season is over. I'll sleep in my bed instead of cramming into yours at night. I'll give you all the space you need."

Her cheeks are streaked with tears and she's biting her lower lip so hard, I'm surprised it's not bleeding. She sniffles and her whole body quakes with emotion.

When she doesn't say anything, I lay it on the line. "I need you to believe in us, Charlotte. To trust me. I fucked up by not talking to you about what Coach said, but I honestly believed it was for the best. I wanted to tell you, but Yvette had been a bitch to you that day, and I didn't want to hurt you more. I promise I won't keep something like that to myself in the future. Let me make it up to you. Let me show you I'm a man of my word."

After the longest minute of my life, she nods, and I'm so relieved I lean down to kiss her, but she turns her face away. I stop a few inches away. It shouldn't bother me that she doesn't want me to kiss her, but it does.

"Okay. I get it." I hold my hands up and step back. "You've got all the space you need." I swallow, hating the mountain range suddenly jutting out between us. Because I have no idea how to scale it.

38

CHARLOTTE

"You know you're always welcome at my place. My bed is too small to share, but my roommates said you can have the couch anytime."

"Thanks, Rox. I appreciate that."

As Roxy and I sit in the cafeteria, I pick at my lunch. I haven't been hungry for the last few days.

"Did you hear they arrested the two girls who harassed you?"

"Great."

That truly is good news. I should be elated, but my emotions have two modes since I got beaned by that Diet Coke. I'm either in tears and falling apart or completely detached from everything.

The head injury might play a role in this. It's possible I have a concussion, but I checked out of the hospital because my parents removed me from their health insurance, and there's no way I could afford an ER visit without it. Guess my parents weren't excited about the bills for my last hospital admission after the fire. Honestly, I'm shocked I had coverage then.

She lowers her voice. "One of the girls was Yvette."

My eyes widen. "Jake fired her after she said that crap to me about Dakota being better-looking."

"Good for him. What a bitch."

"But if he hadn't fired her, I'd probably still be going with the team to the playoffs." Last weekend's game clinched it for the Broncos. "Not that I'm blaming him. I'm not."

Then why are you so upset with him? That I can't explain. Logically, I understand why he confided in Roxy about what her dad asked of Jake, but that doesn't lessen my ire. He should've told me.

"I'm sorry, Charlie. This sucks all around. I tried talking to my dad about it, but he has a bug up his ass about Jake not 'following direction.' Coach is really upset you got hurt."

"I get it." I sigh. "Please tell him I'm fine." I glance around the cafeteria. It's filling with the lunch hour rush. When someone walks by with a plate of fried fish, I gag.

"Gross." I cover my mouth and nose for a minute. "Kinda felt nauseated there for a sec," I explain to Roxy when she asks what's wrong.

She folds her lips, like she has to physically restrain herself from speaking.

"What?" I don't want her to hold back with me.

"Could you be pregnant?" she whispers.

I laugh because no.

Except...

Everything around me slows down and goes a little sideways as a dizzy spell hits me. I suppose that's what I get for checking out of the hospital against doctor's orders.

I can't be pregnant.

I don't think.

"Oh my God. What if I am?"

"When did you get your last period?" she asks as I break out the calendar app on my phone.

Swallowing, I choke out, "Six weeks ago."

∽

I STARE at the pregnancy tests like they're infected with a virus. Roxy and I weren't sure which one might be best, so we got three different brands.

We're holed up in the bathroom at Jake's, but he's at practice, and Buffy is watching cartoons in the other room with Asher.

"Just bite the bullet," Roxy says as she holds my hand. "Here. We'll do it together." She grabs one of the tests and pops open the box.

"In case I haven't told you lately, you're a really good friend. Thank you for doing this with me." I grab a box and break the seal.

"Of course. Us badass bitches have to stick together. Listen, you've been under a lot of stress lately." She shrugs. "You'll probably get Aunt Flo in a few days."

When she says it like that, I feel silly for being so worried. It helps that she's willing to take a test with me.

I read the directions on the box as Roxy pees on her stick and then I do the same.

As I take my turn, she washes her hands and applies lip balm in the mirror, joking, "You know you're besties when you can pee together."

I laugh, so grateful for my beautiful friend.

We place the tests on a paper towel and wait until the timer goes off.

When her phone buzzes, my stomach lurches. I'm not sure how Jake would react if I was, but I'm hoping I don't have to find out anytime soon. We have sex with condoms *and* birth control, so I'm guessing a second kid is not on his agenda anytime soon.

I definitely want to have children together someday. Just not when he's under so much scrutiny. Not when I'm being harassed by idiots at football games. Not when I'm broke.

Hmm. I suppose Jake and I need to talk about how he feels about more kids down the road.

Please, Jesus, don't let me be pregnant right now.

Roxy grabs my hand. "We'll look on three. Ready?"

I nod and she counts down.

When I see the negative sign on my test, I'm hit with a tidal wave of relief. Thank God!

Except when I turn to Roxy, her eyes are wide and her hand is trembling. A second later, her eyes water.

"It's positive."

Positive? As in...

Oh, crap.

She starts to cry. "I'm pregnant."

The second test only confirms it.

39

CHARLOTTE

I TOLD you I'd walk Duke when I got home.

Jake's text annoys me for some reason. When I told him I wanted space, I hoped he'd ignore me for a few days. It's hard to get a lockdown on my emotions when he's so damn considerate.

The streets are eerily empty tonight. Duke and I pause in front of my old apartment. It's being condemned. Some of the charred remains have been bulldozed, but there's a gaping hole in the side of the building where rebar juts out like fingers reaching out of a grave. I get chills when I think of what could've happened that night.

Jake saved your life. He charged into a burning building and saved you and your dog.

It took my whole world going up in flames to find my way back to Jake again.

So much has changed since that day.

Jake is the best thing to ever happen to me. *He's not going to hurt you, Charlotte.*

The wall I started to build in my heart when I found out he'd kept Coach's advice from me begins to melt away.

I love Jake to the bottom of my soul, and I just have to trust that once the season is over, things will settle down. Especially after *The Hot House* wraps up.

We'll be fine.

Maybe by spring, AD Armstrong will see that I'm not some huge liability, and he'll let me shoot baseball after all.

Jake's right. I have to be strong. Everything will work out.

Feeling better, I'm about to turn back to our apartment when Duke jerks and his leash goes flying out of my hand.

"Duke!" That damn dog charges across the street, hopping through weeds to reach the condos next door to my old place.

I run after him, grateful there isn't any traffic.

When I reach my Aussie, he's on his belly, barking and whining, trying to crawl under the dumpster.

"What's up with you?" I grab his leash, but he won't budge.

Praying we're not about to get mauled by rabid raccoons, I bend over to try to see what's making Duke so crazy.

That's when I hear it.

"Meow-eow! Meow-eow!"

I freeze.

"Winkie? Is that you?" Tears spring to my eyes. I've never heard a cat who meows like my fur ball.

It takes another half hour for me to calm down Duke enough for Winkie to emerge. And then he starts purring and rubbing against my legs.

"Aww, I missed you, my one-eyed pirate. I'm so glad you're okay!" I pick him up and he immediately tries to curl around my neck. He's kinda scrawny, but he's obviously been eating out of the trash, and that's better than nothing.

"Good job finding Winkie, Duke. Sorry I freaked." I cradle my cat in my arms, excited to get him back to our apartment.

This feels auspicious. Like the universe is trying to tell me my life is on the right track. That Jake and I will be okay. That we're stronger than the challenges we face.

I'm smiling as I open the door to our apartment.

"I'm home! Guess... what I... found?" The words die on my lips when I see the picture-perfect family in front of me.

Jake.

Asher.

And my sister.

"Kota." In a flash, in the two seconds it takes to cross the threshold into the apartment, my whole world falls apart all over again.

Winkie flies out of my arms and disappears down the hall while I gape at my sister.

"Surprise," she snarks as she bounces Asher on her lap a little too aggressively on the couch. Jake is standing a few feet away with his hands on his hips.

My sister looks absolutely stunning, like she's bathed in the golden California sunset for the past few months. Her hair is a pale blonde and shimmers in big waves. She stands, putting Asher down, and smooths out her minuscule sundress that puts her considerable assets on display. Her nails are done, her makeup flawless. She's every bit the Hollywood celebrity.

I glance down at myself. I'm wearing old sneakers I got at the Goodwill, a Bronco t-shirt, and a pair of shorts I got from a discount bin at Walmart. And let's not forget the bruising under my eyes.

She flicks her hand at me like I'm a gnat. "Wow, it's really true. I didn't want to believe it, but you really have gone *Single White Female*, trying to live my life. Well, minus a sense of fashion and a good skin routine. Anyway, I caught the video of Jake pulling you from that fire." Her eyes narrow to slits. "Did you set it so he'd come to your rescue?"

What an odd thing to suggest. "Um, no, I'm not a psychopath."

Judging by her eye roll, she doesn't believe me. "Whatever, Charlotte. The important thing is I'm back now, so you don't need to be a placeholder anymore."

"Dakota." Jake's jaw is tight.

She ignores him and flips her hair over her shoulder. "Well, Charlotte? What do you have to say for yourself?"

"Wh-what are you doing here? What about your show?" I hate that I stutter, but she brings out every one of my insecurities.

"I'm in Austin for a few days to shoot a campaign. I have a camera crew." She pats Asher on the head like he's a dog.

Duke doesn't like that, and he starts barking at her.

Jake's remarkably quiet. He pinches the bridge of his nose, likely wishing he could run out of this apartment like I want to.

"Come on, Duke." I tug him down the hall where I put him in Asher's room and close the door.

When I make it back to the living room, Jake's pacing like a caged animal. "Dakota, you can't just show up like this. You've had every opportunity to reach out to me over the past two years and never have. Why now?" His voice is a low grumble. I'm honestly shocked he's not yelling.

"Funny you should ask, but one of my fans sent me this hysterical video of you and my sister making out at a football game. And after seeing 'your daring fire rescue,' I figured I need to get down here and save you from my sister before she burned down your apartment building too." She turns to me and cackles. "Charlotte, hot dogs look really good on you. Bet I could get you a sponsorship. Nice job hiding whatever nasty gash you got under that bandage on your head, though."

I close my eyes, loathing that Kota has seen one of the videos circulating from last weekend's game. I'm guessing there's more than one.

Bending over, she basically puts her whole rear and some teeny thong on display while she digs into her bag to get her phone. "Last I saw, this video has over three million views. You've gone viral! Mother hates it, of course. Like, 'Why can't Charlotte go viral for doing something clever?' Do you want to see it?"

Do I want to watch myself get harassed and ridiculed? I shake my head.

"Aww, really? Come on, Charlotte. It's not that bad. Oh, but the memes? You're going to hate them, but they're fucking hilarious. And I know how much you love memes."

"Stop it, Dakota," Jake says between clenched teeth. "Leave her alone. She has nothing to do with this."

Her eyes cut to him. "This has everything to do with my skanky sister who couldn't keep away from you. If you marry her, do you know how embarrassing this will be for Asher someday when kids ask him, 'Is that your mom?' He'll have to say, 'Well, it's my mom, but also my aunt.'" She cringes. "How fucked up is that? If you two have kids, his family tree will look like a damn Christmas wreath."

Oh God. She's not wrong about that.

I swallow, hating the kernel of truth in her vitriol.

My sister taps one of her pointy talons on her chin. "Speaking of kids, I suppose congratulations are in order."

Silence fills the room.

She motions down the hall. "I saw the positive pregnancy tests in the trash."

It takes me a second to figure out what she's talking about.

The pregnancy tests!

"It's not like that," I say immediately.

She smirks. "Are there or are there not pregnancy tests in the bathroom?"

"Yes, but—"

"Aren't there *two* that are positive?"

"Yes, but that's not exactly..."

I turn to Jake, about to explain what happened with Roxy this afternoon, but he's ghostly white. I've never seen him so pale. He staggers to the couch, sits at the edge, and drops his head into his hands.

"Charlotte, Charlotte," Kota coos. "Is this not the reaction you were looking for? You know, when I told Jake I was pregnant in high school, he was *so sweet.* He wrapped his arms around me and told me he'd be there every step of the way. Cradled my face and kissed me. Said that if I wanted the baby, he'd be there for me. Guess he's not so excited to have knocked you up."

My head pounds as I think back to her telling me how supportive Jake was back then. She was thrilled he was so understanding.

The longer I look at Jake, the more my heart hurts. This whole time I told myself one day he'd be over the moon to have kids with me. But right now, he looks like someone sucker-punched him.

My sister just arrived, and she's already destroying my life.

Hot tears well in my eyes as I glare at her. "Fuck you, Kota."

She juts out her bottom lip in a mock pout. "Back at ya, baby sister."

"Why do you hate me so much? What did I ever do but bend over backwards to help you with your career? To help you with Asher? To listen to you complain constantly about whatever didn't go your way?"

She rolls her eyes. "Bitch, please. Do you know how many opportunities I had to turn down when we were growing up because 'Charlotte can't handle another reality show?' You wet the bed for years. You woke up in the middle of the night screaming and freaking out everyone. We had to put everything on pause because you had to see so many shrinks."

"I was afraid you were going to die. I had PTSD from spending so many nights in the hospital. Excuse me for being traumatized."

"Do you know how fucked up it is that I had to curtail *my* career because of *your* neurosis? I got so damn tired of everyone tiptoeing around you like you were so fragile when I was the one who was sick."

My family never catered to me. I have no idea what she's talking about.

"You threw out my letter to Jake, when I left NTU." It's not a question.

"Of course I did. It was such a sad play, like you were begging him to chase after you."

"I never said where I was going, so that would've been impossible."

"The worst part," she continues as though I hadn't responded, "is how you made eyes at Jake the whole time he and I were together. Did you think I didn't notice? Did you think I was okay with you following him around everywhere like some sad little loser? Did you know he once told me there was nothing he could do about that because he didn't want to hurt your feelings? Bitch, you lost your chance in high school. And for the record, on the night we hooked up senior year, he came to my bed all too willingly." Her words slice into me like rusty, ragged razor blades. "Actually"—she chuckles—"we never made it to a bed."

I wait for Jake to say something, anything, but all I get is silence, as he's apparently turned into a statue. His face is still in his hands.

I'm a beached fish. Flopping on the sand and gasping for breath.

I swallow, needing answers from Kota despite how it'll compound the pain. "Did you do it on purpose? Did you deliberately go looking for Jake that night?"

She smirks. "I considered it a fun personal challenge. 'How hard will it be to hook up with that guy Charlotte's been lusting over for years?'" The smug satisfaction on her face tears me apart. "It took me less than ten minutes to get in his pants. A personal record."

I open my mouth, but nothing comes out.

She flicks her fingers at me. "Well, this was a nice reunion, but you need to run along now. Jake and I have to discuss our custody arrangement, which I'm updating. My son shouldn't be around his toxic aunt or any of her spawn."

I look down at Asher, who's quiet and withdrawn. His somber demeanor cuts through my heartache and helps me think more clearly.

Can she do that? Can she make those kinds of demands?

"Dakota, stop twisting everything." Jake finally pipes up. Miracle of fucking miracles.

She turns to him. "I have a few simple demands, the first of which is you cut this slut out of your life. Or I take you to court."

There's no way Jake can afford that. Not right now.

"Why are you really here?" he asks her.

I wait for him to look at me. I need that connection, but he never turns my way.

She drops down onto the couch next to him and squeezes his bicep and her voice gets soft. "I've missed you, Jake. I know things went downhill at NTU, but that was really just a big misunderstanding..."

I don't hear the rest because I can't handle watching them sit side by side. I can't handle her touching him. I can't handle that baby voice she's using. Not when Jake is being so accommodating. Why isn't he flipping out on her? Why isn't he yelling until the roof caves down on her head?

When I reach Asher's room, I grab the bag that was halfway packed with my stuff and sling it over my shoulder. Then I attach Duke's leash to his collar, scoop up Winkie, and head back down the hallway with my two rescue animals.

Jake calls my name, but I ignore him.

I have nothing to say to him anyway.

40

CHARLOTTE

"Th-thanks for letting me cr-crash here, Roxy." I'm a slobbery mess as tears drip down my face and water drips from my nose.

She pulls me in for a tight hug. "Shut up. You never have to thank me."

We're sitting on her couch in her dark living room. Her two other roommates went to bed when I showed up out of the blue. I couldn't call her because I'm not sure where I left my phone. Thankfully, Roxy was home or Duke, Winkie, and I would've spent the night in my car.

Duke is curled up at our feet. Every now and then, he whines like he knows I'm upset. Winkie is sitting in the windowsill and happily ignoring me now that he's had some tuna.

When Roxy lets go of me, I reach for another tissue and blow my nose. "I'm sorry for crying all over you. I know that what I'm going through is nothing compared to what you are right now."

She grabs my hand. "Don't say that. You can't compare people's personal challenges like they're pieces of fruit and one might weigh more than another. This thing with your sister is ridiculous, and when I get my hands on Jake, I'm going to wring his pretty little neck."

"He's doing his best. Now that I've gotten some space from the situation, I know how upset he must be that my sister is bringing up their custody situation. I just... I just wish he'd reacted differently to the pregnancy news. I mean, I'm obviously not pregnant seeing how I got my period the moment I got here —thanks for the tampon, by the way. But you should've seen his face when he thought he'd knocked me up. I swear he looked like he was going to pass out."

Her expression goes flat. "Fine. Maybe I won't strangle him, but it sucks to hear how he was so sweet to your crazy-ass sister when she told him she was pregnant."

"That's what I can't get over." A few more tears leak from my eyes. "I love Jake, but I'm really upset with him right now. We've been through so much together over the years, but I don't want a lifetime of comparing myself to Kota, and it's impossible not to if she's going to rear her head around every corner like a hydra."

Roxy wrinkles her nose. "What's a hydra?"

"From Greek mythology. It was this huge snake with, like, seven heads and razor-sharp teeth."

"That does sound like your sister."

"Right?" My laugh turns into a moan. "What am I going to do?"

We're quiet for a moment, and then she pokes me. "You fight that bitch."

"How? Look at me. I don't even have the money to rent a motel for the night. My sister is rolling in cash, and ugh, Rox, this would be so much easier if she were a troll, but she looked so beautiful tonight."

"But that girl has an ugly soul. No amount of hair product, makeup, or money will ever change that."

She has a point, but I'm not ready to look on the bright side yet. "How many views does that video have now?"

"Nope." She tucks her phone under her butt. "You're not looking at that again."

The one that went viral was taken from the stands. Someone captured the whole thing. Me kissing Jake and smiling like an idiot just before I got a face full of food.

When I got here an hour ago, it had four million views and had been uploaded to all the big gossip blogs. I guess people care since I'm related to Kota, who's one of the most popular celebrities on her dumb show. Plus, Jake is a hot commodity now since his football season is going so well.

But Jesus, the comments.

Why would he dump Dakota to be with that *girl?*

Dakota is a smoke show compared to her sister.

What does Jake see in that bitch? She's so bland!

"Why are people so mean?" I wipe the corner of my eye.

Leaning back, she sighs. "I don't know. Kinda wish there was a bad karma dating app, so you could set up assholes with each other. Because then I'd set up Ezra with Dakota. They're perfect for each other."

I wince. "Did you talk to him yet about everything?" I haven't asked her if Ezra is the father of her baby, but based on that comment, I think he is.

"No, but he's not going to take it well. I suppose he could surprise me. I'm not holding my breath, though."

"If it's any consolation, your father will probably take him out with a shotgun."

"That's an accurate assessment. But I love my father, even if he can be an overbearing ass sometimes. I can't tell him about Ezra, or he'll go ballistic. Ezra is his golden-boy quarterback. It'll break his heart."

I frown. "Are you sure? Doesn't Ezra deserve some payback for being such a dick to you?"

"Oh, he definitely deserves some payback, but it can't come from my father." She lets out a long sigh. "I need to sleep on this."

It's my turn to hug her. "Whatever you need, anything at all, I'm here for you."

"Thanks." For the first time, her voice wavers. "I want to keep it, but that means giving up cheerleading, and I've worked so hard for that."

"I guess you couldn't go back to it in the fall after you have the baby, could you?" The moment the words are out of my mouth, I want to yank them back because I know how demanding a newborn is.

She snorts. "Sure. I'll breastfeed at halftime."

We look at each other and start laughing. It's that maniacal, 'it's too late to be questioning the big questions in life' kind of laugh.

After wiping her eyes, she shakes her head. "Not sure how I'll manage my senior year with a kid in tow."

I grab her hand and give her a gentle squeeze. "It'll be challenging, but it can be done. You're the toughest girl I know."

She sniffles. "I am kinda badass."

We smile, and I give her a hug.

Now I just need to dig deep and find my own badassery.

I hope it's in there somewhere. I'll need it to deal with my sister.

41

JAKE

It's after midnight before I manage to kick out Dakota and get Asher to bed. I immediately reach for the phone and try calling Charlotte, but it goes directly to voicemail.

I'm sick about what happened tonight. I can only pray that Charlotte hears me out.

"Babe, it's me. I'm so sorry for how shit went down. I had no idea Dakota was stopping by. I didn't even realize she was in Texas. And I *know* I didn't handle your... your news... very well, and I apologize. I was caught off guard. We'll make this work. Whatever it takes." I wonder if she'll even listen to my message. "I love you. Please call me back."

I obviously hurt Charlotte's feelings, and the thought keeps me up all night. I don't blame her for being upset with me. She's the last person I'd ever want to cause any pain.

Dakota spewing her nonsense didn't help. She loves to pour salt in people's wounds. I was so caught off guard by the pregnancy tests, I didn't really hear much else in that conversation, but I can guess it wasn't pleasant for Charlotte.

Ironically, last night I'd had some good news. A top-notch

agent had reached out to me. I can't sign with anyone until the playoffs are over, but I'm psyched he wants to rep me.

So when someone knocked on the door, I thought it was Charlie and didn't look through the peephole first.

Big fucking mistake.

Like a record scratch, my head goes there again.

Is Charlotte really pregnant? The thought bombards me for the millionth time. Admittedly, my first reaction was not excitement.

I don't want to give NFL teams the impression I'm the player who goes around populating the earth with my seed. I'm not that guy. I've *always* worn condoms. I figured if I had kids with Charlotte someday, we'd both be well into our careers and settled. Not struggling to afford pull-up diapers and groceries and childcare.

Coach will probably flip out when he finds out I'm responsible for *another* unplanned pregnancy.

I groan, feeling conflicted.

I love Charlotte. With all my fucking heart. Seeing my ex only solidified how I feel about my cupcake. She's amazing. So positive and loving. So sweet and thoughtful. Literally everything I want in a girlfriend.

Definitely everything I want in a wife.

But we're not there yet.

Got to get her to talk to me first.

Have to convince her I'll be there for her if she decides to have this baby.

A baby with Charlotte.

I close my eyes, and I can see it. My sweet woman cradling a little bundle. She'll be a fantastic mother.

Me conmueve. It chokes me up a little.

Because I want that life.

And in this moment, all of my anxiety fades away. So what if this baby pisses off Coach? So what if NFL teams think I'm a jackass?

All that matters is getting Charlotte to understand I love her to the moon and back and I'll be by her side come hell or high water.

All that matters is proving to her that I'm on board for this baby. I'll love him or her and welcome this new addition to our family with open arms.

All that matters is showing Charlotte I'm one hundred percent devoted to her.

Will I be pissed if I don't get drafted? Of course. No one works this hard, this long, to accept defeat. But I guess I could always work for my brothers. Being a mechanic won't have the same kind of paycheck, but it's respectable, steady employment. And it would mean my kids grow up around my family, which I'd love.

Reluctantly, I admit working with my brothers wouldn't be so bad.

My phone buzzes with a text, and I scramble for my phone. Only it says "THE PSYCHO." What the fuck does Dakota want at this hour? She's been radio silent for years and now this?

Good to see you, Jakey baby! I know you're still mad at me, but you'll see this is for the best.

I can actually feel a vessel in my neck throb. This bitch has some nerve. I couldn't bring myself to yell at her in front of Asher. My parents had an ugly divorce, and my brothers and I were privy to their screaming matches. I don't want that for my son. So if I have to bite my tongue until it bleeds when I'm around her, so be it.

But Dakota is batshit crazy if she thinks I'm going to bend over and take this crap.

I just have to figure out how to beat her at this game.

Because there's no way in hell I'm giving up Charlotte. Not when I just got her back in my life.

42

JAKE

"You look like shit, dude." Billy slides into the booth across from me in the study lounge tucked back in the field house and motions to the uneaten chicken burger in front of me. "You gonna eat that?"

"Go for it." I watch him scarf down my food at record speed.

When he finishes, he pulls out a bottle of water and chugs it down. "You gonna dish or what?"

Why is Billy always the guy lurking around when my life gets fucked up? I look around for Cam. He's more normal, but I don't see him anywhere.

I finally relent. "Charlotte's upset with me." That's putting it lightly. The last forty-eight hours have been hell.

"Yeah. I heard."

Of course he did. "What exactly did you hear?"

"That you thought she was preggers and you went full-on mute and hurt her feelings since, apparently, you were a knight in shining armor when it came to your ex baby-trapping you."

My eyebrows lift. "How the hell do you know all this?"

"I have my ways."

Unbelievable. I'm guessing Roxy gave him a play-by-play.

Frustrated, I rub the back of my neck. "Charlie dropped by the apartment and left me a note saying she was staying at Roxy's and needed some space." It also said, *FYI, I'm not pregnant. I never was. Bet you're relieved.*

I deserved that dig.

I'm trying to look on the bright side. At least I got the note this time. And at least she didn't transfer schools to get away from me. And, hey, she didn't tell me to fuck off exactly.

Yes, my sense of humor is grim right now.

"You want my advice?" he asks as he reaches over to grab my granola bar.

"You're going to give it to me whether I ask for it or not."

He wags his finger at me. "You're catching on." After mowing through the rest of my food, he leans back. "Honestly? You're fucked."

I stare at him. "You're a dick."

The asshole chuckles. "I'm teasing. Seriously, man, you got some groveling to do. Charlie loves you. It's in her eyes. Instead of pupils, she has little dancing hearts."

"So what do I do, man? I love her. She means everything to me. She's literally the woman I want to marry someday."

He chokes on his water. "Whoa, bud. When someone says 'marriage,' my balls shrivel up."

It's my turn to laugh. "Didn't realize you had commitment issues."

His head jerks back. "Me? Nah. Just... I'm cautious." I'd call bullshit, but he looks freaked out. "Anyway, is Dakota out of your hair for good or should we expect her to pop out from behind a potted plant with her film crew?"

"Her show wraps up in a few weeks and then she claims she'll be back. This is where things get weird. She doesn't want me to see Charlotte. Says she's gonna take me to court and sue me for custody if I don't comply. I don't have that kind of money.

Neither does my family, and they'd cough it up in a minute to take her down. Plus she wants to hang out 'as a family' with me and Asher, and I get the feeling that if she doesn't get her way, she'll hold custody over my head for that too."

"Are those empty threats or do you think she means it?"

"She has money to burn, so if she wants to blow it on attorneys, she can afford it. Whereas I do not have those kinds of funds." At least, not yet. If I get drafted, then I suppose I'd better hire the best lawyer I can find.

"Fuck, that sucks."

"And I've left Charlie a million messages, begging her to call me back so we can talk this out. She finally texted me and says she thinks Coach is right and we need to chill, and that she'll talk to me when the season is over."

"Regular or playoffs?"

Good question. I'm guessing she didn't mean after this weekend's game. "Fuck. If I have to wait until January to talk to her, I'm gonna lose my mind. I know she's hurt, and it kills me that I'm the source of that pain."

"Actually, Dakota is the source."

I wince. "No, this was my doing too. When I thought she was pregnant, I pretty much almost passed out." I had to sit my ass down and breathe until the spots in my vision disappeared. "There's no way Charlotte's not beating herself up right now. She's absolutely comparing this to how things went down with her sister when she got pregnant with Asher. And when you tack on that stupid viral video and the shit that happened to her at last weekend's game, I'm not surprised she's pulling away."

Which reminds me... "Did you know she got heckled at the NTU game? Did you know when we got back on the field for the third quarter? Is that why you asked me if I was okay?"

He looks sheepish all of a sudden. "Sorry, dude. Thought it would fuck up your head, and you'd been having such a great game. Didn't want you bolting. I heard she got into the ambulance on her own, so it's not like she died."

I roll my eyes. "If I haven't told you lately, you're an asshole."

"Not gonna deny that." He pauses to grab a sandwich from his backpack. "So what's the plan to win back our girl? 'Cause you'd better have a good one."

"No shit."

I'm not totally sure, but I have an idea where to start.

43

CHARLOTTE

Two girls walk up to the table and pick up a calendar. "Holy shit, these guys are hot. Are they all football players?"

I shake my head. "Some are from the baseball team. There are cheerleaders too."

I'm sitting at a small table outside the student union, selling calendars for Second Chances. I've been so wrapped up in my own personal drama this fall, I hadn't realized how much work it was going to take to actually *sell* all of these calendars. I'm not sure how I'm supposed to offload them by next month. I didn't really have a plan for getting them into people's hands. Merle has sold a few at the animal rescue, but we're nowhere close to having enough revenue to save the shelter. He's already told me they're preparing for the worst-case scenario, which breaks my heart.

I'd ask Roxy to help me, but she has so much on her plate right now, and I'm already sleeping on her couch. *And* I brought my two pets. I don't want to take advantage of our friendship.

I just finished making an order form. My only hope is that people will purchase them online. Maybe I can talk to the school newspaper about doing a pro-bono ad.

And as worried as I am about Second Chances, I have another pressing issue I need to deal with ASAP.

As soon as someone buys the last calendar I have on hand, I tuck away the money and book it to the photo lab, which is pretty empty. After I log into a computer, I jog out to my locker, but first, I look up and down the dark hall to make sure no one is following me. I don't know why, but I have this fear my sister is going to jump out and catch me.

Creaking open the locker, I reach up to the top cubby, under some spiral notebooks and an old sweater, to pull out a dusty rectangular-shaped metal hard drive.

I'd forgotten it was here until I came to clean out my locker yesterday. I figured, why hang out in the photo lab when I don't have a camera? Yes, it was a pity party, and I'd fully planned to top it off with a giant slice of pizza and a shot of something strong.

Only when I got here, I found this—a hard drive with all of the old footage of my sister. Outtakes from shoots and images I'd taken for her social media posts.

My fingers are twitchy from excitement, but I don't want to get ahead of myself. I almost called Jake to tell him my idea, but it's possible I'm misremembering those videos, and I don't want to get his hopes up.

He might not even like my idea. Plus, we have so many other issues to wade through, which I'm not ready to do just yet. I want to get my emotions in check so I don't blubber all over him.

I also think he needs time to decide if this relationship is what he wants. We happened so fast this fall. It's been a whirlwind, starting with that fire. With the way Kota is threatening him, he might think having a relationship with me isn't worth the hell he'll catch from my sister.

Will it break my heart? Absolutely. Listening to all of his voicemails this week almost had me reconsidering.

But I don't want to be a knee-jerk reaction. I don't want Jake to pick me simply because he doesn't want Kota dictating what he can do. I want him to be clearheaded if he chooses to be with me.

Which means we both need some space to calm down and think rationally. So I'm going to embark on this little mission on my own.

The silver lining is knowing he'll never go back to my sister. That blunts the pain a little bit. It's not like he'd be choosing her over me. The question is whether he will pick me despite the wrath she'll send his way.

As I plug the FireWire into the hard drive, I check behind me to make sure I'm alone. God, I'm paranoid, but my sister has this effect on me. It's like she's the leader of a cult, and I'm a runaway member in hiding.

Well, no more. It's time to get some leverage. I'm tired of her pushing me and Jake around like she owns us. If Jake and I don't work out, it'll be because *we* decide to go separate ways, not because Dakota is pulling our strings like puppets.

An hour later, a grin spreads on my lips.

That bitch is going down.

44

JAKE

THE BAND PLAYS our victory song, and my teammates celebrate. Sure, I'm happy about beating TCU. I played like the hounds of hell were on my ass and had my best game of my college career. I needed a stellar performance so no one could say I was distracted.

Now that it's over, though, I know what I have to do.

Coach is gonna be pissed.

I brace myself for his reaction as I head toward the post-game press conference—one I haven't been invited to.

When I open the door, Evelyn's eyes go wide, and she stalks over to me. "Jake, we talked about this," she hisses as she tries to usher me out into the hall.

Reporters start shouting my name.

I hold up my hands because I'm not about to manhandle a woman, but I look to Coach. He knows what I want.

He stares at me in that ice-cold way he has and finally waves me in, thank God.

Some of the guys scoot over to make room for me. I'm grateful to sit a ways down from Santos so he doesn't reach over and strangle me.

"Sorry for interrupting, Coach," I say into the mic in front of me. "But there are some things I'd like to clear up."

Coach clears his throat. "Any more questions for Thomas or Smith?"

The room goes silent, and I mentally note I should apologize to the guys for hijacking this press conference.

Ezra and Diesel head out, and Coach waves me closer.

Damn.

I grab the seat next to him and pray he doesn't choke me out.

Reporters start shouting questions and I answer several about the game, grateful that my performance is taking center stage.

But then someone asks about Dakota's accusations that I cheated on her.

Fuck her stupid NDA. Pretty sure signing that doesn't mean she can outright lie the way she has on her show.

I lean forward to talk into the mic because I don't want anyone to miss this. "Let me put it this way. *I* wasn't the one who cheated. And just to clarify, I've been best friends with Dakota's sister Charlotte since we were fourteen. Charlotte and I were one hundred percent platonic until we met up this past fall. In fact, it wasn't until I pulled her out of a burning building that I realized she meant more to me. Life-or-death situations tend to crystallize things for you. By that point, I hadn't heard from Dakota in two years. We broke up when I found out that she was"—I debate how to phrase this next part—"that she was seeing one of my NTU teammates."

"Why do you think she made those accusations?"

"Frankly? For ratings. That sounds harsh, *pero es la verdad.*" I clear my throat. "It's the truth."

Will Dakota lose her shit when she sees this press conference? Definitely. But I'm done letting her have her way. Because if I give in, I'll never be rid of her. This has to stop. I can only hope to postpone any custody hearings until after I'm drafted, when I'll have the money to fight her. If worst comes to worst, my brother told me he can front me a little cash if I'm desperate and need an attorney immediately, but I hope it doesn't come to that.

"Are you still dating Charlotte? And is that the same girl who got harassed at last weekend's game?"

"Yes, I'm dating Charlotte. And if I'm being honest, I hope to wife her up someday." My ears go hot at the thought she might be watching right now, but it doesn't matter. I fucking love that girl. "She's an amazing woman and my best friend. I'd be lost without her. And this might shock some of you, but I love her more than football."

People chuckle, and I brave a glance at Coach, whose icy demeanor is thawing. Weird that my statement about loving something more than football does the trick.

I return my focus to the room of reporters. "Unfortunately, she was the same person who was bullied at the NTU game. Speaking of Charlotte..."

This is the part that might get me in trouble, but fuck it. We're a goddamn team, and it's about time someone stands up for her the way she's always there for everyone else in her life. "Some of you might have seen her on the sidelines because she's been covering our home games. She's an incredible photographer. But due to the harassment from some of Dakota's fans, Charlotte wasn't allowed to attend today's game and her invitation to cover our playoff games has been revoked. I'd like to respectfully ask the team to reconsider. I don't think it's fair to punish the victim for being harassed and bullied. The Broncos need the best photographers to cover our games, and that should include Charlotte Darling." I hold up my hand. "I swear I'm not being biased. She kicks ass."

I refer everyone to her website to check out her work and

explain how she volunteers at Second Chances and is raising money to keep them open. I give her calendar a little sales pitch and hope it helps the effort.

"Jake, why haven't you been available to the press?" another reporter asks.

"Coach and I thought it best to hold off so the team could focus on finishing strong. Neither of us want to turn this fine program into a circus." I clear my throat. "I also want to thank the Lone Star State coaching staff for their support this season. It's been a wild one, but thanks to this man sitting next to me, I can also say it was the best one of my college career. That never would've happened if I didn't have Coach Santos in my corner."

Braving another glance at the guy who has my career in his hands, I lay it all out there. "Coach, I know you would've preferred that I not make a statement today, so we could focus on the playoffs. Generally, I would be on board with that one hundred percent. But you once told me you brought me into this program despite my baggage because I was honest with you and leveled with you about what I had going on. That's precisely why I needed to get these things off my chest. That's why I had to stand up for Charlotte and make sure everyone knows she's not the home-wrecker people are making her out to be."

"I know, son," he says quietly with a nod.

Turning, I face the reporters again, letting out a sigh of relief to have this over. "Thanks for coming today. I won't be making more statements about my personal life anytime soon. I'd much rather focus on football and the playoffs."

"Jake! One more question. What's your dream NFL team? If you could get drafted by anyone, who would you want?"

I chuckle. "My dream team is the one that wants a kid from Texas who loves the game as much as I do." A team that knows my family—my son and Charlotte—are the most important people to me.

I'm almost light-headed by the time I hit the locker room. Between the exertion of the game, the stress of the press conference, and the chaos of the last two weeks, I'm surprised I'm still standing. But now that I've hopefully set things right, I need to find Charlie. She needs to know she's the girl for me and I'll do anything to have her in my life.

Unfortunately, the bus ride home from Fort Worth will take at least three hours. *Probably the longest three hours of my life.*

After a quick shower, I reach for my phone, hoping I can track her down and make plans to see her tonight.

Only there's a text from her.

Maybe she saw the press conference. I close my eyes and pray the things I said made a difference. That she knows I'll always choose her.

Strangely, the message is addressed to me and her sister, one Charlotte sent around the time we finished our game.

Kota, I found an old hard drive the other day. You might be surprised to see what's on it. Before you even think about pressuring Jake to do your bidding, you might want to watch this highlight reel I put together. If you don't back the fuck off, I wouldn't be surprised to find this circulating online.

I click on the link.

It's a video of Dakota applying gobs of makeup. "They're all brainless little bitches. Good thing they're willing to spend twenty bucks a pop to get my bracelets."

The camera pans across the room to a table overflowing with pink Little Darlings jewelry.

Oh, shit. She's talking about her fans.

Segment after segment follows, obviously outtakes, moments when Charlotte kept the camera rolling between shoots. Candid moments where Dakota criticizes her fans or sponsors. Her parents. Her professors. Her friends. It's an endless stream of complaints.

It's nothing like the face she showed on *The Hell House* this season.

Finally. The true Dakota Darling.

Billy stops at his locker, which is across from mine. "Crashing Coach's press conference was pretty ballsy."

"Wasn't trying to challenge Coach. Just needed to set the record straight."

"Hope it gets you your girl."

"Thanks, man."

He motions to my phone. "Whatcha watching?"

The video is paused on a shot of Dakota sneering at something.

I replay the video for him, and his eyes widen as he realizes what he's seeing. I explain Charlotte's text with a laugh. "My cupcake is fucking fierce."

I was a dumbass to think I needed to keep that stuff Coach said from her. I've learned my lesson. She doesn't need my protection. Just my support.

All of a sudden, text after text from Dakota pops up on my phone. She's obviously freaking out.

I don't bother looking at them. I'm happy to let her stew in her own mess for a while.

The only thing I care about right now is Charlotte, who texts that she'll meet me at the park. I'll take whatever time I can get with her, frankly.

The second our bus pulls into campus, I'm ready to bolt and find my girl. After I gather my crap, I wait for the doors to open.

I nod at Billy. "I'm meeting with Charlotte. Wish me luck."

He slaps me on the back. "I have a feeling you don't need it."

45

CHARLOTTE

As I sway in the swing, I scan the park. It's dusk, and as the sun sets, the breeze gets colder. I shiver and pull my coat tighter. I needed to get some fresh air after I saw Jake's press conference. Roxy had called me as it was going down and demanded I turn on the local TV affiliate, which covers the games.

I still can't believe he did that after knowing how much his coach wanted him to stay quiet and keep his head down.

If I wasn't already in love with him, that would've done it.

But I've been so worried about Coach's reaction to making that statement that I needed to get outside. After walking Duke for a while, I headed out again by myself, wanting to get my thoughts together.

Hopefully, Jake's not upset about the video I sent Kota. I'm not sure, since he hasn't mentioned it yet even though my sister has been calling and texting nonstop. I finally blocked her number. I may need to talk to her eventually, but not until I touch base with Jake first.

I waited until his game was over to send the video. Today was his last regular season game, and I didn't want anything to mess with his focus.

I pull out my phone and read his message for the tenth time.
I'm on my way. Don't move.

I've been going crazy waiting for him to get back from Fort Worth. Is he mad about the video? Could it affect his custody arrangement? I hadn't really considered that until after I sent the text, and then it hit me—Dakota might take out her wrath on Jake, which is the opposite of what I intended.

I bite my thumbnail again and scan the gentle sloping hills in front of me. I'm sitting just a few yards away from where I did that photoshoot months ago for the calendar. I hope Jake and I have a very different kind of reunion today.

Movement catches my attention across the park, and I jerk my head up.

It's him.

My heart batters my rib cage as Jake gets closer.

The sun sets behind him, and his thick, dark hair blows in the breeze. He's wearing jeans, a t-shirt, and his letterman jacket. He looks so handsome, and I've missed him so much. It takes everything in me not to jump up and run to him.

When he reaches me, I smile hesitantly. "Great game today."

The words are barely out of my mouth when he grabs me by the lapels of my coat and yanks me up into a fierce kiss.

Everything I'd planned to say to him blows away in the crisp breeze. I toss my arms around his neck and hold on as he threads his fingers in my hair and holds me to him.

His tongue battles with mine, but after a minute, he slows down until he's pressing tender kisses to my lips.

"I fucking love you, Charlotte. Please don't be upset with me anymore." I open my mouth, but he places a finger over my lips. "Hear me out."

I nod and reluctantly let go of him. We sit side by side on the swings, but he swivels around to face me, and I do the same.

He exhales. "I'm sorry for how I reacted when I found out

you might be pregnant. I can't explain why I had an out-of-body experience. I think one of the biggest shocks was hearing it from Dakota instead of you."

"I'm guessing she used the bathroom before I got there?" I ask. Nodding, he reaches over to grab my hand. "She obviously saw them in the trash."

"I just felt really fucking overwhelmed. I thought, 'I'm stretched so thin as it is with Asher. I never get enough time with him. Every moment with you feels stolen. Some days I'm barely awake in class. Football consumes all of my energy. And I have a mountain of laundry and no time to do it.'"

I squeeze his hand. "I get it. I'm sorry you misunderstood. Only one of those tests was mine. The negative one." I explain the situation with Roxy. She's given me permission to tell Jake what's going on with her.

"Jesus. I feel dumb." He lets go of my hand to scrub his face.

"But I will admit it's been hard not comparing that night to how you responded to my sister when she told you she was pregnant. And the fact that you didn't flip out on Kota when she was saying all of those horrible things? It felt like you weren't defending me."

"Baby, *lo siento*. I'm sorry. When I thought you were pregnant, my brain short-circuited. I guess I needed a few minutes to process it. And once the blood flow reached my brain again and I could focus on your conversation, I couldn't just tear her up. Asher was right there. I won't yell at Dakota, even when she deserves it, when Asher's around. I remember my parents screaming at each other, and that shit fucks you up."

I never thought about it like that. I remember him sharing those details with me when we were in high school. How awful it was to hear his parents fight.

He leans forward. "Did I have the best reaction to a potential pregnancy? No. But here's the truth—when I found out you *weren't* pregnant?" Pressing a hand to his chest, he swallows. "I was disappointed. Because there's no one else I want to have a family with. The thought of you having my babies?" He shakes his head, his eyes a little glassy. "That would mean the world to me."

I wipe the tears that leak from my eyes. "Really? You're not just saying that? You want to have kids with me someday?"

He pulls me out of the swing and into his lap. "Did you watch my press conference?"

I nod.

"Then you know what I want to do, right?"

He said a lot to the press, but with the way he's looking at me right now, there's only one thing he can mean.

Smiling, I laugh as another tear slips out. "You want to wife me up?"

"Damn straight. And I definitely want to have our own little brood together down the road. I don't have the money to get you the kind of ring you deserve, but when I do, you can bet that will be the first thing I buy."

I grab his handsome face and press a kiss to his lips. "I don't care about a ring."

"But you deserve the best."

"I'd say I'm getting a pretty great deal regardless." I kiss him slowly. "We've only been dating a few months."

"Cupcake, you've been burrowing your way into my heart for years."

We kiss, and it suddenly feels like all of our stars align.

But there's still one thing I need to ask.

Leaning back, I ask, "You're not mad about the video I sent Kota?"

He kisses my forehead. "How could I be upset? Honestly, you're a genius. Dakota deserves everything coming to her. And if that video gets her off my back for a few months, even better."

He explains how his brother can float him a little money if he needs an attorney, but Jake hopes he gets drafted, and then he'll have an advance to afford it himself. "Should we call her and get this over?"

"I'm dreading it, but yes." My stomach twists with anxiety, but he grabs my hand and brings it to his lips.

As he dials, I get out my phone and hit record. He nods in approval.

Texas is a "one-party consent state," meaning at least one person who's being recorded has to approve. I checked before I sent her that video compilation. I even have her recorded as saying I should record all the time, even between shoots, because "there's no telling when I'll say something funny or do something cute."

Insert eye roll.

When Dakota answers, all she does is screech like her hair's on fire. "What the fuck, Jake? How could you let Charlotte make up those lies? How could you say all that shit at the press conference? Don't I mean anything to you at all?"

Jake and I look at each other. His eyes bug out comically as he circles his finger around his temple in the universal sign that Kota's crazy.

He clears his throat. "Charlotte and I have you on speakerphone. You should know we plan to hire an attorney if you don't cut your crap."

She starts crying. "Please promise me you won't release that video. If my fans see that, I'll be over. Please."

Irritated she's trying to be a martyr, I lean forward. "Kota, take a good long look at that video. That's the real you—snarky, mean, and selfish. None of your friends really like you. They only want to hang out with you because of your fame. All I ever did was support you even though you treated me like your slave. Go get some therapy. Stop trying to use Asher for your social media, because I know that's why you're suddenly interested in him again."

When she doesn't say anything, I know I'm right.

I finish unleashing. "As long as you leave us alone—me, Jake, and Asher—you won't hear from us. But if you slander us again or try to manipulate us to get to Asher, I swear to God, I will fuck up your career so hard, starting with that modeling sponsorship you might land. Because I have a lot more footage. What I sent you is just the tip of a big-ass iceberg. There are so many more clips, including a lovely little bitchfest you had about Gypsy Glam one afternoon."

That's the clothing brand offering a modeling contract to one of *The Hot House* contestants. I know Kota won't want to piss off the sponsor before the show's finale.

She sniffles, and for a minute, I feel bad. Because deep in my heart, I wish my sister and I were close and that she loved me like I always loved her.

But then she opens her mouth again. "Fine. Whatever. Just remember that I had Jake first."

I smile at my beautiful boyfriend and take his pinky in mine. "Yeah, but he's mine now, and I'm not dumb enough to let him go."

$\sim$

JAKE and I walk hand-in-hand to his car. After we pick up Duke and Winkie, we head to Jake's apartment, where Buffy gives me a hug and takes off. Asher squeals when he sees me.

"Charwotte! I missed you!"

I cry when he wraps his arms around my legs. "Hey, Ash. How's my favorite boy?" Kneeling, I hug him to me. It's only been a week since I saw him, but that felt like an eternity.

Jake makes a face and playfully grumbles, "I thought I was

your favorite boy."

Over Asher's shoulder, I smile. "You're my favorite *man*."

He waggles his eyebrows at me, and I chuckle. I'm sure both of us are counting down the minutes until we can be alone tonight, but I also want some time with Asher.

Jake kneels next to me and whispers, "Let's make things official." Then he presses a kiss to his son's forehead. "Ash, how would you feel if Charlotte was my girlfriend?" He winks at me and adds, "I know we're well past this part, but I want him to know you're going to be a permanent fixture in our lives."

Asher yells in excitement before he hugs me tight. "Aruuu my mommy now?"

Oh, my heart. I blink furiously to stem the tide that wants to erupt. I glance at Jake, who's giving me a soft smile.

My voice cracks. "I hope to be someday, baby."

After I introduce Ash to my one-eyed pirate cat, who he's really excited about, we order pizza and watch one of Asher's movies. He snuggles up between me and Jake while Duke sprawls at our feet and Winkie stretches out in the windowsill. It's absolute perfection.

When it's bedtime, Jake tucks in Asher, and I take Duke out to potty one more time. The moment I return, Jake grabs my hand and walks me to his bedroom where he locks the door and flips on the monitor. "Finally."

As I look up at Jake, I'm all up in my feelings. After everything that's happened, we somehow made it to this point.

He grabs my chin and tilts my face up. "I love you, cupcake, and I've missed you so much."

My voice cracks once more and my eyes turn into faucets again. "Lo-love you too."

"Everything's okay now, baby."

He holds me as I sob against his chest. I cry for the time we lost in high school and for the years he dated my sister and for the pain we caused each other this last week. And when the last tear falls, I promise myself I'll never shed another one over the past.

"Let's start with a clean slate, okay?" I ask.

His thumbs slide against my cheek as he dries my face. "Clean slate." But then he smiles and whispers in my ear, "I can still get you a little dirty tonight, though, right?"

I laugh and squeeze him tight. "So, so dirty."

"Filthy," he growls as he takes my earlobe between his teeth.

He pulls me closer, and I feel that giant bulge against my stomach. It feels so good to know he wants me as much as I want him.

Using that to make me brave, I step out of his arms and tug off my t-shirt and slide off my jeans, so I'm just standing in a sheer bra and a tiny pair of panties.

He takes my hair out of my ponytail, and I shake it loose. My body heats under his slow perusal.

"Fuck, you're gorgeous."

I unsnap my bra and let it fall to the ground. Wiggle out of my undies. The whole time, he watches me with those blazing hot eyes.

And then, because I feel so sexy under his gaze, I crawl onto the bed and glance back at him. "Are you joining me?"

I curl up with a pillow as he curses under his breath and tugs off his t-shirt, putting all of those rippling muscles on display. Next, he pops open his jeans and slides them down with his boxer briefs.

His hard length springs forward, and he runs his hand up and down his cock.

Goosebumps spill across my body as I watch, and I squeeze my thighs together.

"Touch yourself." His low command makes my nipples pebble.

This might sound crazy, but I love when he tells me what to do. It makes all of my anxiety melt away.

I roll onto my back and spread my legs. His eyes are riveted to my hand as it slowly moves down my body. Pausing to pinch one nipple. Then the other. Down my stomach. Finally dipping between my thighs.

"Good girl. Are you wet, cupcake?"

I nod and swirl my fingers faster.

"Fuck yourself with your hand," he adds as he palms his cock faster.

Bending my legs, I dip one finger, then two inside of me and arch my back to reach deeper.

"That's it, baby. Use a third finger. Get yourself ready for me."

My clit throbs when I do as he instructs, and I moan.

"That feel good?" he asks as he gets on his knees at the other side of the bed.

"So good."

I should be embarrassed. He's *right there* with a clear view of me getting myself off, but all I want to do is please him the way he pleases me.

He slowly removes my hand and sucks each of my fingers before he replaces my hand with his. Suddenly I'm stuffed full. His fingers, so much thicker than mine, work in and out of me, and I spread my legs wider so I can take it.

"I fucking love watching you like this. Your pretty wet pussy stretched wide." Lightly, he traces my seam with his tongue. So gentle at first. Just enough to drive me out of my mind as he pushes against this magical spot inside me.

With each thrust of his hand, the fireworks get brighter. More intense. I start chanting his name, and by the time his tongue lands on my clit, I nearly fly off the bed. Quaking around his fingers, I press my fist to my mouth so I don't wake up the entire apartment building.

I'm still fluttering when he crawls up my body a minute later and slowly starts to work his cock into me.

"Wait. Don't you want a condom?"

He pauses, a furrow in his brow. "You're on birth control, right?"

I nod. I already know he got tested after he found Troy and Dakota messing around, and he hasn't been with anyone since except me.

He smiles. "I trust you."

Never have sweeter words been spoken. I yank him down to kiss him, and he groans as he burrows deeper into my body. He's never gone without condoms, and since I've never been with anyone else, obviously I haven't either. I love that we're each other's first.

"Goddamn, you feel amazing bare. Fuck."

"It's even better without condoms. Don't stop." I'm stretched so full and out of breath and frantically trying to get him to move.

He chuckles as he holds himself still. "I need a sec, baby."

That thick part of him lodged between my thighs pulsates, and I shiver. "I felt that."

Groaning, he drops his head to my chest and exhales. "Trying not to come."

I thread my fingers through his thick hair and wrap my legs around him. "I love you, Jake. I've always loved you."

When he lifts his head, his eyes meet mine. "I love you too, Charlie. You're it for me. You know that, right?"

My God. How did I land Jake Ramirez?

I kiss his rugged cheek. Thread my fingers through his hair. Squeeze him between my thighs, and smile. "Good, because I meant what I said. I'm never letting you go."

His weight feels so good. I breathe in his masculine scent, and when he somehow sinks deeper, I bite his shoulder.

He chuckles. "I know, baby."

And then he starts to move.

We're tangled limbs and low grunts and moans. He nibbles and licks and bites my nipples. I want all the marks.

Lifting up on his knees, he raises my hips, and that angle has me gasping.

"Too much?"

"No! Don't stop." It's hitting the perfect angle—something deep in my body, a spot that has me arching into him as he watches his length slide in and out of me.

I reach between us and run my fingers over his thick erection, loving how his eyes go a little wild and he starts pumping faster. Deeper. I press my palm into my clit and grind.

"That's it, baby. Get there."

My legs start to quake, and I feel him jerk inside me as we detonate together.

I yank him down to me, holding him close as heat sears through my body. He burrows his face in my neck. Holds me tight as he comes.

After a minute, he rolls us to the side, and I laugh. "You're dripping out of me."

He lifts his head, his hair a sexy, disheveled mess. "That's the hottest thing you've ever said."

My smile is so wide, even after we clean up and he spoons me from behind.

"Love you, my sweet cupcake," his low voice rumbles in my ear.

Reaching back, I run my fingers through his hair. "Love you too, Romeo. Thanks for coming to my rescue freshman year."

Squeezing me tighter, he whispers, "My Juliet never needed me to rescue her."

I close my eyes, but the smile on my face remains.

46

EPILOGUE

CHARLOTTE

THE STADIUM IS ABOUT to erupt. Riveted, Bronco fans count down the clock. We're up by four points, but LSU has the ball with thirty seconds left.

It's been a high-scoring game. Jake and Ezra have been on fire today, connecting for three touchdowns. Jake's rushing stats are going to be off the charts. Even though I'm not Ezra's biggest fan because of what's going on with Roxy, I'm thrilled it's not affecting his performance. Because the team deserves this victory even though I want to punch him in the throat.

I peer over at Roxy, who's doing a non-tumbling routine on the field. She finally came clean to her cheer coach about being pregnant, but told her squad she's recovering from a bad stomach virus so they wouldn't question why she's not at the top of the pyramid. It's nobody's business anyway. This is the championship game, so she'll have time to figure out what she's going to do.

Houston is a lovely fifty degrees. Since we're only about four hours from Charming, I swear half the town drove out here.

Those who couldn't get tickets are having the tailgating party of their lives.

The best part is Jake's mom, brothers, and Asher are in the audience. Jake hasn't mentioned it, but I know it means the world to him to have his family here. Since he finally opened up to David about the crap going on with my sister, they've both realized there's been a lot of miscommunication messing up their relationship.

David swears he's never been down on Jake playing football and that he's proud of him. Jake realizes David missed his games in high school because he was always working and trying to keep their family afloat. They have a long way to go before they're close, but I'm hopeful it's on the horizon.

When the other team snaps the ball, my heart pounds as the Tigers find an opening in our defense.

"No!"

I remind myself to take photos and thankfully capture the moment Billy takes that dude down.

After Jake's public request to reinstate me as one of the team's student photographers, I sought out AD Armstrong to argue my case. Jake is helping me realize I need to advocate for myself more. Getting pushed around by my sister for so long taught me to give in whenever someone gets bossy. I'm planning to see a therapist soon to try to work through some of my issues.

But the silver lining is the athletic director relented on the condition I have an escort on the field in case any weirdo gets out of hand. I glance at the enormous lineman who's been my shadow all day. Otto is a redshirted freshman, who's psyched he gets to attend the playoffs. It's a win-win for both of us.

In return for his company, I've promised to introduce him to some of Roxy's friends. Despite his size, he's a shy guy. I can relate.

Jake says Coach isn't mad at him for that impromptu press

conference attendance. Since Kota's last episode aired, she's been surprisingly quiet on social media, so things quieted down for the team. Which was exactly what they needed as they headed into the playoffs.

Miraculously, Kota did not win *The Hot House*. Somehow "America's sweetheart" didn't nab the grand prize, but she did win a modeling contract with Gypsy Glam, the company she tore to shreds on my old video.

I'm ridiculously pleased with myself for finding that little treasure because it'll keep her out of our hair for a while. At least long enough for Jake to enter the draft this spring.

Although... it might be a moot point now.

Last week, it was unusually warm in Southern California, which was likely why Kota was driving down Rodeo Drive in Beverly Hills with the top down on her convertible. It gave bystanders a clear view of her texting when she ran a red light and got T-boned by an SUV.

She's fine. I mean, except for that broken leg, which jeopardizes the modeling contract. She's lucky she wasn't arrested, although that's still a possibility, especially after video of her texting as she sped through the intersection went viral.

Maybe that's karma kicking her ass.

It still pisses me off to remember how she gushed on TV about being a mom after abandoning Asher.

With Kota not winning the big prize on *The Hot House*, it makes me wonder if she had an inkling that loss was on the horizon and was getting her ducks in order to update her social media with pics of Ash. She used to say mom influencers got the best sponsorship deals.

But she did drop one more bomb on her show.

In the final episode, she claimed our mother deliberately poisoned her when she was little. Dakota said our mom made her sick for the attention after she met that producer in the hospital. Since doctors could never figure out why Kota got progressively worse, there may be some truth to her allegations.

There's a name for when parents do that kind of heinous thing to their children. Munchausen syndrome by proxy.

If it's true, that would explain why our parents always let Dakota get away with murder. And why they had so many secrets.

The possibility that happened breaks my heart. Kota was an innocent little girl, and I know how much she suffered.

But that doesn't excuse her for being such an asshole now as an adult.

I pause, wondering if this is why she asked if I had set my apartment building on fire. Because she learned how to fabricate drama from our mother.

Speaking of the woman who spawned me, I think it's time to get the rest of my royalties back. I'm planning to talk to an attorney about it next semester.

My phone buzzes, and I check the message. I have to hurry because LSU's timeout is almost over.

It's Merle.

Guess what just sold out? You did it, girl!

I cover my mouth, overwhelmed. I threw the calendar order form online as a sort of Hail Mary, hoping and praying we'd make a little more money. Never in my wildest dreams did I think they'd all sell.

Jake did this. I mean, yes, I coordinated and shot it, but Jake pimping out the calendar at that press conference is what drove so many people to the Second Chances website. Roxy has been helping me package them for the last two weeks.

So many more animals are going to get the love and attention they deserve because of this. Just like Duke, who we formally adopted right before the holidays. It was one of our Christmas gifts to Ash, who is ecstatic we're keeping his best buddy. Ash is a natural with animals. Even my pirate cat adores him.

The teams set up on the line of scrimmage. LSU has to pass on fourth down since they're almost out of time. A field goal won't tie the game.

I'm so nervous, I want to puke. And no, I'm not pregnant. Apparently, I get nauseous on game days. I'm learning to live with it.

With ten seconds left, they snap the ball. The QB hurls it high. I'm watching through my viewfinder as my shutter whirs. It's so tempting to set down my camera and enjoy the game, but this is an incredible opportunity and I want to make the most of it.

An LSU receiver reaches up, looking like he's going to make the catch. I hold my breath. If they score on this down, the Broncos won't have time to recover.

Out of the blue Billy cuts in front of him, leaping and stretching like a panther about to kill his prey, and bats the ball out of his opponent's hand.

Game over, baby!

Otto and I scream and jump and hug each other.

Fans rush the field, and I hop up and down and look for Jake.

"There's no way I'm going to find him in this!" I yell to Otto.

The longer I stand here, the crazier the fans get. I'm about to give up and go meet his mom like we planned, but then someone taps my shoulder.

I whirl around.

And then have to look down.

Because Jake is down on one knee, but he's motioning to Otto.

My bodyguard whips out a black box from his jacket and hands it to my boyfriend.

I cover my mouth as my eyes sting.

Jake gives me the most breathtaking smile. "Charlotte Anne Darling, we've had a long and winding road together, and throughout that time, you've become the most important person in my life. You're the woman I want to grow old with. The one I want to kiss first thing in the morning and come home to every day. I'm a lucky man to call you my girlfriend, but I'd be even luckier to call you my wife. Would you do me this honor?"

Pretty sure I scream my answer because I have no chill. I barely notice when he grabs my hand and slips a gold band on my finger.

When he stands, I leap into his arms, not caring who sees me kiss him.

When he puts me down, he whispers in my ear, "I'll get you a bigger ring as soon as I can."

My heart swells with love for this man, who really can't afford this kind of gesture. I'm guessing his brother loaned him the money.

Holding my hand up, I take a look. It's a simple, thin band with a small cluster of diamonds. And absolutely perfect.

I grab his handsome face in my hands. "But I love this one. Don't you dare replace it."

Several news networks catch Jake's proposal that day, and it runs on all of the local affiliates. There are pics of us everywhere.

And for once, I don't mind.

Miracle of miracles, I don't blink in those photos.

I guess when life is this good, you don't want to miss it.

BONUS SCENE

JAKE

The angry cry from the crib has me leaping out of bed. Who says football isn't good for families? I bet I have the fastest reflexes in the neighborhood. Fortunately, the noise doesn't wake Charlie, who's sleeping soundly.

I peer over the crib. "What's wrong, sweetheart? Need Daddy to change your diaper?"

Mackenzie doesn't stop fussing until she's changed and fed and burped. Afterward, I sit and cradle her in the rocker by the window where Winkie is soaking up the sun. "Is that better?"

She finally makes a happy gurgle, and her tiny hand wraps around my finger. My heart melts into a giant puddle. "Look at you. *Fuerte*. Strong. Just like your mama."

I kiss her fuzzy head. Run my finger over her button nose. She's a beauty. *And definitely not a morning person,* I chuckle to myself. Asher was all smiles in the morning, but not my little petunia.

The rustling of blankets makes me look over my shoulder to find a sleepy Charlotte smiling at us.

"Morning, cupcake. How'd you sleep?"

She covers her mouth as she yawns. "So well. I almost forgot we have a baby."

That was my goal. "You needed some rest."

"You really got up for the night feed?"

"I told you I would." It's my turn to yawn.

She sits up slowly and peers down at her damp nightgown. "Leaking all over the place is the only drawback to not getting up in the middle of the night."

I hand her the roll of paper towels we have on the bedside table.

After she cleans up and pumps, she leans over to kiss me and then takes the baby. "How's my girl? I should've gotten up to do your morning feed, but my God, I was tired."

"Kenzie took the bottle like a champ last night and this morning."

Several hard thumps land on the bedroom door.

"Come in," I call out, surprised Asher remembered to knock. Although that sounds more like a Viking invasion.

"Mom! Dad! Look what Duke can do now!" Asher storms in wearing his pajamas and a magic cape. Duke follows on his heels and sits at our son's feet. From the windowsill, Winkie looks over with mild interest.

Ash holds up his hand like Moses about to part the Red Sea. Duke sits at attention until Asher lowers his hand, and that crazy dog lowers onto his belly.

"Nice job, bud." I give him a high-five.

Charlotte laughs. "Honey, that's so cool! Maybe you could teach him to poop the first time I ask instead of him needing to walk all over town first."

Asher hops onto the bed and clambers over to Charlie, who holds Kenzie in one arm and opens her other for him. He tucks himself against her for a morning snuggle as he tells her how he taught Duke the new trick.

I'm so grateful for my wife. She's such a good mama.

Sometimes it's hard not to compare this experience to what happened with Dakota, who rarely held Asher and complained about everything.

It makes me really fucking grateful for what I have now.

Thankfully, Dakota has stayed out of our hair.

And yeah, I've had moments of doubt, where I've wondered if we're doing the right thing by keeping her out of Asher's life. Because of my experience with my parents' divorce, sometimes I worry. Charlotte and I have spent long nights discussing it because we both want the best for our son.

Our doubt came to a screeching halt last summer when we ran into her sister at a restaurant. Dakota barely glanced at Asher, much less expressed any kind of interest in him. That only solidified our belief that he's better off without her. We work hard to maintain our kids' privacy, and that woman doesn't understand the meaning of the word. She still insists on living her life on social media and uses everyone around her as fodder. And I refuse to let her use Asher.

But if we had any question whether she's reconsidered her toxic ways, her reality show last spring put her vicious temper on display for the world.

Dakota's also suing her mother in a civil court for emotional and physical abuse.

Charlotte researched Munchausen syndrome by proxy and said cases that don't result in death are often difficult to prove. No formal charges have been brought by the state, possibly because of the statute of limitations.

I feel bad for Dakota and for the suffering she went through as a child, but it sheds light on why she's such a train wreck now.

She had to pay a huge fine after that car accident a few years ago and barely avoided jail time, but she ended up losing that modeling contract because of all the bad press. Honestly, Dakota deserved it for the way she treated Ash and Charlotte.

Right after we graduated, Charlie finally got the rest of her *Little Darlings* royalties back from her mother after she threatened to sue her.

I'm just glad that chapter in our lives is over, and we can move on.

Reaching into our closet, I grab our suitcase and start packing for our trip.

"Did you get the message I left for you yesterday?" I ask Charlotte. "Rider confirmed the photoshoot with his family."

Charlie had a close call last year and almost got smashed on the sidelines of one of our games when a linebacker got pushed out of bounds and hurdled over her. Nearly gave me a fucking heart attack when I saw a replay of it. Fortunately, that video didn't go viral. No one really expects the wife of one of the players down on the field.

As a result of that close call, she decided she'd rather not end up in traction and hung up her NFL media credentials, but not before winning Sports Photographer of the Year. I was afraid she'd regret not shooting professional football anymore, but she said she has nothing to prove.

Damn right, she doesn't. I bought her a trophy case to hold all of her photography awards. I'm so proud of my wife.

She hasn't left the field entirely. My coach gave her an open invitation to return anytime. Plus, since she knows the guys on the team, they've been coming to her to photograph their families, and she's having a blast doing engagements, baby showers, and weddings.

Our QB Rider Kingston, a fellow former Bronco, booked an appointment as soon as I mentioned what she was doing.

It's been cool as hell playing with him in Dallas. I was lucky to get drafted by such an incredible team. I'd like to take some credit for our Super Bowl win, but really, it was mostly due to having a kickass quarterback.

Charlotte yawns again. "I can't believe Rider and Gabby are having twins. I'm so excited for them. I love that our babies will grow up together."

"They already have two. Talk about exponential growth," I tease. "I almost forgot, he said he also wants to book a pregnancy shoot for Gabby."

"That's great! I'm so excited."

"Babe, you sure you're not overdoing it?"

She lifts her face to me, and I see it now, how her eyes go all soft and dreamy when I say something protective. "I promise I'll take care of myself."

My wife somehow wrangles our kids and balances her photography business with my crazy schedule. It helps that my family is nearby and offers a hand, but I'm still in awe of her.

"Babe, David and I are finishing the rebuild this week. Think you could take some photos of the car before we give it to Mom for her birthday?"

Over the last several months, my brothers and I have been renovating a 1976 Gran Torino for my mother, who's only ever driven beaten-up clunkers. She refused to let me buy her a house or a car after I signed with Dallas, but she never said I couldn't restore something. I'm shocked to say that I've had the best time working on this project with my brothers. We've even talked about taking on another restoration when this one is done.

"I'd love to take photos. Do you want some large prints?" Her eyes light up. "Because my handsome husband gave me an incredible present, and I love having reasons to use it."

Last Christmas, I built her a custom darkroom with all the bells and whistles.

I wink at her. "If you have the time to do prints, we could give them to her at the restaurant and surprise her there before we drive her over to see it."

"That car is gorgeous. She's going to love it."

I glance at the clock. "We'd better get a move on things. My mom will be here soon."

She's watching Asher for the weekend while Charlotte and I drive down to Charming for a little reunion before training camp starts this summer. The drive from Dallas isn't too bad. I'm praying Kenzie sleeps most of the time.

Traveling with a three-month-old isn't ideal, but Charlotte really wanted to go, and I didn't feel right attending without her.

We're planning to stop by Second Chances while we're there. My wife just helped raise money to rebuild their aging facility. Seriously, the woman is amazing.

I dig out the baby carrier I bought the other day. "Can you help me figure this out before we leave?"

It's one of those weird contraptions that straps a child to your chest. I never thought to try this with Asher, but now that we have two kids, I can see the value.

Charlotte puts Kenzie in the crib and sets up Ash with a small stack of his favorite books on the bed. Then my beautiful wife wanders over to me and whispers, "Have I told you how sexy you look first thing in the morning, snuggling my baby? Watching you with our kids is literally the highlight of my day."

I waggle my eyebrows at her. "You can prove it to me tonight."

Her cheeks flush, and she tries to hide her grin, but I know she's excited to get away for a few days.

We only recently started having sex again after Kenzie was born. It was slow going at first because even though Charlotte's doctor gave her the thumbs-up for that kind of activity, her body wasn't ready for it yet. And I'd rather take a sharp poker to my eye than do anything that would hurt her. So we've mostly been doing a lot of foreplay and oral. We've turned it into a game. I guess you'd call it roleplay because we pretend we're dating again. It's hot as fuck.

I nuzzle my face against her neck as she reaches around my waist to help me strap into the baby carrier. "You smell good," I murmur before I nip her earlobe.

"Do you ever get tired of being the sexiest dad in the neighborhood? Is being a hotshot wide receiver not enough?" she asks cheekily as she snaps the carrier into place.

I steal a boob squeeze, and she sneaks a cock grab. Judging by the look in her eyes, we're gonna have all kinds of fun tonight once the baby is in bed.

No question about it. I love my life.

WHAT TO READ NEXT...

Thanks for reading! If you enjoyed Second Down Darling, I hope you'll consider leaving a review. I try to read each one.

To stay up-to-date with my new releases, be sure to subscribe to my newsletter, which you can find on my website, www.lexmartinwrites.com.

Next up in the series is Roxy and Billy's book! Billy is a player with a capital P, which means he's going to fall hard for Roxy. Of course, she's pregnant with Ezra's baby, so there will be lots of angst and drama! You can also get your copy of Heartbreaker Handoff from my website.

And if you want to start at the beginning of the Varsity Dads series, be sure to check out The Varsity Dad Dilemma, which is a USA Today bestseller. Keep flipping to read the synopsis.

THE VARSITY DAD DILEMMA

A USA TODAY BESTSELLER

What's worse than having Rider Kingston, the star quarterback, give you the big brush-off because he doesn't want to get serious? You'd probably think living across the street from him where you get a firsthand view of his hookups, right?

That's what I thought. Until someone drops off a baby with a note pinned to her blanket that says one of those jocks—either Rider or one of his roommates—is the father. The problem? Baby mama doesn't mention which of these numbskulls is the sperm donor.

I wouldn't care about their paternity problems—not the slightest bit—except my brother lives there too. Which means that adorable squawking bundle might be my niece, and there's no way I'm leaving her unattended with those bumbling football players.

They need my help, even if they don't know it yet. Once we solve this dilemma and figure out who's the daddy, I'm out.

I'll just ignore Rider and those soul-searing looks he gives me every time I reach for the baby. He broke my heart three years ago. He won't get a second chance.

∾

The Varsity Dad Dilemma is a sexy, small-town sports romance novel from USA Today best-selling author Lex Martin. Readers are raving about this passionate, angst-filled enemies-to-lovers romance, and the smoking-hot chemistry between Gabby, the slightly nerdy Latina with a take-charge attitude, and her surprisingly sweet former fling, Rider. Who knew that he actually had a heart of gold underneath that deliciously ripped, well-defined exterior?

"Gabby and Rider have great chemistry and their banter is HOT. While she had loathed everything about Rider since freshman year, there was no denying the physical attraction they had towards each other... If you are looking for a college romance that brings the laughter, with loads of sexual tension and plenty of heart melting moments, check this book out!" – Reader Review

ACKNOWLEDGMENTS

I hope you've been enjoying my Varsity Dads! As much as the focus in this series tends to be on the fathers, I had a lot of personal inspiration for Charlotte.

When I was growing up, writing used to frustrate me. My mom always told me I was a writer, but when I read my work, I never felt like it was good enough. I always agonized over my diction and felt like there was some elusive word in the ether I could've used but didn't and so my writing was lacking. (If I could go back and tell teenage Lex that she would be a romance novelist, that would blow her mind! *Also, yes, Mom, you were right.* She likes to hear this from time to time.)

But that's one of the reasons I was attracted to photography. I ended up majoring in photojournalism in college and became obsessed with the dark room. There, surrounded by Dektol and developer lights, I didn't need to find the perfect words.

The assignments, however, took me far, far out of my comfort zone, and that landed me my first job as the in-house photographer for one of the largest performing arts theaters in New England. I eventually went on to teach photography and journalism as a high school English teacher, but I never would've made it to the front of a class without the courage photo first gave me.

Photography made me brave when I would've preferred being a wallflower at times, and that was the perfect vehicle to draw out my sweet little Charlotte.

That's just one of many tidbits from my life I used for this book. The holes in the floorboards of Jake's mom's vehicle come compliments of the car I had right out of college, and Duke was inspired by my finicky Shih Tzu Teddy.

Also, I'd like to note that North Texas University is entirely fictional. It's not intended to be a reference to the University of North Texas, which is UNT.

Speaking of colleges, I figure someone out there will question the odds of how Jake ended up at the same school as Charlotte. To that, I want to say, it's a small world.

When I was in 8th grade, my dad and I drove from Texas to New Mexico for spring break to go skiing. When we got to the resort, we parked right next to a boy I went to school with. We had a small grade with maybe 20 kids, and I'd known Colby since pre-k. He and I never discussed our plans for spring break, and he was just as shocked to see me as I was to see him. I had a blast skiing with Colby and his brothers, and whenever I think of strange coincidences in my life, that day always stands out. In a world where I can run into one of my childhood buddies on spring break in another state, I figure Jake and Charlotte can find each other again at a different college. And in honor of my friend, who sadly passed long ago, I named Jake's younger brother Colby.

With each book, there are always so many people to thank, and I have to start with my awesome husband Matt, who recently leveled up by learning how to cook! He's so extra these days. It's official—I married the perfect book boyfriend! He and my girls are my entire world, and I'm so grateful I can work from home and annoy them every day.

I have a great team of people who help me reach the finish line: my agent Kimberly Brower, editor RJ Locksley, proofreader Julia Griffis, photographer Lindee Robinson, cover designer Najla Qamber, alternate cover designer Janett Corona, Kylie and Jo from Give Me Books, and Candi Kane PR. Thank you for everything you do for me!

I'm sure the wheels on this bus would fall off without my PA and dear friend Serena McDonald, who not only cheers me on but kicks my ass when I need it. She's my beta reader, my sounding board when I'm debating a story, and the best comic relief when I need a laugh.

Along with Serena, I have a fantastic team of beta readers who are so generous with their time and help me craft the best books possible. Leslie McAdam, Victoria Denault, Kelly Latham, Amy Vox Libris, Maddie Hewitt, Christine Yates, Jess Hodge, and Jan Corona (who also helps me with my Spanish!)—thank you for all of your input and love!

A huge thanks to my dad, who double checks my football scenes, brings me iced tea and tacos at all hours of the day, and is the best sidekick ever. He also hands out my swag unprovoked, so if some random guy hands you one of my pens or magnets when you're shopping for groceries, it's probably my dad!

My mom has always had an unwavering belief in my writing. Not sure what inspired this, but I'm so grateful!

Hugs to my cousin Lisa, who proofs my Spanish. Thanks, *prima*!

And my childhood bestie Angela always answers my weird legal questions. I blocked her view in middle school with my big, poofy hair, and we've been friends ever since.

Lastly, a huge thanks to my readers in Wildcats, my ARC

team, author friends, fans, bloggers, and influencers who've spread the word about my books. You have my deepest appreciation. I hope you love these college dads and the women who set them straight as much as I do. Thanks for picking up my books!

Next up is Heartbreaker Handoff. Get ready for Billy and Roxy's story!

ALSO BY LEX MARTIN

Varsity Dads:

The Varsity Dad Dilemma (Gabby & Rider)

Tight Ends & Tiaras (Sienna & Ben)

The Baby Blitz (Magnolia & Olly)

Second Down Darling (Charlotte & Jake)

Heartbreaker Handoff (Roxy & Billy)

Texas Nights:

Shameless (Kat & Brady)

Reckless (Tori & Ethan)

Breathless (Joey & Logan)

The Dearest Series:

Dearest Clementine (Clementine & Gavin)

Finding Dandelion (Dani & Jax)

Kissing Madeline (Maddie & Daren)

Cowritten with Leslie McAdam

All About the D (Evie & Josh)

Surprise, Baby! (Kendall & Drew)

ABOUT THE AUTHOR

Lex Martin is the *USA Today* bestselling author of Varsity Dads, Texas Nights, and the Dearest series, books she hopes readers love but her parents avoid. A former high school English teacher and freelance journalist, she resides in Texas with her husband, twin daughters, a bunny, and a rambunctious Shih Tzu.

To stay up-to-date with her releases, **subscribe to her newsletter** or join her Facebook group, **Lex Martin's Wildcats.**

www.lexmartinwrites.com

Made in the USA
Columbia, SC
27 July 2024

39446685R00186